BLOOD, LIES & SISTER WIVES

MYSTIQUE

TEXT UCP TO 22828 TO SUBSCRIBE TO OUR
MAILING LIST
If you would like to join our team, submit the first 3-4
chapters of your completed manuscript to
Submissions@UrbanChapterspublications.com

1

JULES

"Where the towels that's on sale?" a loud, crass voice, yelled behind me.

Sighing to myself, I stood up from where I was organizing video games on the lower shelf at Walmart, where, unfortunately, I worked. As soon as I turned my attention to the loud woman who was balancing a snotty nose baby on her hip, while holding the sales flyer for the store, a group of teenagers zipped behind me and began fucking up everything I'd just organized.

Taking a deep breath, I counted backwards from ten in my head. It was a technique they'd taught in my court-appointed Anger Management class.

"Is you slow or something?! Where these towels!?" the headscarf-wearing woman yelled at me, while tapping her, in need of a fill, acrylic nail on the paper.

I wanted to snatch her ghetto ass up, but she was holding that baby, and I needed my job. The holidays were coming up, and I wanted to buy my mom something real nice this year. So instead of fucking this hood rat up, I mustered up a smile.

"They should be in the home décor section, ma'am. Right down that way," I said politely, pointing towards the big ass sign that clearly said *Home Décor.*

Bitch probably can't read.

Sucking her teeth, she bounced her child up onto her hip and rolled her beady eyes, while I prayed that the black hair glue she used for her lashes would get in her eyes.

"I was just over there! It's none out! Can you check in the back?"

"We put all of the sale items out, so if it's empty, I'm sorry, but we're all sold out," I explained, feigning sympathy.

"Uhn uhn! See, this is why I don't normally shop at this ghetto ass Walmart! So what y'all gonna do?" she ranted.

I stared blankly at her for a moment before responding, "Ma'am, it says *while supplies last,* that means once it's gone, it's gone. I can check with another store to see-"

"Fuck that! I don't like your attitude! Where's your manager!?" she shouted, cutting me off.

"Bitch, she on lunch! And she only gonna tell your dumb ass the same shit I just told you!" I screamed, unable to control myself.

"What's going on?!" my coworker and the only person that made this job bearable, Tracy, asked, hurrying over to us.

"Are you her manager?!" the enraged woman inquired, sitting her baby down on the dirty ass floor and patting her dirty ass weave through her scarf.

Glancing between us, Tracy assessed the situation quickly from the angry snarls on both of our faces.

"Yes I am. Now, what seems to be the problem?"

I glanced at Tracy, happy that she was lying for me, but nervous that she might lose her job. Hopefully, this bitch was as dumb as she looked.

"I asked this girl a simple question, and she's been giving me nothing but attitude!"

"I'm very sorry, ma'am! Unfortunately, Jules has just switched medications, and the side effects can be quite irritable, but that's no excuse for mistreating our customers! Jules, go wait in my office!" Tracy reprimanded, pointing towards the restrooms.

Holding in my laugh, I nodded, trying to look ashamed, while the woman looked at me with a smug expression. As I walked towards the bathroom, I heard Tracy tell her that we would ship her the items and not charge her for shipping as if that was something special. We never charged shipping anyway but if the bitch was appeased. Then whatever!

Inside of the restroom, I finger combed my thick, cherry-colored hair, which had a fresh Dominican blowout, and applied a coat of lip balm to my full, pink lips. I stared at myself in the mirror, disappointed. Here I was, two years away from thirty, with a degree in Ethnic and Civilization studies and can't find a job in my field. Four fucking years wasted! I should've listened to my mother and went for something simpler, but I wanted to travel, be glamorous and make a difference for people in need along the way. Now look at me. Working at a job I hate, putting up with the attitudes of stupid customers, barely making enough to survive, and just recently got put on probation for latenesss.

And that's just my work life! My personal life is worse!

I was with my boyfriend...well, EX boyfriend, for five years. Five years of being lied to, cheated on and manipulated. Rich had all the qualities of a Grade-A fuck nigga, but my silly ass chose to look the other way. I turned my cheek more times than Jesus and all his disciples.

He was fine as fuck. *Check one.*

Had a fade on the sides with a high moisturized curly top. *Check two.*

Didn't have a job, but hustled and had just enough money that he could fraud like he was a cartel nigga. When in all actuality, he never left the block. *Check three.*

Had three baby mamas. *Check four.*

Kept his phone locked at all times. *Check five.*

Wore Polo Black cologne. *Check six.*

Listen, his fuck boy credentials could go on forever!

Anyway, he's the reason I ended up with that court-appointed anger management! Had me out in these streets fighting bitches like I ain't have no damn sense! Like I'm not going on thirty! Like I don't have a whole ass degree, (albeit not useful) but still!

But he'd always hit me with some quick game and devil dick. Then I'd forgive him, be in the kitchen cooking tacos and shit. That was until this last time. I'm on the fifth day of my seven-day treatment for Chlamydia. This nigga actually burned me! Laying in the bed of that free clinic, thinking I had a yeast infection and finding out I really had Chlamydia, was the most humiliating experience of my life. Of course, I felt the need to explain to the nurses that I'd gotten it from my boyfriend, so they wouldn't think I was out here fucking every Dirty Dick Dan that crossed my path. But shit, thank God it was something I could get rid of.

The geek though, is that when I confronted Rich about it, he tried to turn it around on me! Talking 'bout, *"The few times I cheated, I used a condom."* Nigga please! Take that bullshit on, 'cuz in five years, his is the only dick I had; despite the many offers. Hell, the way he treated me, you would think I was busted, but that was far from true.

I had caramel skin that was as smooth as butter and a face that the best plastic surgeon couldn't build! I used to be slim thick, but after years of doing nothing but fuckin' that nigga and laying up eating in bed, I'd gained some weight. I like to call it my grown woman weight, and baby, I was thicker than a snicker!

Even this lame ass blue shirt and khaki pants couldn't contain my curves. Just as I stuck a piece of Big Red gum in my mouth, the bathroom door swung open. Tracy rolled her eyes at me before going in.

"Girl! Why you arguing with these customers?! You know Samantha got it out for your ass! That's all her ugly ass woulda needed! A customer complaint so she can fire your ass! You not leaving me here with all these weirdos!" she huffed, throwing a hand on her wide hip.

I laughed, "I'm sorry, boo but she was a bitch! I couldn't with her! And the way I'm feeling, Sam's ass coulda got it too! Knock them whack ass clip-in hair-pieces right on the floor!"

Now we were both cracking up, because those clip in tracks was often the butt of our jokes about our pathetic manager. She was a nuisance. Bitch acted like she was running the Whitehouse instead of Walmart. Girl bye! I assumed she didn't have any dick in her life because she was always miserable. Gawd, I hate this job! I couldn't blame anyone but myself. My bad decisions throughout the years had landed me in this position.

Even though the rest of my shift crawled by, Tracy made it slightly entertaining until it was time for me to clock out. After grabbing my coat and scarf from my locker, I speed walked outside to the parking lot. I was so ready to take a hot bath and wash the stench of retail off my ass! Jumping in my '06 Explorer, I rubbed my hands together.

"Shit!" I yelled, as my breath fogged up.

It was colder than an Eskimos clit out this bitch! Wishing I had one of those push to start thingies so I could have warmed this bitch up, I fumbled with my keys, sticking it into the ignition.

"Noo!" I whined, when nothing happened.

I tried again, but the engine wouldn't turn over.

"Fuck!" I yelled, pounding my fist against the steering wheel.

I didn't have enough money in my account to call Lyft or Uber. Steadying my shaky hands, I thumbed through my contact list, looking for anyone who would be able to come get me. The only reliable person I had was my best friend, Tash. I hated to bother her, knowing she was probably laid up in a warm bed with her man. I paused, teeth chattering from the cold.

Just as I started to press her name, a knock on my window startled me.

"Oh!" I said, throwing a hand over my chest.

I calmed down when I noticed it was only Stefan from

work. I opened the door since I couldn't roll down the window.

He smiled, "Hey. Everything cool? I saw you crying and punching the wheel and shit."

Smirking, I sucked my teeth, "First off, I was not crying! My stupid truck won't start!" I explained.

He nodded, "Get out for a second. Lemme check it out."

Gratefully, I slid out and let him climb in. I knew he was checking for me because he'd told me so numerous times. But since at the time I was with Rich, every time he took his shot, I knocked it away from the net. He was definitely a cutie though, with his smooth brown skin and deep dimples.

"I think it's just your battery. Sometimes the cold weather drains them. I'mma pull my car up and give you a jump."

"Oh my God, thank you so much!"

He simply smiled as he jogged off down the almost empty parking lot. Checking the time, I saw that it was only 10:30. Soon the store would be staying open later for the holidays. I wasn't looking forward to all the extra hours and crowds of people, but I obviously needed the extra money. Sighing, I pulled my scarf tighter around my neck and tucked it into my coat before climbing back inside of my car and pulling the lever to pop the hood, praying Stefan was right and it was only the battery.

Lord knows I couldn't afford to put it in the shop right now. Sighing once again, fighting depression, I rubbed my hands over my arms to keep warm inside of my freezer on wheels. A car pulled up in front of me, headlights blinding me and Stefan hopped out. I watched him get the jumper cables from his car until he lifted my hood completely, blocking him from my vision.

I sat there for what seemed like an eternity, feeling frostbite beginning to creep in through my Ugg boots, freezing both of my big toes. He tapped on my window again, this time motioning for me to start the car. Turning the key, pure joy coursed through my body as it started up. Quickly, I turned on the heat, which came out in a blast of cold air.

Rolling down the window, I said, "Stefan, thank you so much! I really appreciate this!"

"Its light work," he grinned. "You can sit in my car until yours warms up."

I wasted no time hopping out of my icebox and making my way to his...Audi?! Stopping in my tracks, I gawked at the black matte paint and black rims. I know for damn sure he couldn't afford this on Walmart salary.

"You got another job or something?" I asked as he opened the door, revealing the custom blue leather interior.

I didn't wait for him to respond before I slid my ass inside and shuddered from the heated seats.

He grinned, "I do a little something on the side," he said before closing the door.

Because I was book smart and street smart, like Drake wanted his women, I knew that meant his ass probably sold drugs on the side.

"Fuck boy, check one," I mumbled to myself as he walked around to the driver's side.

He hopped in and I watched as he changed the XM stations until he found one he liked. I noticed how deep his waves were.

Fuck boy hairstyle.

"Why you ain't call your nigga, since you always talking 'bout him?" he asked, reaching over me.

I quickly moved my thigh, thinking he was trying to touch me, but he reached past me to the glove compartment and pulled out some pre-rolled weed. He watched me, waiting for me to answer his question as he sparked up.

"We not together anymore. Fuck that nigga."

"Oh yeah?" he asked, his eyes lighting up.

I held up my hand, "Yeah, but I'm not tryna talk to anybody right now. I just wanna be by myself for awhile."

"He musta really fucked up, huh?"

Talking about Rich irritated my soul, so I changed the subject as I felt my body beginning to thaw out.

"You got kids, Stefan?"

"Nah," he replied, inhaling his smoke.

My eyes widened in surprise. Maybe I was wrong about him being a fuck boy.

"I mean, it's a few bitches claiming they kids is mine, but I ain't feeling it."

I sucked my teeth. *Here we go...*

"Seriously?! You know you can buy a swab right from here!" I spat, pointing to Walmart.

He remained silent, passing me the weed, which I smelled to make sure it wasn't laced, before puffing.

"Nah. They shoulda been on birth control or something."

"Nigga, you coulda wore a condom!" I snapped.

"I did! That's how I know they lying! But I don't wanna talk about them. I wanna talk about me and you."

Exhaling the smoke, I passed his weed back and shook my head, "I just told you–"

"I know, I know," he interjected. "Damn, we can be friends though," he said, staring at my thighs lustfully.

"Stefan, thanks for the jump, but I really should head home. I need to make sure my mom ate," I said, climbing out of his car, without giving him a chance to respond.

I could feel his eyes on my ass through his tinted windows as I switched to my car. Hopping in, it wasn't as warm and comfortable as Stefan's Audi, but it wasn't below zero anymore. I couldn't wait to get home and in my bed. I was so thankful that I only worked about fifteen minutes from my house. I'd lucked up on that house. It was one of those big, old houses, situated in a nice neighborhood in Brookhaven, Pennsylvania. I bought it about four years ago with the settlement money I'd gotten from a bad accident I was in when a drunk driver ran a red light and plowed into me. The owners were in a rush to sell and sold it to me for half of what it was worth.

Anxious to buy, I quickly signed my name on the dotted line, but before the ink could dry, I realized why it was so cheap. The pipes were old and rusted, the electricity was faulty, and I pretty much shared the house with mice! Thank goodness my Uncle was good at repairs and the cat I adopted cleared away all of the vermin. But on top of all that, I think the damn place is haunted!

I know it sounds crazy, but I swore I would hear all types of whispers in the dark, things constantly went missing, and a few times I'd wake out of my sleep and feel like somebody was watching me. At the time, my mother was living alone in her small apartment and had just been diagnosed with diabetes. I ain't waste no time packing her ass up and moving her in with me! It was a perfect solution to both of our problems. I didn't have to be alone in that big ass house and I was also able to monitor her diet.

Because her diabetes was so bad, she wasn't able to work, but she got a disability check every month, which against my wishes, she used to help out with the bills. The only thing I didn't like was that she insisted on her sister's daughter staying with us until *"she got on her feet."* Whenever that would be. My cousin Nikki was a piece of fuckin' work! She refused to work, well except her mouth. I mean that literally too. The bitch had the nastiest attitude and made a living out of sucking random dick.

Just a few days ago, I had to cuss her the fuck out for sneaking randoms in and out of my house where me and my mom lay our head! Me and Nikki used to be close when we were kids, but after her mom got killed, she changed. She withdrew from the family and found solace in the streets, determined to be somebody's trap queen. I can't lie and say she didn't get under my skin, but I felt sorry for her more than anything.

She was a beast with fashion. When we were younger, she wanted to be the next Versace or Louis Vuitton, and she had the skills to do it. But now, it seemed as if she was content with laying around finessing niggas. Pulling into my space in front of the house, I turned off the car, that had just started to really heat up, and walked up my driveway. When I opened the door, I was met by my black kitty, Egypt.

"Hey boo," I greeted her, scratching her back.

She purred, rubbing up against my leg, before

following me to the kitchen. An empty pizza box sat on the table.

"I know she didn't feed my mom this shit!" I said to myself, folding the box and putting it in the trash.

Snatching open the refrigerator door, I saw the meal I made for my mom still in the Tupperware. Sighing, I made myself a sandwich, trying to get a quick energy boost before I went upstairs and punched this bitch in her face! Scarfing down the turkey and cheese on wheat, I fed Egypt and marched back through the house, heading upstairs to the attic where Nikki had made herself at home.

Pulling open the wooden door, I stomped up the stairs, only to find her room empty, while her TV blared *Black Ink*. Grabbing the remote from her messy bed, I shut off her TV.

"That's why the bitch so ratchet, watching these silly ass bitches all damn day!" I spat, turning to leave out of her room.

Downstairs, I calmed myself before lightly knocking on my mother's door.

"Come on in, Jules," her voice sounded through the door.

Opening her door, I glanced around, immediately spotting a plate on her nightstand, with pizza crust and crumbs. Sitting on her bed, I waited for her to come out of the bathroom. When she moved in, I gave her the master bedroom, which was spacious and equipped with its own restroom. The cream and brown color scheme she'd decorated in, reminded me of our home when I was a little girl. I stared at her TV screen, that was playing the ID channel. She loved those crime dramas.

Finally, she emerged from the bathroom, wearing a housecoat and slippers. Her long black hair pulled back into a ponytail. At fifty, she still looked youthful with smooth, brown skin and bright eyes, except she was about twenty pounds thinner. She smiled when she saw me.

"Hey, baby. How was work?" she asked, making her way over to sit next to me.

"The same as always. Horrible. Mom, why did Nikki order you pizza when I made baked chicken and lima beans for you?" I asked, pointing at her plate.

Frowning her face, she looked at me, "Juju baby, I appreciate you looking out for my diet, but I'm tired of eating that white people food."

My mouth fell open, "White people food?! Mom, stop! It's seasoned!"

She chuckled, "With sea salt."

I sucked my teeth, "I'm just tryna keep you healthy! You know what the doctor said!"

"I know, but one cheat day won't hurt! Can I just have that?"

"Fine," I huffed, standing.

"Jules, stop being like that! I get you're only trying to help, but let me live a little, baby. Speaking of, you need to live a little too. You too young to be looking so tired. It's Friday; you going out?"

I plopped back down, "Mom, I've been at work all day. I'm tired."

"That's what I'm talking about. You never have any fun. And I hope you not back with that boy. He stopped by earlier," she informed me.

I shook my head, "Believe me, I'm done with him! Did you talk to him?"

"No, I was up here, but I heard his voice. Nikki told him you weren't here. Humph, if I was you, I'd be on a date with a new nigga!"

Laughing loudly, I said, "I'm not hot in the ass like you!"

"Back in my day, I was fine! Had my pick!"

"You still fine, mom," I said, smoothing her ponytail. "But I really am tired. All I do is work."

"Jules, go out and have some fun. Ain't you off tomorrow? I worked two jobs and still found time to enjoy myself!"

"It was different back then. An electric bill was like five dollars," I said, laying my head in her lap.

She plucked my ear causing me to giggle, "Hussy, I'm fifty, not a hundred!"

"Seriously, mom, I have no idea what I'm doing," I confided.

"Baby, even people that seem like they have it together, have no idea what they're doing. We all just out here winging it. You can make all the plans you want, and one little thing can change everything. Long as you're loved, got a roof over your head and food to eat, you're doing fine. And don't let nobody make you feel differently! Not to mention, where would I be without you? You've always been my blessing," she said, rubbing my hair.

I smiled, feeling a little better, "Thank you, Mom. I love you. Let's go to the movies or something tomorrow," I suggested.

"You really gotta get a life."

"Mom! You know what?! Never mind!" I squealed, jumping up as she laughed.

"Love you too!"

I closed her door, chuckling to myself, "Mean ass lady," I mumbled, making my way to my own room.

Sitting in my soft recliner, I pulled off my boots and socks and wiggled my toes, happy to have them freed. Pulling my phone from the skin tight khakis, I went through my news feed, but quickly exited when I saw half of my timeline was posting pictures from tropical looking vacation spots.

"How the hell is everybody affording this shit?" I wondered out loud.

Noticing a text from my bestie, I opened it.

TASH: HEY BOO! PARTY TONIGHT! OUR HUSBAND VENOM IS PERFORMING!!!!

Venom was a local rapper that we were kind of obsessed with. Whenever he released a mixtape, we were quick to download it from Sound Cloud... along with every other chick in a twenty-mile radius! Biting my lip, I smiled, as my finger hovered over the text, but the pill bottle on my dresser caught my eye and my smile faded.

Instead of responding, I backed out of my texts, put my phone on the charger and grabbed the bottle of antibiotics for my nasty woman's disease, and my bottled water next to it. Quickly, I swallowed the giant pill and frowned my face, sticking out my tongue. Undressing, tossing my work clothes in the hamper, I threw on a large t-shirt, making my way out of my room and down the hall to the bathroom.

Turning on the shower, making sure the water felt like the seventh circle of hell, I carefully stepped in and began lathering myself in my Cherry Blossom body wash under the scalding water. My mind wandered again to the mysterious rapper.

Shit, shoulda brought my phone in here, so I coulda listened to his song, "Fuckin Your Soul."

Oh well, my sex drive was gone anyway, thanks to dirty dick Rich. I felt disgusting and never wanted to have sex again. I swear, I didn't understand men. What little mind they had was more difficult to decipher than Chinese math. They be having a woman that's pretty, ambitious, chill, got good sex, and still will run the streets looking for the next best thing, only to end up with the drip dick.

These hoes. I stood under the water, thinking and scrubbing until my skin was red and the water ran cold. Stepping out, I grabbed one of the fluffy blue towels I'd gotten on sale from work, and patted myself dry. Wrapping it tightly around myself, I went back to my room, lotioned myself down and grabbed my remote, turning on some old *Martin* reruns. Clicking off my light, I climbed in my soft bed and finally relaxed. I ignored my texts that seemed to be constantly going off while laughing at Martin's stupid ass.

"I could not have kept a straight face working with this fool!" I laughed.

My blaring phone caused me to suck my teeth and throw the warm covers off of me. Stomping over my cream carpet, I snatched up my phone from the dresser.

"Nigga what?!"

"Can I come-"

"Hell no, drippy! Call whoever festering pussy you was in!"

"Jules-"

"Stop calling me, stupid!" I yelled, clicking off the phone, blocking yet another random number.

Putting the phone down, I started back to bed, but it rang again.

"BITCH, I WILL CUT YOUR DISEASED DICK OFF AND FEED IT TO YOU!"

"Hoe, I ain't got no dick! And if I did, I'd come over there and fuck you up for threatening my shit!" Tash yelled through the phone.

"Girl! Shut up! I thought you was that nigga Rich!" I laughed.

"Obviously! He still stalking you from different numbers?"

"Um hm. Nigga ain't call me this much when we was on good terms! Tuh!" I huffed.

"I been told you get rid of that dog! You already got a cat; fuck you need a dog for?!"

I couldn't do nothing but laugh at her stupid ass.

"Anyway...I know you got my text."

"Hmm? Oh girl, I ain't even check my phone."

"Bitch, you know it says *read*, right? Get your shit together 'cuz we going to this party!"

"Tash nooooo!" I whined. "I'm exhausted. We can do something tomorrow."

"Girl, it's Venom! Shid, I'm tryna get bit!"

I laughed, "Ok, first of all, he's not a real vampire! It's no such thing! It's his gimmick! Second of all, you got a whole man! A faithful one!"

"I believe that nigga! I'mma *true* Venom fan, k?! And fuck Tyriq, that nigga ate the last of my Lucky Charms knowing I gotta have a bowl before I go to sleep!"

"I can't! I can't and I won't with you!"

"You can and you will! I'm outside; open up!"

Rushing to my window, I moved my curtains, and sure enough, her red Charger was parked right behind my car. I was about to tell her ass to go home, but she hung up. Throwing on some sweat pants over my panties and pulling on an old wife beater, I walked out of my room and jogged down the steps, not wanting her to be out in the cold for too long. Unlocking the door, I swung it open and made a face at her shivering on the porch.

"Yea, this is the type of weather where your hot ass should be in bed!" I scolded, opening the screen door for her to come in.

"Girl, shut up and move!" she spat, damn near knocking me down.

I looked her over, once I closed and locked the door. She looked cute as usual, but not like she was going to a party. Her bundles were long and flowing down her back with freshly cut layers in the shiny, black curls. Her creamy dark skin was makeup free, except for the lash extensions we'd both went and got together. Her slim frame housed some simple jeans, UGGs, and a little leather jacket with a fur hood.

I gave her a confused look until she held up a big bag and waved it in my face.

"It's a costume party! I ordered these last week!"

"Costume party?! Bitch, it's December! Halloween been over!" I protested.

She simply waved me off and headed upstairs like she lived here.

"It's Venom! You know he into that weird shit!" she giggled as I begrudgingly followed behind her.

"Tash, I don't know about this. It's cold and I'm tired. I'm just not in the mood."

"Uhhh," she twisted up her face as we entered my room. "You've been so...blah lately! You really let that nigga steal your joy!"

"It's not just him. It's everything!"

"What happened at your job today?" she asked knowingly, starting to unpack the bag on my bed.

I filled her in on today's events, and she chuckled, shaking her head, "I knew I liked Tracy! I don't know why you won't just quit and come work with me! I told you I can get you into the home health aide program! And they pay more!"

Sitting down, I watched her unpack and sighed, "Boo, you know I appreciate you and no shade, but I just can't wipe no grown person ass unless they birthed me or birthed the person that birthed me. I would seriously get sick."

"Suit yourself." She smacked her lips.

When she unfolded a pair of giant black wings, I looked at her, "What the hell is all this?!" I asked, staring at piles of spandex, lace, and leather.

She grinned, "We gonna be angels! I'm the good angel," she paused, holding a white catsuit up to her body, "and you're the bad one!" she exclaimed, tossing me a similar bodysuit, but in black, stretchy leather.

I couldn't contain my laughter, "Oh, you serious serious! I thought you might've had some cat ears or something!"

"That's basic! We 'bout to turn heads, boo!"

"Well, I think I should be the good one. You the one

dragging me out of the house," I said, reaching for the white catsuit.

She smacked my hand away, "No, bitch! This white gon' be everything up against all this chocolate! Plus, they different sizes, all that ass you towing around is not fitting in this size six um kay?!"

I rolled my eyes so hard they almost got stuck in the back of my head.

"Fine. You gotta curl my hair though," I said, carefully untying my scarf and walking to my closet to start looking for a good pair of shoes.

An hour later, we were dolled up and ready to go! Tash had my hair in big barrel curls, which I fluffed around giving me a wild sultry look. I opted on dark makeup, since I was supposed to be the bad angel. The dark eye shadow looked great against my brown eyes and caramel skin, and the wine-colored lipstick accentuated my pout. This outfit was a bit much though, just barely fitting. If I ate one sandwich, I would burst out of it like Ursula burst out of that wedding dress at the end of *the Little Mermaid.*

The black leather stretched tautly over my ass and hips, while the bustier-like top had my titties pushed damn near up to my chin. Thank God for Spanx! I blew a curl from my eye as Tash adjusted the giant black, lace wings behind me. Watching her in the mirror, I admired the way the gold metallic makeup she wore complimented her deep skin tone, making her look more like an Egyptian goddess than a good angel. The white one-piece flattered her modelesque frame.

"Yasss, bitch! You better look like one of the devil's

sexy helpers!" she shouted, looking me over, causing me to laugh.

"Let's just go before I pop out of this shit!" I said, while carefully exhaling, something I didn't plan to do a lot of tonight.

She laughed, grabbing her purse and keys from my bed. "I'm sure niggas won't mind if you pop out!"

"Umm..." I paused, trying to get my coat over the colossal wings.

"Girl, be cute about it. Drape," she instructed, draping her coat lightly over her shoulders.

I sucked my teeth, "Bitch, it's cold!" I complained.

"We only gotta go to the car," she insisted.

Giving in, I imitated her, gingerly placing my coat over my shoulders, and grabbed my things.

"Oh shit! Wait!" she said, digging inside of her purse.

I watched as she pulled out a black tube and drew a little 'V' at the base of her throat. On Instagram, Venom always posted his female fans with the marking, signifying that they were marked for him. He took this vampire theme a little too far at times, but he was sexy enough to get away with it.

"Your turn!" she said, nodding towards my dresser.

"Tuh! Girl please! I wish I would waste my Ruby Woo!" I laughed.

"Suit yourself!" she grinned, making a face at me before checking herself out in my mirror once more.

2

JULES

WORKIN' me, she workin' me (work, work)
  Urgin' me, it be urgin' me
  Just let up the top and close the curtain please (skrr, skrr)
  I decided to go up like Major League (goin' up)
  She just popped the perky just like pork and beans (perky)
  She just popped the perky, say I hurt her knees (perky)
  She hurtin' me, wrist strong, Hercules (hurtin' me)
We listened to Quavo's "*Working me*," as we sped up 95, in Tash's red Charger.

"So, you really gonna cheat on Riq?" I inquired, already knowing that she wasn't.

Grinning sheepishly, she took her eyes off of the road for a split second, glancing at me, "No. But maybe he needs to think that!" she yelled over the music.

Sucking my teeth, I reached over to turn the volume down, "Why?!" I asked, genuinely befuddled.

Her and Tyriq were couple goals in my mind. They both had good jobs, but still made time for each other. You rarely saw one without the other, and there had never been any accusations of him running around. Sure, sometimes they argued like an old married couple, but even that was cute.

She sighed, "Jules, we been together four years. Don't you think he should have proposed by now? He won't even talk about marriage or kids! I blame myself. When we moved in together, my grandmom told me I was giving him the milk for free, so why buy the cow? I'm not getting any younger and I'm starting to think we want different things."

I bit my tongue, not wanting to tell her that Riq had asked me for help with ring shopping. He was planning on proposing to her on Valentine's day!

"I mean, you see that ring Porsha got?!"

My mouth dropped, "Bitch, I know you not comparing your real ass relationship to a fucking reality show?!" I snapped at her for bringing up some damn Atlanta housewives.

"No!" she laughed, "but...that ring though!"

Shaking my head, I laughed at her, "You stupid! Seriously though, just be patient. That man loves you. Putting up with all your crazy. Don't throw away gold, searching for gold plated," I advised, pursing my lips, wishing I could be in a relationship just *half* as perfect as hers.

"I know. I just needed to blow off some steam. Besides, I'm really hoping to hook you up with Venom. You know he just got signed to a major label! Hurry up and get yo' ass in on the ground floor, bitch!"

We laughed our asses off, cracking jokes the rest of

the short ride to Philly. My boo could always cheer me up. When we arrived at our destination, the *G Lounge,* in Olde City, of course, we couldn't find parking. We ended up a few blocks away in a parking garage. Deciding to leave our coats and purses in the car, I grabbed my phone, lipstick, and my ID and some cash, shoving everything down inside of my cleavage, and prepared to brace the cold.

"Goddamn!" Tash shouted, as we hit the street and a gust of wind whipped around our bare shoulders.

"Uhm hmm," I mumbled knowingly. "Tryna be cute!" I exclaimed, rubbing my arms and putting some pep in my step.

My feet were already sore from my ten-hour shift earlier, and these four-inch, black, over the knee boots weren't helping, but I was tired of complaining, so I sucked it up, and powerwalked next to Tash. People in costumes were everywhere. Nurses, vampires, cats, and zombies paraded around the area. The thing they all had in common was they were all dressed sexy and scantily. Even the zombies. And they all had those dumbass 'V' marks on their necks.

"I can't!" I said, chuckling.

"This jawn litty!" Tash squealed, as we noticed even more people gathered around the club.

I frowned noticing the line, "I don't suppose you know somebody at the door?" I asked, hoping to cut the line.

"No. But it shouldn't be that long," she insisted.

"Ohh, y'all look cute!" a voice behind us exclaimed.

"Thank you," I said, turning around, spotting two

girls dressed like they were from Wakanda. "So do you!" I complimented, looking at their colorful makeup.

Tash started chatting it up with them, like usual. The girl could run her mouth non-stop to anybody. She's the one who should've been in customer service! I stood there, trying to keep warm while the line slowly inched up. That's when I noticed two big men, dressed in black, slowly surveying the long line. Tapping Tash, I nodded towards them, and we watched as they pulled two girls out of line. The girls squealed with joy, while I watched on, confused as fuck. As the men, followed by the two girls dressed as cats, got closer, they stopped at the Wakandians in back of us.

One of the men grinned, "Wakanda forever! Y'all wanna skip the line and possibly meet Venom?" he asked.

"Do it for the culture," he joked, still surveying their outfits.

The girls looked at each other and smiled, shrugging their shoulders and jumping out of line. I noticed one of the men staring at me and Tash.

"Angel and devil, y'all wanna come?"

"Angel. Devils not marked," the one who thought he was funny looked at my throat.

Tash cut her eyes at me with a *Bitch, if you fuck this up* look.

"What?! I was marked; it must have rubbed off!" I lied, quickly.

"You can't come without it," he insisted.

Digging in my cleavage, while they watched with raised eyebrows, I pulled out my wine-colored lipstick.

"That's not red," one informed me.

I sucked my teeth, "It is! It's just a darker red," I irritably informed them.

"Nah. Angel, you coming?" They looked to Tash.

"No," she said, clearly disappointed, but standing next to me.

"Wait!" one of the Wakandians said, reaching into her colorful Kenta head wrap.

She fumbled around until she pulled out a tube of lipstick and quickly walked over to me, drawing a *V* on my neck.

"All good?" she asked, looking to the men in black.

They shrugged, "Let's go!"

Tash jumped up and down in excitement, while I mouthed a *thank you* to the girl. Tash would have probably killed me if I had cost her getting to see Venom up close and personal. We fell in line, following who I now figured were probably Venom's bodyguards or something. My bestie squeezed my hand excitedly, and I couldn't front, I was a little geeked up too, that was, until a familiar voice called out to me.

"Jules!" my cousin Nikki called from her place in line.

I turned, just as she flung her long, red, Poetic Justice braids over her shoulder. She wore a pair of cat ears, a black see-thru top and leather pants. Her friend Stacy, stood next to her, dressed similar.

"Hey, Nikki," I said blandly.

"Where y'all going?! Can you get us in?" she pleaded.

I didn't really want to, but this was my cousin. Sighing, I called out to the men, causing them to stop and focus on me.

"Is there room for my cousin and her friend?" I asked.

They looked over Nikki and Stacy as they tried their best to strike sexy poses.

"We already got cats. Just one of y'all."

I looked at Nikki and shrugged, expecting her to stay with her friend, but instead, she spat,

"Bye gurl! I'll see you inside!" she said, practically running over next to me, leaving her friend with her mouth gaped open.

"Um mmmm," Tash whispered next to me, shaking her head.

I don't know why Stacy or I was shocked. Nikki always been about Nikki. We marched along, with Nikki's giant heels click-clacking behind us.

"Girl, I'm too hype!" Tash whispered excitedly as we bypassed security and headed downstairs to the main floor.

"Me too!" I admitted, giving her hand a tight squeeze.

"Where's Venom?!" Nikki asked, damn near yelling, while rubbing her hands together like Birdman, causing me to roll my eyes.

No matter what she did, she managed to get under my skin.

"You can go mingle. If he's interested, he'll come find you," we were told.

I can't even lie and say I wasn't disappointed.

"What?! How is he gonna even know who we are?! Just take me to wherever he at and I'll handle it from there!" Nikki insisted, sounding thirstier than usual.

"We didn't even pick you! You in here as a favor! So chill the fuck out! He sees everything. Believe me; he's watching right now. So go fall back and get a drink or something," one of the men snapped.

Nikki folded her arms across her chest and rolled her eyes. The man dipped off, obviously annoyed, disappearing into the thick crowd, while the other was shooting his shot with one of the girls from Wakanda.

"This shit wack! I shoulda went to one of my nigga's cribs!" Nikki pouted.

"Why don't we just get some drinks, dance and have fun?" I suggested, trying not to let her ruin the first night I've been out in what felt like forever.

She looked at me and Tash with the stank face, "That shit lame. I'mma go bag a baller until I find Venom. Y'all have fun though," she finished sarcastically, switching her surgically enhanced cheeks away from us.

"That bitch really blows me, man!" I said, balling up my fist like an Arthur meme.

"Don't worry 'bout Raggedy Ann. Let's turn up until your man come find you," she said, waving her fingers around magically.

I laughed, "Nigga probably somewhere getting lit and y'all trying to make the shit seem mystical."

We laughed, and danced our way over to the bar, and waited to order drinks, while twerking to the bass-filled *Mo Bamba* by Shek Wes. This beat was sick and I lost it every time it came on. Before I knew it, a nigga was dancing behind me, and I was enjoying myself, so I let him. Of course, he tried me, whispering sweet Henny in my ear. Laughing lightly, I politely declined his offer and turned to at least see what he looked like.

I laughed harder when I saw his son's Batman mask sitting tightly over his face. I could tell he was about to be persistent and make me get rude, but thank God Tash yelled my name over the music. She was at the other end of the bar, holding up a drink.

"Be right back," I lied quickly, hurrying away, trying to get lost in the crowd.

"Girl," I said, placing a hand on my friend's shoulder, while taking the drink from her.

"I saw," she laughed.

Looking at the drink, I noticed it was red, and raised a brow. "What's this?" I asked, swirling it around and noticing that there were tiny pieces of something floating around.

"They tailored all of the drinks to fit Venom! I got you a blood orange Nightingale! Mines is called Victim's Last Sunrise," she said, holding up her black, orange and yellow drink.

Chuckling, I shook my head, "Does everybody know Halloween is over or am I in a time warp?" I questioned, downing the drink, which burned slightly but had a surprisingly sweet after taste.

Shrugging her shoulders, Tash sipped hers, while I looked around, taking in the Décor. I'd only been here a few times before, but it definitely looked different in here. All of the lights were red, giving everyone a crimson glow as they danced shoulder to shoulder.

"Damn, that was good. Let me get another one," I said, digging inside my large cleavage for my cash, that was now sticky with sweat.

Tash nodded in agreement, waving her hand at the cute, chocolate bartender. Once he noticed her, he smiled, revealing straight white teeth and dimples. I'll be damned if he didn't look like fine ass from *Queen Sugar* and *Girls Trip*. When he walked over, Tash batted her lashes and requested two more drinks.

When he walked away to prepare them, I said, "Tyriq gon' fuck you up!"

She laughed, waving me off, "I'm just flirting. He'll be aight!"

When cutie pie came back, he sat our glasses on a napkin in front of us and waved off the twenty I tried to hand him.

"Venom said y'all drink free."

My eyes widened as I quickly looked around, but I didn't see him anywhere. He walked away to help other customers leaving Tash and I shocked.

"Bitch, is he watching us somewhere?!"

"I don't know," she shrugged, "but shit, drinks on him!" she cheered, holding up her glass.

Catching a glimpse of myself in the mirrored wall behind the bar, I couldn't help but admire how fly I looked...except for the damn 'V' on my throat. I know it was all in fun, but to me it symbolized me waiting for some man to pick me. I'd wasted enough years being dumb over a nigga. *Never again.* Picking up the napkin, I dipped a tiny piece inside of my glass and scrubbed my neck until the red lipstick faded from my skin.

After the second drink, I was feeling it! I was hot, damn near overheating, but still tryna dance. Glancing around again, I did a double take, thinking the liquor was causing my eyes to play tricks on me. Squeezing them shut, I looked again. Sure enough, it was Rich, with his corny ass! Judging by the black Kangol he wore and the heavy gold chains, I knew he was supposed to be Nino Brown.

Watching him all in some girl's face, after what he did to me, had me pissed! No, pissed wasn't even the word to describe my anger. I was enraged and ready to pull a real-life Nino and cancel that bitch nigga! Snatching Tash, who was dancing next to me, I pointed through the crowd. Once she saw what I was pointing at, her confused expression turned to shock.

"Jules, don't–"

"Uh uhn!" I cut her off, marching over to my target.

I could feel her following behind me, but the blood rushing in my ears wouldn't let me hear, feel or focus on anything other than Rich. When he finally noticed me marching towards him, his eyes widened in surprise, before he tried to play it off.

"You calling me from anybody phone that'll let you use it, begging like a simp, but you out here at somebody party in the next chick face?!" I screamed at him, so close I could smell the Queen Helen lotion he piled on underneath that damn Polo Black.

He looked like a deer in headlights for a second before he regained his fake ass composure.

"Look ma. I'ont know what you talking about, but that shit we had is dead," he lied, trying to save face.

My mouth dropped, but I quickly picked it up, snatched the cup from his hand and threw the drink in his face, attracting attention from the crowd.

"Yeah! That's how you feel?! Nigga, did you even take your antibiotics or you still out here spreading chlamydia, you fuckin' wildfire!"

"Bitch, you tripping!" he snapped, tightly gripping my arm.

I smiled, 'cause he knew good and well that was the

wrong move. A lesson that everybody should have learned early on is don't push a motherfucka when they close to the edge, and baby, my ass was free falling! Tash stepped in, trying to push him off of me, while I calmly snatched up the bottle that he, no doubt, was trying to fraud with and cracked him over the head with it. The music stopped, and the sound of the shattering glass made its own rhythm. He fell to the floor as his blood ran from his shiny, curly hair and down the side of his face.

Some people gasped while others laughed. Looking over at the girl he was talking to, to see if she wanted this smoke, I noticed her slowly backing away and disappearing into the crowd. Smart girl. Holding onto a chair, Rich tried to regain his balance, but I kicked it, causing him to fall again.

Suddenly, I was gripped up from behind and lifted off my feet. Security snatched up Tash as well, and she automatically started swinging, catching one of the big, burly men in the eye.

"GET OFF HER!" I screamed, as they started to grip her more roughly.

"Get them the fuck outta here!" the one carrying me yelled, as I twisted and turned, trying to get out of his grasp.

We were carried through the club towards a back entrance with us screaming, kicking and biting the entire way.

"Yo! Big Mike, they cool," a voice spoke, but because I was thrown over someone's shoulder, I couldn't see who was speaking.

"Nah. Venom, man, I know you paid for all this, but I gotta follow the rules."

Did this nigga say *Venom*?! Struggling again, I was able to turn my head slightly, enough to see some fresh black, red and green Gucci sneakers and some fitted black Balmain jeans. Turning my head the other way, I saw Tash, who was in the middle of being dragged out, on the floor, mouth wide open, staring in the direction of who I was pretty fucking sure was Venom!

"I hate to repeat myself, so this gon' be my last time. I said, they good."

It was silent for a moment, before I felt myself being lowered back to my feet. The blood that rushed to my head from being upside down had me slightly dizzy, but I quickly shook it off and focused on Venom. His neatly manicured dreadlocks were freshly twisted and hung to his waist in long, black waves. The smooth brown skin that covered his handsome face was so flawless it looked filtered. A neatly trimmed beard and mustache framed his thick, wet looking lips and the fang grill he always wore. His eyes...well, of course, they had to be contacts the way that the green, gray and purple swirled around, but they were burning a hole through me, almost as if he could see my soul.

Tattoos covered almost every inch of his lean but muscular body. As he stepped closer, the smell of Sandalwood, Jasmine, and something earthy that I couldn't quite place, began to permeate my senses. He grinned as he looked at me, while I'm sure I looked as stuck as I felt. Grinning, he bared his fangs completely, before reaching out a hand to pull Tash up from the floor. It felt as if I was in a trance, seeing Tash smile, while Venom spoke to the security team. I could see everyone's lips moving, and the security eventually leaving, but I couldn't hear a thing. I wasn't even sure if I was breathing. All I could do was stare at Venom in awe.

Finally, his attention landed back on me. He sized me up, starting at my feet, trailing his eyes up my body until his sight stopped at my face. I felt Tash nudge me, but I still couldn't move, staring at the unreal sexiness in a six foot three package standing in front of me. Snapping his fingers in front of my face, the light flickered off of the gold and diamond encrusted skull ring that he wore, shaking me from my paralyzed state.

Music and voices from inside of the club immediately pounded in my ears, and I exhaled, feeling like I'd been holding my breath the entire time.

He chuckled, "You aight?" he asked in his deep, raspy voice, so close I could smell the peppermint on his breath, from his gum.

"Y-yeah..." I mumbled, before clearing my throat, "I mean, yea I'm straight," I spoke with a little more confidence, nervously finger combing my curls.

He nodded, "So y'all ready?"

"Ready for what?" I asked.

Tash discreetly pinched my side, "To go to VIP! Security said we can't go back inside the main part, but we can stay as long as we don't leave the VIP area," she informed me.

"Oh! Oh ok. Um, sure, I guess."

Venom nodded and led the way. Instead of going back through the club, he led us to a small stairwell and gestured for us to go up before him. Tash led and I followed behind her, careful not to trip in my heels. I looked over my shoulder and caught Venom watching my ass as I climbed the steps in front of him. Feeling myself blush, I quickly turned my head and put a little pep in my step.

Tash stopped at a door, and we waited for Venom to walk past us and use his VIP key card. Opening the door, we slid past him and entered the room, which was decked out like a cute little cocktail lounge. As we stepped further inside, heads spun in our direction. Good looking guys were scattered about, and a few cute girls were dancing. The alcohol and good times seemed to be flowing plentifully.

"Bitch, I think that's Meek Mill! And is that Lucky Farigamo he talking to?!" she whispered excitedly, nodding towards the far corner. "I'm 'bout to go see if they hiring!"

"Hiring for what!?" I responded, confused as hell.

Last time I checked, this bitch cleaned ass and portioned out pills!

"I pick out all of Tyriq's clothes. If I can style him, I can style them niggas! Tuh!" she replied, flipping her hair over her shoulder and sashaying over.

Laughing, I shook my head at her shenanigans and glanced around. Fluffing my hair and straightening my skin tight outfit, that had gotten slightly twisted from the earlier manhandling, I prepared to go have a drink.

"Oh!" I said in surprise.

Venom had appeared right in front of me, which was weird because he wasn't there half a second ago. Nervously, I took the drink he was offering, from his hand and downed it, trying to calm my anxiousness. With a serious face, he watched me the entire time. Finally, I mustered up the courage to speak,

"What?" I asked, referring to him staring at me.

Reaching out his hand, his finger brushed my neck. I almost jumped from the icy chill of his touch, which for some odd reason, felt electric against my hot skin.

"Where's your 'V'?" he inquired, with a hint of a smirk.

It took me a moment to realize what he was talking about. Placing a hand on my hip and putting all of my weight on one foot, I looked up at him and frowned,

"It's in my pants where it belongs," I said with attitude.

His eyes widened before he threw his head back and laughed, showing off his pretty white teeth. I marveled at how realistic his fang grill appeared, prompting me to ask about them.

"How do you eat with those?"

"I eat fine. I've never gotten any complaints," he responded seriously, running his tattooed hand over his lips and beard.

Catching on to the innuendo, I felt my face flush with embarrassment, "I didn't mean–"

"I know what you meant, but I said what I said," he shrugged. "What's your name?"

Am I really standing here flirting with Venom?! I thought to myself, trying to remember what my mama named me!

"Jules. Now what's yours?"

"You came here to see me and you don't know my name?"

"I meant your real name. I know your mom didn't name you Venom."

He nodded, but instead of answering my question, he asked his own, "What's up with you and ol' boy that you smacked up?"

Fidgeting with my hair, I shrugged, "Just an ex."

"Like, an ex ex, or just an ex?"

I laughed, "Definitely ex ex! Why you wanna know?" I flirted.

"Shit, 'cuz its probably a warrant out for your arrest and I don't need the cops bustin' up my party."

Not expecting that response, my eyes widened, and I sucked in a breath in surprise, "I can leave your little fuck ass party!" I snapped, spinning on my heels, feeling played.

Marching back towards the way we'd entered, I shook my head, "Nut ass nigga!" I mumbled to myself.

Just as I reached the door, a cold hand grasped my wrist, "Yo, chill! I was only joking!"

I turned, staring at his handsome face, "Not funny. I really might have a warrant," I said, the realization that I'd cracked somebody over the head with a bottle starting to sink in.

"My fault. You was with me in VIP all night," he said.

I smiled, "You gon' lie for me?" I asked, raising my brows.

"On God, I will... if you chill with me for the rest of the party."

Smiling even harder once I realized that he was still holding onto my wrist, I pretended to think about it, even though in my mind it was a closed case!

"Fine, but no more jokes. Leave that shit to Kevin Hart and them. Focus on rapping," I told him, patting his chest and internally rejoicing feeling his toned muscles.

"Damn! Most women laugh at my jokes," he said, pretending to be hurt.

"That's 'cuz they dick riding. Don't expect that shit

from me," I said, switching away from him, heading back inside of the lounge.

"That's cool. You ain't gotta ride it," he spoke behind me.

Sucking my teeth, I looked over my shoulder at him, giving him a warning look.

"What?" he asked, innocently.

Shaking my head, I laughed at him, and took a seat on one of the small red couches. Plopping down next to me, he placed an arm behind my shoulder. I was feeling real comfortable next to him, and was about to start asking him questions about his personal life, like what the hell prompted this whole vampire image thing, but Tash and Lucky Farigamo, the East coast Suge Knight, walked over. Glancing from Venom to me, Tash smiled brightly and took a seat on the arm of the couch near me, while Lucky was watching her like she was his next meal.

"I hate to interrupt," Lucky said, eyeing me. "but it's about that time."

Venom grinned, "Word? Let's do this shit then."

Leaning towards me, he whispered in my ear, "Wait right here or I'm turning your ass in," he said.

Laughing, I fake pouted, as he stood and dipped off with Lucky.

Tash quickly took his seat and we looked at each other before letting out excited little shrieks.

"This is the best night ever! I got a picture with Meek, Lucky's thinking about hiring me as an assistant, and you cozying up with Venom!! Girl, is it a full moon or something?!"

"Bitch, I don't know but it's definitely crazy! And

umm, Lucky big ass looking at you like you a whole meal, bih! I bet he is thinking about hiring your ass!" I smirked.

"Well, you know, had to turn the charm on!" she smiled broadly.

"So what is the fucking deal with Venom?! Y'all looked booed the fuck up over here!"

"We just chilling. He's different than I thought he would be. He's actually cool!"

"Yasss! I like it! Jules Venom."

"Girl, that is not his last name!" I screamed in laughter.

Suddenly the music stopped, causing us to look around.

"Yo! If I didn't tell y'all yet, some of you ladies looking right in these costumes! And some of y'all, I'm glad you got a costume on!" the rude ass DJ spoke into the mic, causing the crowd to go crazy with laughter.

"My man Venom got a few good ones to pick from!"

At the mention of Venom, the crowd went crazy, and for some reason, I got pissed.

"Come on!" Tash said, pulling my hand, leading us towards the small balcony, so we could look into the club.

Squeezing past plenty of groupies, we looked out at the hyped crowd. Spotting Nikki, I frowned as she pushed her way closer to the stage.

"We got a special guest in the building! Head honcho Lucky Farigamo!" he yelled into the mic as Lucky walked onto the stage, looking like money in his tailored, burgundy suit, and jewels blinking heavily in the flashing lights.

Crime Boss, a single from one of the artists on his label

who'd been gunned down years ago blasted as his theme music, while we all went crazy reciting the lyrics.

Once he grabbed the mic, the DJ cut the music again.

"Appreciate it, fam," Lucky spoke.

"If y'all don't know, I only move for a reason. I'm making a big move tonight, if you didn't figure it out yet. I'm here to formally introduce my newest artist. The newest member of the family!"

We all cheered. I don't know why it took me so long to put two and two together! Venom was signing with Lucky! Shit, I was cheering like I was shooting with him in the gym!

"Aye Venom! Come grab this chain, nigga! This shit heavy!" Lucky shouted, holding up the trademark, *Nightmares On Wax Record Label* iced out chain, which was a platinum skeleton spinning a diamond encrusted record.

In a cloud of smoke, Venom appeared on stage, leaving everyone baffled, but soon the uproar started again, as he smiled handsomely, and approached Lucky so he could put his chain on him.

"Lucky, this the best move you ever made!" he shouted, using both hands to hold up his chain.

The club went completely dark, and loud thunder crackled, before red lights flashed, and a deep booming beat poured through the speakers.

PULL UP IN A ROASTER WIT' *Lucky/*
Get wit' me, girl, you lucky/
Cause my power so ancient got the opps tryna duck me/

. . .

NIGHT ON ME, girl got you/
  Didn't know I been spot you/
  Take over Philly now they down wit' that Nosferatu

HE BEGAN HYPNOTICALLY RAPPING the lines to a new song, and Tash and I twerked, enjoying the fire he was delivering. We laughed and danced for the next hour as he performed banger after banger. Feeling someone staring at me, I turned, noticing a tall, honey-colored woman with long, black hair watching me intently. Even when I caught her looking, she continued to peer at me until finally, she rolled her eyes and walked off.

"Did you see that bitch?!" I asked Tash, who was still engrossed in the free concert below.

"Who?" she asked, giving me her undivided attention.

"Nothing," I said, not wanting to get us kicked out for a second time that night.

Finally, Venom finished, and the DJ made the closing announcement. People began filing out, and I didn't know if I should leave or wait around for Venom. The fantasy of being with him was beginning to wear off after the way that chick looked at me earlier. I was tired of fighting over niggas, and I was only fooling myself if I thought anything serious could come from me and Venom.

"You ready?" I asked Tash.

"You not gonna wait for your boo?" she asked in disbelief.

I shook my head, "Nah. I had fun, but I'm ready to go."

"Okayy," she spoke, drawing it out, while giving me a confused look.

Most of the VIP crowd were still lounging around, probably waiting on Venom. I glanced around for the bitch with the eye problem, but I didn't see her. Opening the door, I gasped, seeing Venom standing there, looking dead at me.

How the fuck does this nigga keep popping up?!

"Thought I asked you to wait for me, Jules?"

Oh my God, my name sounded like butter, flowing from his tongue.

"I was but, but I didn't want you to cut your fun short. Congratulations on signing!" I said, glancing at the giant medallion laying against his chest.

"Yes! You did that shit! Just be careful! Lucky artists always getting shot!" Tash spoke next to me.

Venom chuckled, "Thanks. I ain't worried about that though," he said, turning his attention back to me.

"You was really gonna skate without giving me your number?" he asked.

Trying to suppress my smile, I was just about to give in and give it to him, when the woman from earlier walked up behind him. My smile faded as we made eye contact.

"Venom, baby, I'm ready to go home," she said, playing in his hair.

Chuckling, I shook my head.

"Home?!" Tash spat.

"Let's just go," I said, trying to push past him.

"Serina, take your ass on!" he yelled, moving his head away from her hands.

"Venom! You fronting for this bitch?!" she said,

turning her misplaced anger on me.

"Bitch, I'm not the one you wanna see!" I spat, balling up my fist, ready to fuck her silly ass up if she jumped bad.

"Serina! You heard what the fuck I said!" Venom shouted, causing her to jump.

Tears welled in her eyes as she looked from me to him before turning and running down the steps. I took that moment to pull Tash and brush past him.

"Jules!" he yelled, following us down the stairs.

"What?!" I shouted once we got to the bottom.

"How I'mma get in contact with you?" he asked.

Rolling my eyes, I stared at him in disbelief, "Nigga, you just chased your girlfriend off and you still tryna get my number!? You niggas are unbelievable!" I spazzed, shaking my head.

"It's not what you think. Let me take you out and I can explain everything," he said, following us outside into the cold, early morning air.

"Nah. I'm not with it. You Dracula or whatever, do some mind tricks and figure out my number," I replied smartly.

"Jules!" he said, grabbing my arm to stop me from walking. "I promise it's not like that. Fuck with a nigga and find out," he insisted.

Looking up into his colorful eyes, I saw a hint of sincerity, and as stupid as I felt, I was close to giving in. Folding my arms across my chest, I looked around at people stumbling to their cars, probably ready to hit a diner for a late-early breakfast. I did everything I could to divert my eyes from his, until he placed his heavy, leather jacket around my shoulders.

"Umm, I'mma go warm up the car," Tash said, making an excuse to exit.

"You gon' give me a chance?" he asked, cupping my chin with his fingers so that I had to look at him.

"I guess." I sighed.

He smiled as if he'd accomplished a goal, "Give me your number," he demanded.

"Nope. I was serious. If you want me that bad then find me," I told him, smirking and walking away with his jacket.

He stood there, and I could feel him watching me. Putting the jacket all the way on, I turned to say something about him staring at my ass, but stopped when I noticed a black car with tints slow rolling towards us. Something about it didn't feel right. Slowly, the window lowered, and the barrel of a gun poked through.

"VENOM!" I screamed.

POP!

POP!

POP!

Quickly, he turned, spotting the approaching danger. He jumped on me just as the shots rang out. I hit the cold concrete hard and heard the screeching of tires and the screams of the party goers who were still milling about.

"VENOM!" I screamed, scared because he wasn't moving.

I breathed a sigh of relief when he slowly lifted himself.

"Oh my God!" I shouted.

"You aight?!" he asked, slowly standing and pulling me to my feet.

I nodded, still in shock. Looking at the ground, I

noticed the blood and began frantically patting myself. I'd heard stories about people who were shot, but because of an adrenaline rush, they didn't realize it until they'd practically bled out! When I was sure it wasn't me, I looked at Venom. Blood was beginning to seep through his white shirt.

"Venom! You've been shot!" I yelled, trying to find his wound so I could apply pressure.

"V!" the men from earlier came running up.

I'd rightly assumed they were his bodyguards.

"Man, you dipped out without us! Oh shit, he's hit! Go get the car!"

"I'm cool!" he said, as we all fussed over him. "It's just my arm," he informed us.

"We gotta get you outta here before the cops come!" his bodyguard said, as the other one pulled up in a black, Cadillac truck.

"Come with me," Venom said, holding out his hand.

Just as I reached for it, Tash's Charger came squealing up, causing Venom's bodyguard to reach for his hip, until he saw her behind the wheel.

"Oh my God! I heard gunshots! Boo, you okay?!" she asked, her eyes big as she watched the bodyguard wash Venom's blood from the ground with a bottled water.

"I'm good," I told her, wondering why washing the ground was necessary.

"Well shit, come on! Let's go!" she exclaimed.

I looked to Venom as I walked towards her car. He smiled, holding his thumb and pinky finger to his face, gesturing that he would call. I just looked at him as I hopped in her car. When we pulled off, I remembered that I never gave him my number.

3

VENOM

"Why would you leave without us?!" Corey yelled, while driving recklessly down Claremont Avenue.

Unable to answer him, I gritted my teeth as Sypher dug around the burning hole in my shoulder, pulling out the bullet that struck me in front of the club. Breathing a sigh of relief, I leaned back into the leather seats, feeling the burning beginning to subside.

"Because I don't need fuckin' bodyguards!" I gritted.

I hated that my Father insisted on 24/7 security for me. Corey and Sypher were cool, but they were pretty much hired, human babysitters. Unnecessary for a hundred-year-old vampire.

"Its silver," Sypher said, grimly, after rinsing the bullet off with water and examining it.

I made a face at his obvious conclusion. I already knew it was silver from the way it easily pierced my flesh and caused my blood to boil. A regular bullet would have simply bounced off of me like they had plenty of times before.

"Silver?! Man, your pops gon' dig in our asses behind this!" Corey said, making a sharp right turn, beeping his horn at drivers in his path.

"Nigga, man the fuck up! Shit's healing already!" I snapped, watching my seared flesh piecing itself back together like Humpty Dumpty.

"Man, I know you can handle yourself, but silver? You know that's gotta be the Rogue Vampire Squad," Sypher spoke next to me, still examining the silver bullet with a frown on his face.

The squad that he spoke of were basically a bunch of lame, immortal, haters that didn't have the balls or the charisma for the limelight like I did, so instead of staying in their own mediocre lane, they insisted on trying to dim my light. Always worried about what could happen if the humans ever figured out I was a real vampire! I hid in the shadows for most of my life, and I was tired of it! Shit, my first twenty years I didn't even know I could go out in the sunlight. Fuck outta here if they think I'mma keep hidin'!

"I know who it was and fuck them niggas!" I said.

"Venom–" Corey started.

"I SAID FUCK THEM NIGGAS!" I shouted, causing him to shut up and shake his head silently.

Taking a few minutes to calm myself before I did something I would regret, my mind wandered to Jules. Shorty probably saved my life. If that bullet would have hit my chest, instead of my shoulder, I'd be dust right now.

"Where's Serina?" I asked, pissed at the way she acted tonight, but still concerned about her safety.

"She's good. We sent her home with Lexi," Sypher responded.

I nodded, relaxing the rest of the quiet ride to the Vampire court. I'd deal with Serina when I got home. When we finally made it to Germantown, it was close to five a.m., and my shoulder had completely healed. Corey parked in front of the large home on West Washington Lane and killed the engine.

"Hold on," Sypher said, wrapping the bullet in tissue and pushing it down in his pocket, before grabbing the gun from his waist and cocking it.

Stepping out, he went to the back of the house, making sure the area was secure before letting out a high-pitched whistle, letting Corey and I know it was safe to exit the vehicle. Sighing, I swung open the door and stepped out, followed by Corey, who still hadn't said a word since I snapped on him earlier. He and Sypher had done security for me for almost three years now, and we had formed a bit of a friendship.

I knew he was genuinely concerned about my well-being and I was starting to feel a little bad for not controlling my temper better. Corey had taken two bullets for me in the past, and I knew he wouldn't hesitate to do it again.

"You cool?" I asked him, trying to strike up a conversation before I had to sit with the Court.

"Straight," he responded, tight-lipped.

I sighed, 'cuz he wasn't gonna make this shit easy.

"Corey, man, I ain't mean no disrespect back there. You know how I get. I don't like to keep talking about the same shit," I explained.

"I feel you, brother. I'm just concerned with these attacks becoming more frequent."

"I'mma handle it. Long as you still got my back."

"Say less," he said, holding out his fist.

I dapped him up, before jogging up the stairs. Now that the sentimental shit was out of the way, it was time to explain to my Father and the rest of the Vampire Court, that I'd been shot at, yet again. Knocking on the security door, I waited, hearing the quiet footsteps of Butch, the house caretaker. He was a quiet, older man, that took care of little things like cleaning, and making sure that the blood from the donors was well maintained and kept at body temperature.

Opening the door, he peered at me with his large brown eyes, trying not to stare at my blood-stained shirt.

"Sup, Butch?" I greeted, stepping past him.

"Venom," he spoke, giving a small bow of his head.

Sypher and Corey followed behind me as I climbed the stairs inside of the modernly decorated family home, while Butch locked up downstairs. The bedrooms had all been converted into offices since most of the Court chose to sleep in the basement. Advancing towards my father's office, his door swung open before I could even knock.

My dad, Xavier, was tall, about my height exactly and brooding. He was the type that would always lose at poker because you could always make out his mood from his facial expressions. He was old as millenniums, but didn't look a day over fifty in human years. Because he was one of the oldest remaining vampires on the planet, he was the head of the Vampire Court in this chapter. Different areas had different courts, but they all worked in tandem with each other.

Lifting a large, glass mug of blood to his lips, he frowned as he surveyed me from head to toe, before giving a death eye to Corey and Sypher behind me.

"Come on and explain to me why you're covered in your own blood!" he growled lowly, stepping to the side.

We entered the large office, and I nodded at Talia, my stepmother and Clay, also members of the Court. Talia gasped, jumping up from her seat in front of my father's desk and rushed over to me, lifting my shirt, examining me for wounds.

"It's healed," I told her, touching my shoulder.

I liked Talia, maybe even loved her. She was the only mother I'd known, since my own human mother died during childbirth. It took a lot out of humans to give birth to a vampire, because we required so much energy. Which is why I made sure all of my women were on special birth control, but I'll get to that later.

"Where in the hell was Tom and Jerry!?" my father yelled, looking at Corey and Sypher.

"Dad, it's my own fault. I got preoccupied and left without them. They found me shortly after and Sypher got the bullet out before it could get infected," I explained.

They gave me a grateful look, but still seemed terrified of my pops. Probably because he'd ripped his old security team apart in front of them.

"Preoccupied?" my father shifted his attention to me. "That can only mean a woman! Don't you have enough?! More than enough?" he grilled me.

"That's besides the point! I'm a grown ass man, and the Court is not here to run my life! You can only give me direction! I ultimately make the last choice! What we should be focused on is the Rogue vamps that keep coming for me! Why haven't they been found!?" I yelled.

Everybody always wanted to harp on my choice of lifestyle instead of handling real business.

"Don't be ungrateful, Venom," Talia whispered in my ear.

"Let me make something clear. THE ONLY REASON YOU HAVE SO MUCH FREE REIGN IS BECAUSE OF WHO I AM! YOU WANTED TO PURSUE THIS LIFE AND THE ONLY REASON YOU ARE FREE TO DO SO IS BECAUSE OF WHO I AM! DON'T YOU EVER FORGET THAT IT'S BECAUSE OF ME AND MY POSITION THAT YOU ARE WHO YOU ARE!" My dad shouted, causing the other Court members to leave their offices and come see what the commotion was about.

This was nothing new; my father hardly ever let me forget his position. Gently moving Talia from in front of me, I walked up to my father and stared in his eyes, which were identical to mine, and clenched my jaw.

"How can I forget when you constantly throw it in my face! I'm grateful to the Court for allowing me to pursue a dream, but I no longer want to be under the protection of the Court," I announced, causing gasps around the large office.

"I'm out," I spoke with finality, taking off the black and gold band from around my middle finger and placing it onto his desk.

Me pretty much leaving the Court meant that I was Rogue, something frowned upon in the vampire community, because we heavily lived by the motto: Family is everything.

"Don't be stupid, Venom. Without the protection–" my father started, but I cut him off.

"WITHOUT THE PROTECTION, WHAT?!" I

snapped, ripping off my shirt and holding it up in front of his face, making sure everyone got a good view of the blood. "THIS IS THE FUCKING PROTECTION?! FUCK THIS SHIT! I'LL CATCH THEM NIGGAS MYSELF AND IN THE MEANTIME, I ANSWER TO NOBODY!" I spat, tossing the shirt at his feet.

I saw the crimson slowly beginning to cloud over his eyes, before he quickly charged at me, but since I knew it was coming, I disappeared swiftly and reappeared behind him.

"You getting slow, old man," I said to his back.

"Stop it! Xavier, Venom, you don't mean this!" Talia shouted, placing a hand on my father's shoulder to calm him.

"Talia's right! Why don't we all take a few days to cool off, and have this discussion again...in a *civilized* manner?" Clay, my father's oldest friend, and my godfather, suggested, giving both of us a look.

"Fine. I'm out," I said, storming past the Court, and down the stairs, Corey and Sypher hot on my trail.

Butch, who was waiting at the door, opened it and I marched through, pausing on the sidewalk, patting my pockets. Pulling out my weed, that was laced with blood to boost my high, I flicked my gold lighter and began to puff. After exhaling a large amount of smoke, I looked to Corey and Sypher as they leaned, uncomfortably, against the truck.

Offering them the blunt, Corey made a face and shook his head, while Sypher reached out to take it.

"Shit, I need something," he said, inhaling.

"Listen, I know the Court pays you, but I'm 'bout to be on my own mission. Y'all pay will come out of my pocket from now on, but I need complete loyalty. You will only answer to me. Communication with the Court is dead! If you not down, let me know now," I said, looking at them both.

They were both quiet, until Sypher finally spoke, "I'm wit you, man. Let's take these Rogue niggas out!" he said, holding out his hand, which I dapped.

I looked at Corey, waiting for his response, while he shook his head and looked towards the sky.

"You do realize what you saying? Disconnecting yourself from the Court means you're a sitting duck! If you think that hit squad was gunning for you before, without the Court, they'll come full force!" he reasoned.

I sighed, "Cor, I know that! You think I'm supposed to be scared?! I want these niggas to come harder! Let them make themselves known! Is you with me or not!?"

"You know I am! I'm just wondering if you thinking this shit through!"

"I always think shit through, but I'm ready to act! Enough of this sitting still bullshit!" I spat, taking my blunt back from Sypher.

"Fine," he said, opening the door and climbing in behind the wheel.

Raising a brow, I shot Sypher a look.

"He cool. You know he always got your back. Nigga just like bitchin'," he laughed.

I laughed too, because I could already start to see the effects of the laced weed on him by his half-closed eyes. After we jumped in the truck, I started to feel tired. The sun would be coming up soon, and that meant it was time for me to lay my neck. I could go out in the sun without turning to dust and shit like that, but the rays still drained my energy. During the short ride to my crib, I checked my phone. My notifications were blowing up as usual, but something stood out.

I was tagged in a few posts. Going to the page, I saw Jules' girl. She had posted pictures with my niggas, Meek and Lucky. She also posted videos of me performing and a picture of me and Jules sitting on the couch. Using my fingers, I enlarged the picture and studied the beauty next to me. She was thick as hell, and had the face of an angel, except those lips. Those lips were straight from Hell.

Tapping the photo, I saw she was tagged and quickly went to her page. Disappointed that it was private, I requested her and went back to the picture.

"Yo, I need you to find out everything you can on her," I said, handing my phone to Sypher.

He looked at it and nodded, "The devil from the party... I'm on it," he said, taking out his own phone and typing something into it. "I'll let you know what I find out tonight."

WE PULLED up to my own house, which wasn't too far from where the Court resided. I said my goodbyes before hopping out and walking up my large stone steps, framed by stone Lion heads on either side. Opening the door, I quickly hit the alarm code so as not to wake up any of my girls, even though I could sense that Serina was up, no doubt in my room. Though I'd told her time and time again that I didn't want anyone in my space unless I invited them.

Walking quietly up the stairs, I checked in each room,

one by one. Opening the first door, I noticed Savalia and Kember, their toned, chocolate bodies tangled around each other as they slept, wildly. Kember had her own room but most of the time she slept in here with Savalia. They'd formed a relationship of their own, which didn't bother me, considering they constantly invited me to join or watch. Savalia was my newest girl, and she was somewhat of an airhead, but very soft spoken and sweet. A genuinely kind person. Rare. The fact that she was beautiful only added to the appeal.

Kember, on the other hand, was overtly sexy, being an ex video vixen. Everything she did or said, made my dick hard. Closing their door, I skipped the next one, since that was Kember's. Moving on, I opened Lexi's door. Lexi was the only one of my girlfriend's who opted to keep her job. She owned a small boutique, that sold crazy accessories. Her shit was popping too. Her drive and her determination to succeed made me crazy over her. Her smooth cinnamon skin and long, bright red hair turned me on too. She was what I call sneaky thick, meaning she was extremely tiny and petite, but when she turned around, her ass was out of this world. She had a pretty face to match and I especially liked when she wore her glasses instead of contacts.

Gazing around her room, I saw that she'd fallen asleep with her laptop open. Shutting it down, I placed it on the charger, before leaving out and shutting her door behind me. Walking past Serina's room, which was right next to mine, I opened my door, not surprised to find her ass naked in the center of my large bed. I could never deny how beautiful she was. It was just lately, her attitude was making her unattractive to me.

She was my first girlfriend and I still had love for her, but I'd fallen out of love with her a long time ago. And she knew it, which is why she came up with the idea for this *cult*, as she called it. Thinking that by bringing in other women, it would somehow keep me satisfied with her. And for awhile, my interest in her did seem to be renewed, but it didn't last long. Serina was a user. She used her looks and intelligence to get everything she desired and for awhile, I played right into her hands, giving her whatever she wanted. That is, until she wanted everlasting life.

She knew that I was not in the business of making new vamps. When a new vamp was made, they and their creator would have a strong mental and emotional bond until one of them died. It was a heavy commitment, and I didn't feel strongly enough about Serina to want to be bonded with her forever. Nonetheless, she continued to apply pressure about it, thinking I would give in.

"Venom! Are you ok?! I heard about the shooting!" she spoke, her large green eyes looking me over.

Damn, she was beautiful. Like Tyra Banks in her prime beautiful. When she licked her soft lips, my dick got hard, but I'd refused to fuck her in months. Her manipulative personality was seeming real suspect to me and I didn't trust that she was still taking the vamp approved birth control my doctor gave all of the girls.

"How did you hear about the shooting?" I asked, looking at her sideways, as I lifted my new chain over my head and shook out my dreads.

"Umm, I do have a phone, Venom! Shots were reported, and I knew it had something to do with you! And where's your ring?!"

I hadn't seen anything about no fuckin' shots fired, but I guess it would be out there. Ignoring her, I undressed and headed to my bathroom, and she hopped up following me.

"What's happening to us?" she asked, watching me turn on the faucet.

I chuckled, "Now you wanna have a talk about where we stand?! When I wanted to have this talk two years ago, you know what your solution was?! To bring more bitches into the relationship!" I snapped, turning to face her.

"I was only trying to make you happy! I didn't expect for you to develop real feelings for them!"

"Well, I have. I feel more for them than I do for you! At least their shit is genuine! And what the fuck was that stunt you pulled tonight?! I invited Lexi and you insisted on coming with her, then you don't even know your place!" I shouted, closing the bathroom door so the other girls wouldn't wake up.

"Know my place?!" she repeated, "I think I've played my role better than good! That's what this is about?! Another little bitch that you wanna add to your harem?!" she questioned, tears running down her cheeks.

"You started the fucking harem!" I snapped.

"Well, I want to end it! No more! And I want all of these bitches out of here by next week!" she demanded.

I looked at her a moment before laughing in her face, "Fuck outta here! They ain't going nowhere! You can go though. Ain't nobody keeping you here by force! Matter of fact, I want you out my shit tomorrow!"

"No! Venom, why won't you just turn me, and we can–"

"NO!! HOW MANY TIMES DO I HAVE TO SAY IT?!

I'll never turn you, and if I find out you on some scandalous shit, I'll fucking kill you, Serina," I told her, fighting back my slowly extending fangs.

I could feel that something wasn't right with this bitch, but I didn't want to think the worst.

"V, let's calm down and not say anything we'll regret," she said softly, running her blood red nails over my chest.

She slid her fingers down and caressed my dick, causing him to harden and betray me. Before I could move her hands, she dropped to her knees and gobbled me up. Her lips and tongue worked magic, as I let my guard down and enjoyed the sensation of being swallowed down her warm throat. She increased her speed and I gripped her soft, black hair and began fucking her face. I was tryna speed this nut up because although physically it felt amazing, my mind wasn't into it. My thoughts drifted to Jules and her big juicy lips and sultry voice had me close.

"Oh shit!" I shouted, pouring my seed down her esophagus.

She smiled up at me, licking her lips, before slowly standing. She moved her long hair to one side and bared her neck so I could feed. Watching her, I roughly grabbed the back of her neck, pulling her closer as my fangs extended fully. I thought about ripping her vein out, but quickly got myself in check, and plunged my teeth into her skin, savagely biting and sucking the blood from her in the steamy bathroom.

After I'd gotten enough, I forced myself to stop, biting my own lip and sealing her skin with my blood. She looked at me, expecting more, but I opened the door so she would leave.

"Venom, what about me?! You haven't touched me in months!" she whined.

"Go play with a toy," I said, gently pushing her out of the bathroom and locking the door behind her.

She stood there a few moments, before I finally heard her stomp across the room. Shaking my head, I pulled the glass door back and stepped inside of the shower.

4

TASH

"Let me get two number fives and two shrimp eggrolls," I spoke to the Chinese lady in back of the thick bulletproof glass.

You could always tell a hood Chinese spot by that thick ass glass and the niggas runnin' in and out buying grape, cherry or vanilla Dutchies. I got off work early today, thank God, because Ms. Williams had a doctor's appointment that her daughter insisted on taking her to. Fine by me! That meant I could pick up lunch for my bestie, 'cuz I knew she was tired of eating that nasty ass Subway inside of Walmart, and I could get home early and surprise my man with some quality time.

Taking a seat on the graffiti-covered bench, waiting on my order, I texted Jules to let her know that I would be to her in a few minutes. Before she could respond, a call from Lucky came through. I wasn't sure if I wanted to answer. Yes, I had taken my shot, my *professional* shot, but after the first phone conversation I had with him, it was obvious that he was interested in me in a non-professional manner. Lord knows my man got on my last nerve at times, but I loved his dirty drawers and I would never cheat on him.

Clearing my throat, I decided to answer and try and steer the conversation in the direction I wanted it to go.

"Hello," I spoke, trying to sound professional.

"Why you tryna sound like a white girl?" his gruff voice came through the line.

I laughed, even though I didn't want to. "Why does a proper or professional voice have to sound white?" I questioned, rolling my eyes as if he could see me.

"It's a difference between professional and valley girl," he chuckled. "What you doing next weekend?"

"Uh, hold on, let me check my calendar," I told him, frauding like I was busy.

Putting my phone on mute, I grabbed the bag that the little Asian lady was holding up and left out, ignoring the catcalls from the groups of dudes huddled around the front of the store and got inside of my car.

"Looks like I'm free," I said.

"Perfect. You flying to the Bahamas with me," he told me.

"Wait, what?! Is this for business, Lucky? Because I told you last time, I have a man."

"You gotta what?" he asked.

"A man!"

"Oh, I thought you said something important. Anyway, you down or what?"

I sucked my teeth, knowing he had no plans on hiring me for an actual job. He wanted to fly me to some tropical destination, wine and dine me, and probably try to get his dick wet.

"Nah. I'm straight. Bye Lucky," I said, disconnecting the call and shaking my head.

Sighing, I finger-combed my long, high ponytail as I pulled into the parking lot at Jules' job, disappointed that I wouldn't be starting a new glamorous job that would allow me to stunt on hoes. Shooting her a quick text to let her know I was here, I began unpacking the food, pulling out my sweet tea, taking a long sip. Finally, I spotted her walking through the parking lot. She looked tired and those fuckin' khakis was blowing me! I wished she would just come work with me, but her fake bougie ass was determined to stick this shit out. Quickly opening my door, she let in a gust of wind before slamming it and rubbing her hands together.

"Yass bitch! You are a blessing, because I was starving!" she exclaimed, unwrapping her eggroll.

"It ain't about nothing. You would do the same for me." I shrugged.

Jules and I had been besties since our days at Pulaski middle school. We'd grown to be more like sisters. I considered her family more than the bitches that had the same blood as me running through their dusty veins. My mom was a crack fiend and gave me to my grandmother when she decided that the streets were more important than her baby girl. When I was seven, she cleaned herself up, got married and had another daughter.

I remember crying to my grandmother, asking her why the new baby got to live with my mom and not me? My grandma, known as Ms. Sonia around the neighborhood, would hold me until I was all cried out. One night, I heard her arguing with my egg donor, downstairs.

Tiptoeing towards the stairs, I listened, careful not to make a sound, for fear of my grandma catching me and scolding me for being in grown folk's business.

"Trisha! That child is going to grow up to hate you! How do you think she feels, knowing you have another child, but refuse to take her?!"

"Mom, stop it! She's fine here with you! David doesn't think it's a good idea to bring her with us."

"Fuck David! Tasha is your flesh and blood! Where in the world did I go wrong with you?! You getting high again?"

"I'm leaving!"

"Of course you are! That's all you been good for! And don't you worry about Tash! She's better off with me! But you mark my words, you'll need her before she needs you!"

I jumped, hearing the door slam and hurried back to my room, heartbroken that my mother and her new husband didn't want me. Climbing under the covers, I clutched my stuffed Minnie Mouse doll and sobbed, wetting the soft fur. Hearing my door creak open, I tried to hold in my cries.

"Girl, I know you up. I heard your little butt runnin' cross the floor."

Slowly, I turned over as she clicked on the lamp that sat on the dresser next to my bed.

"I'm sorry, mom mom. I heard her voice and-" I stopped, bursting into tears.

She cradled me in her Donna Karen Cashmere Mist scented house coat, "Don't you shed one more tear for her, you hear me? That's your mother and my daughter, but what she's doing ain't right. You gonna be fine. Mom mom loves you and

I'll always want you with me. We fine," she consoled me, forcing me to look into her large, brown eyes, that always reminded me of Diana Ross.

Wiping my face, I nodded my head.

"Want some cookies?" she asked.

Grinning, I nodded my head harder, as she fixed one of my braids that had come loose.

"Tash, you ok?" she asked, pulling me from my memories.

"Yeah... just thinking about some stuff. Lucky called again," I informed her, shaking off the pain of my mother's rejection.

"Oh Gawd!" she spoke with a mouth full of beef and broccoli. "I wish he'd just accept the fact that he ain't getting no ass! Like damn! I guess he's not used to the word *no*, huh?" she asked, swallowing her food and reaching for her tea.

I chuckled, "I suppose he's not. So, have you heard anything from my brother in-law?" I smirked, batting my eyes at her.

She sucked her teeth, "Bitch, no! He requested me on Instagram, and I accepted, but he's done nothing but like random pictures late at night like a damn weirdo."

"Why don't you slide in his DMs?" I suggested, nudging her shoulder.

"I think the fuck not! I refuse to be one of his little occult groupies, with his weird ass!" she announced, twisting up her face, causing me to spit out my tea.

"Stop frontin'! You like his spooky, things that go bump in the night ass!"

She laughed, folding her arms across her chest, "I do not!" she insisted, sounding like a child.

We teased each other for a little longer before she had to clock back in. After cleaning the containers from my car and throwing them in the trash, I pulled out of the parking lot, ready to go spend some time with my man. Driving down one of the streets that was a popular haven for dope fiends, I swiveled my head as I noticed some commotion on one of the corners.

One of the dealers was smacking up a woman who was obviously on drugs from the looks of her uncombed hair, dirty mismatched clothing that was hanging from her undernourished body, and bad skin. A group of guys stood around laughing and recording the foolishness. Shaking my head, I peered over, while at the red light, trying to get a better look.

My mouth fell open when I made eye contact with the familiar face of my mother! My grandmother told me she was supposed to be in a rehab facility up in Connecticut, so what the fuck was she doing here?! I was torn between getting out to help her or pulling off as fast as these four wheels would take me.

When she made eye contact with me, I quickly turned my head and prayed for the light to change.

"TASH!" she screamed in her raspy voice; I assume from years of sucking the pipe.

Nervously, I gripped the steering wheel, refusing to look over, hoping maybe she would get the hint. Nope. She darted away from her dealer and zoomed over to my car like Hussain Bolt and began banging on my window so hard I thought she might crack my glass.

Sighing, I cracked my window, "What do you want, Trisha?"

Scratching her arm, she said, "Baby, can I borrow a few dollars? I promise I'll pay–"

"Hell no!" I yelled, cutting off her lies. "I ain't giving you shit!"

"Tash, just give me ten dollars! I owe that man! You want him to kill your mama over ten dollars?!"

"I don't care what he does to you! If you live or die, it won't phase me!" I spat, ready to pull off.

She gave an evil, toothless grin, looking like a riled-up Jack o Lantern, "What about your grandmother? It would break her heart if something happened to me!"

Sucking my teeth, I pulled over to the side and snatched my purse from the back seat. My love for my grandmother overrode my hatred for my mom. My grandmother hadn't been feeling well for awhile now and she didn't need this bullshit on her plate. I became even more frustrated when I realized I didn't have anything smaller than a fifty-dollar bill.

"Who this?" her dealer asked, walking up behind Trisha as she pressed her dirty face against my window.

She jumped hearing his voice, while I stared at this little young nigga, that looked like he should've had his ass in somebody's biology class instead of out here on the corner, ruining people's lives.

"This my daughter! Ain't she pretty?"

He stared at me, licking his lips, as I got out of my car, heading to the little corner store to get some change. Quickly, I bought a candy bar and a pack of gum while watching over my shoulder, keeping tabs on Trisha and her shady dealer. I didn't trust either one of them! As they talked, they both glanced in my direction, making me feel uncomfortable.

Taking my purchase and my change, I shoved everything inside of my purse except the ten dollars for Trisha. As I walked out, she came rushing up to me on her stick thin legs. I shook my head in disgust at the way she looked and smelled. It was the winter, and nobody had any excuse to be smelling like this!

"Tash," she whispered loudly, glancing around.

"Listen, that's Mike," she nodded towards the young hustler. "He wanna talk to you! Just go back there with him for awhile and then all my shit is free," she smiled, rubbing her hands together.

I looked towards the abandoned houses that she wanted me to go and *talk* and my body trembled with rage, knowing that this woman, who carried me for nine months, was trying to set me up to get raped. Digging in my purse, I pulled out my keys and wrapped my fingers around the small bottle on my key chain, and proceeded to mace the woman that created me.

"AHHH!!" she screamed.

The bitch stopped, dropped and rolled as if she was on fire. Looking towards the dirty dealer, I watched as he shook his head and chuckled, dipping off. Squatting next to my flailing mother, I gripped my fingers in her knotted hair,

"Bitch, next time you see me on the street, act like you don't know me," I gritted, before giving her one more petty squirt, but ended up inhaling some of the shit.

Powerwalking to my car, I put my arm over my nose and mouth so I wouldn't breath in anymore as I coughed. I drove for a couple of blocks before pulling over again.

"AHHHHH!" I screamed, banging on the steering wheel.

There were no words to accurately describe the way I felt. I felt empty and hollow inside. The only thing that let me know I was still alive was the rage coursing through me that was causing my hands to shake. Still, I refused to cry over her. It would be a cold day in hell before another tear would ever slide down my face because of her. After taking a few minutes to get myself together, I called my grandmother, not to tell her about her worthless daughter, but just to hear the voice of someone who actually loved me.

"Hey, mom mom. How you feeling?" I asked.

She let out a phlegm-filled cough before answering, "I'm getting along. Why you sound like something wrong?" she asked.

"Nothing's wrong," I said, attempting to sound normal. "You had that cough for two weeks now and it doesn't sound any better. You make a doctor's appointment yet?" I inquired.

"No, but I will. Now what's the matter? Lord, I hope you didn't let that boy get you pregnant and he ain't put nothing on your finger!"

"Mom mom, no! I'm not pregnant! Nothing's wrong! Will you just focus on making an appointment?"

"I will, I will. Now let me get back to my stories!" she said, talking about her soaps that she watched religiously.

I giggled, "Fine. Go watch your stories. I love you."

"Love you too, baby. Come over for dinner tomorrow, I wanna see you."

"I will," I told her, shaking my head, knowing her newsy ass just wanted to see if I was pregnant.

Hanging up, I just sat there for a moment, trying to wrap my mind around Trisha's actions. It made me wonder about my little sister. I'd reached out to Talonda numerous times, but she never responded back, which made me say fuck her too. I had my grandmother, Jules and my man. They were all I needed. Fuck everybody else.

Sighing, I pulled back onto the street and headed towards my house. Tyriq should be home, and I couldn't wait to let him know what the hell just happened. He and I met five years ago, but were just friends for the first year. At the time, he was the person I would call and vent to when I needed a man's opinion about the fuck shit the dude I was talking to would do. You know what they say: An ear to listen soon becomes a dick to ride or whatever.

Tyriq was a pretty boy, but he wasn't cocky, and he wasn't one of those guys that spent more time in the mirror than their woman. He was down to earth and not afraid to show his love and adoration for me in private and in public. I smiled, thinking about his smooth, caramel skin, dark bedroom eyes, and of course the big dick that I was ready to bounce on and relieve some stress!

As I rounded the corner, I paused at the stop sign, and watched as Riq's new charcoal colored Maxima, turned off our street without stopping, seemingly in a rush and texting at the same time. My spidey senses began tingling as I wondered what in the world had him so distracted that he didn't even notice me at the stop sign?

Allowing my curiosity to get the best of me, I followed him, telling myself how silly I was being. After a few minutes, he turned onto second street and headed north. I sucked my teeth, realizing that he was probably going to one of the diners near the airport to pick up some food, but when he drove right past Denny's, I scratched my head.

I weaved in and out of traffic, trying not to lose him while staying a few cars behind. He put on his left turn signal and I did too, grinding my teeth as we both turned into a hotel parking lot near the airport. He parked in the front row while I parked a few rows behind him. He couldn't see me, thanks to the SUV in front of me, but I could see his dumb ass!

"Nigga, please just be here applying for a second job or something!"

Dialing his number, I calmed my breathing, watching him exit his vehicle and glance at his phone before looking around.

"Sup, love?" he answered in his usual greeting when I called.

"Hey baby, what you doing?" I asked trying to sound normal.

He cleared his throat, "Uh, you know, nothing much. Running to the store to grab some food. How's work?"

I burned a hole through him with my eyes watching him lie to me with ease as he stood in the parking lot.

"You know, same ol' same ol'. Cleaning ass and dishing out pills. Where you picking up the food?"

"Uh, I don't know yet. I don't know what I got a taste for."

"Oh. Okay. Well text me when you get to wherever you going, so I can tell you what I want."

"Of course. I love you."

I hung up without responding and watched as he looked at his phone in confusion. He tried to call me back, but I sent him to voicemail, so he would think my phone died. Finally, he gave up and walked to the door marked *606,* and knocked. It opened but I wasn't able to see who was behind it before my man disappeared inside. Waiting a few minutes, I got out, ducking behind cars until I made it to the room.

Thankfully, the blinds were kind of fucked and they allowed me to peek inside. Crouching down, I looked through the dirty, probably cum-stained, window. Tyriq sat on the edge of the bed looking pissed, while a girl stood in front of him in her bra and panties. She had her back to me, but I knew those red braids and fake ass anywhere! This nigga was cheating on me with Nikki! I watched through angry, squinted eyes as she rubbed his shoulder. He started to move but she quickly straddled him and his hands went right to her ass. I guess he was finished putting up his fake resistance!

When she unzipped his pants and pulled out his dick, I'd seen enough! Standing, I marched to the door and kicked that bitch open with my work Crocs.

BOOM!

Tyriq looked like he shit his pants while Nikki's face was frozen in fear.

"Tash! It's not what you think!" he shouted.

My eyes darted to her hand wrapped around the base of his dick with her panties pulled to the side. Quickly, he pushed her off of him and she tumbled to the floor.

"NOT WHAT I THINK?! SHE WAS A SECOND AWAY FROM RIDIN' YOUR DICK! Y'ALL PICKED THE RIGHT BITCH ON THE WRONG DAY!" I shouted, attempting to pick up the TV and throw it at them, except it was nailed down.

Switching my focus, I grabbed the mirror from the

wall and smacked him with it, shattering it over his head. Nikki scrambled out of the way as I hopped on him and began throwing punch after punch while he tried, unsuccessfully, to block me.

"TASH, STOP!" he yelled.

But I was seeing red and I had no plans of stopping. Hell, I was just getting started! I continued to beat his ass until my fucking knuckles felt raw, so then I tried to dig my nails in his eyes until I felt myself being pulled back.

"GET OFF ME!" I screamed, elbowing whoever was in back of me.

Spinning around, I saw a middle-aged man, with a bald spot, doubled over, clutching his stomach where my hit had connected. There was also a crowd of people that had gathered around the broken door.

"I call police," the man said in a thick accent.

Pushing him out of the way, I spotted a half-naked Nikki, hurrying away. Sprinting from the room, I began chasing her through the parking lot. When she turned and noticed me on her ass, she took off, sliding over cars and shit. I guess the bitch was used to running from nigga's girls!

Before I could catch her, she hopped in her car, which was parked right next to mine and I hadn't even noticed it, and quickly locked her door. Kicking at her door, I yanked on her handle as she swiftly backed up and raced out of the parking lot.

"I KNOW WHERE YOU LIVE, BITCH!" I screamed after her before hopping in my car.

Shit! I needed to get the fuck outta dodge before the cops came. Bursting into tears, I wondered why I was never good enough? What was so wrong with me?! I needed a break from the dumb shit, and somewhere to go, just in case the police came looking for me. Snatching my phone from the passenger seat, I dialed and waited for an answer, hoping I hadn't fucked up my chances.

"Sup, ma?" he finally answered.

"Hi Lucky...you still hiring?"

5

JULES

"I see you was at the *G Lounge*," Stefan spoke behind me, as we both walked through the parking lot.

Stopping, I turned around to face him, "You must be stalking my Instagram," I smirked.

He shrugged, "Nah. Just scrolling. Tell me you not fuckin' with that weird nigga?" he asked, raising his brows.

Throwing a hand on my hip, I gave him a stank face because he was coming off as a hater, and responded, "Not that it's any of your business, but no. Me and my girl met him and took a few flicks. Nothing major," I told him nonchalantly, trying not to sound like a groupie, or a silly star struck broad, even though I was low key in my feelings that he hadn't reached out to me except for liking a few of my pictures.

He held up his hands in defense, "I wasn't trying to be all in your business. I'm just looking out. I heard he got a bag on his head. You don't need to be getting caught up, you feel me?"

"How do you know this?" I asked curiously.

"The streets talk. Anyway, enough about that. I still can't get your number?" he asked.

I paused, feeling a little worried for Venom, but quickly caught myself remembering that I hardly knew him.

"Um, we work together, Stefan, I don't think that's a good–"

"Just as a friend," he interjected.

Sighing, I gave in and put my number in his phone. He was cute but I wasn't sexually attracted to him, so I wasn't worried that I'd end up doing something with him that I would regret. What the hell, why not? Besides, it might be nice just to have a male friend to talk to from time to time.

He grinned widely as I handed him back his phone. After saying goodbye, I headed to my car and dialed Tash, anxious to tell her what I'd just heard about Venom having a hit out for him, but, surprisingly, her phone went straight to voicemail. Her and Riq were probably spending some quality time together and didn't want to be bothered. That was cool, 'cuz I had a date with my Kindle. Shit, at least I could read about somebody having a good man because it damn sure ain't no real ones out here!

I wasn't used to being single for this long. It was almost a month and this shit felt real unfamiliar. But it was something I was going to have to get used to, because like I said, I wasn't ever going to play the fool again. Hooking up my Bluetooth, I smiled to myself as I listened to my guilty pleasure. Venom's deep voice eased through my speakers and surrounded me. His lyrics giving me ammo for later tonight, when I felt like getting lost in my fantasies.

Inside of my home, after the short drive, Egypt greeted me as usual in the living room. My mom peeked her head out of the kitchen, surprising me. She usually stayed upstairs, but whenever she ventured down here it meant she was feeling good that day, which made me happy.

"Hey baby. How was work?" she asked, dressed casually and opening a bottled water.

"It was ok," I said, not in the mood to complain about my ignorant customers and incompetent managers. "How was your day?" I inquired.

"I felt like my old self today. Walked down to the grocery store and got myself some nice, healthy salmon to cook," she smiled.

I narrowed my eyes, "Uhn huh. Did you happen to pass the deli?" I asked, more so referring to the tall, handsome older guy that worked there, that would always flirt with her.

"Actually, I did," she smiled, combing her fingers through her hair.

"And what happened?" I asked.

"Grown folks' business. Stay in your lane," she told me, holding up her hand.

Doubling over in laughter, I said, "Mom, you don't even know what that means! You been watching them reality shows with Nikki?!"

She chuckled, "I watched a few. Now go shower and come on back down and eat," she told me, switching back to the kitchen.

Shaking my head, I marched up the stairs, "My damn mom got more of a social life than me!" I mumbled.

After showering and changing into some comfortable lounge clothes, I ate the food my mother prepared for me, of course teasing her about her market man the whole time, and made myself comfortable on the couch with my Kindle and a blanket. I was reading *If I was your girlfriend* by *Thea*, and just as I started really getting into it, the front door burst open and Nikki barged in, breathing heavily as if someone was chasing her.

"Nikki! Why you running in here like that!?" I questioned, putting down my Kindle and sitting up, pissed that she just interrupted the most peaceful part of my day!

Instead of answering, she quickly put both locks on the door and leaned against it, catching her breath. Her behavior was making me nervous. Knowing her ass, she probably robbed some dude and now he was after her ass! I started panicking as I jumped up, thinking she might've led some crazy nigga straight to me and my Mom!

"Is somebody following you?!" I yelled, taking in her disheveled appearance, just as my mom entered the room.

"What's going on in here?" she asked, looking between me and Nikki with a confused expression.

"That's what I'm trying to figure out!" I spat, exasperatedly staring at my cousin.

Flinging her braids back from her face, she looked at us and I could see her visibly trying to calm herself.

"Aunt Nia, Ju, my bad. I, um, it was a stray dog outside. A big one!" she explained.

My mom laughed, "Girl, that's what got you scared like this!? Probably the Jacksons down the road, dog got out. Calm yourself and come on and eat," she said, heading back inside of the kitchen.

"Uh, thanks, auntie, but I'm not hungry. I'mma pack a bag and go stay with Stacy for a couple days! She's having a bad time and needs some company," she replied, heading upstairs.

"I ain't hear no dog barking," I said, halting her in her steps.

My mom might've bought that bullshit, but I didn't! I could smell the sex and bad decisions all over her.

"Not now, ok Jules!? I don't have time for your grandma lectures!" she snapped, stomping up the stairs.

My mouth fell open as I looked down at my plaid pajamas, "You older than me, bitch!" I yelled after her.

A loud door slam was her response.

"Ay Juju! Stop all that cussin' and fussin' and sit your ass down!" my mom hollered from the kitchen.

Sucking my teeth, I marched back over to the sofa and plopped down, trying to get my zen back. I was glad the bitch was leaving for a few days. Maybe I'd luck up and she'd decide to move in with Stacy permanently! The thought brought a smile to my face as I, once again, got comfortable with my Kindle. No sooner had I picked up where I'd left off in my book that my phone rang.

Leaning over to grab it from the table, I studied the unknown number. I swear, everyone around me was trying their damnedest to push me over the edge. Declining the call, because I knew it had to be dirty dick, I closed my eyes and took a deep breath, wishing I had some weed. I hadn't heard from Rich since I busted that bottle upside of his head and I couldn't be happier about it, but I see he was about to start his shit again!

The phone rang again, forcing me to open my eyes and grit my teeth. It was the same unknown number.

"WHAT!?" I snapped, answering.

"Damn, that's the greeting I get? You make a nigga do magic tricks to get your number and you pick up the phone like that?" the deep, familiar voice on the other line spoke.

I sat straight up, eyes wide and heart pounding, "Venom?" I asked, shocked as hell.

"Who else was you expecting?" he asked.

"I, uh, nothing. Nobody. What... how did you get my number?" I asked, trying to gather my thoughts.

"I'm a vampire with a wide reach."

I laughed, "Righhtt. I forgot about that. So how can I help you?"

"You dressed?"

"Umm, no. I just got home from work a little while ago."

"Ok. Well, you can help me by getting dressed and coming to see me."

"What?! Yeah, that's not going to work for me. How about another day?" I requested.

"I don't do days. Only nights. Tonight."

"Ok, listen here, Dracula. I know you're used to women doing whatever you say, but not this one. Another *night* or nothing," I told him, putting my foot down.

"Nah. Be ready in a few minutes. I'm sending someone to come get you."

"Didn't you hear– Wait, you don't know where I live!"

He chuckled, "I see listening is not one of your strong

suits. Get dressed," he said, before hanging up.

"Hello?!" I said, but I was talking to myself.

Staring at the phone, I finally got my life and called Tash to tell her about the weird phone call and get her opinion on what she thought I should do, but got her voicemail once again. Getting up, I moved my curtains back and peeked out of the window looking up and down the street. It was clear except for the normal cars.

I tried to call him back, but he sent me to voicemail. I could tell because it rang twice before the automated voice came on.

"This nigga can't be serious," I mumbled to myself, confused about what I should do.

There was no way he could know where I live, but shit, how'd he even get my number? Maybe he contacted Tash and she gave him the info. That's probably why her ass not answering the phone!

"That sneaky hussy!"

"Who?!" Nikki asked, coming down the stairs.

"Nothing," I answered, refusing to tell her my business. "You gonna tell me what's really going on? I don't know what you got yourself into but if me and my mom could be in danger behind it, you need to–"

"Y'all good! It's not what you thinking!"

"So what is it!?" I demanded. "And don't tell me nothing bout no damn dog!"

"Its none of your business! It doesn't involve you and you ain't nobody damn mom in here!" she shouted, tossing her overstuffed duffle bag to the floor.

"I ain't nobody mom, but this my damn house and I'm sick of you acting like it's not!"

"Man, fuck outta here, Jules! I pay rent in this bitch,

so I give no fucks that it's your house!"

"Girl bye! You only give up two hundred dollars a month! Why don't you do us both a favor and keep your whack pussy popping coins and get the fuck out of MY HOUSE?!"

"Hey! Y'all need to calm down! We are family in case you forgot!" my mom intervened, hurrying from the kitchen.

"It's her! She always doing some dirt and bringing it to the house! I'm sick of it! What?! You done finessed some nigga out of his stash or something?! He probably on his way here now to put a bullet in all of us and this bitch runnin' out, leaving us to try and clean up her mess!" I snapped.

"Jules!"

"No, Aunt Nia! Let her get it off her chest! You telling me how you really feel! I told your dumb dramatic ass it wasn't nothing like that! But you just can't take my word for it! Your judgmental ass just leaping to your own conclusions! What if I judged you for bringing Chlamydia up in here?! Shit bitch, I was scared to use the fuckin' toilet after you!"

"Oh hell no, bitch! I'mma fuck you up!" I yelled, lunging for her and wrapping my hands around her throat.

"Aunt Nia! Get her crazy ass before I hurt her!" Nikki choked out as I squeezed tighter and we tripped over her duffle bag, falling to the floor.

We rolled around with me throwing fucking haymakers at this bitch while she desperately tried to block them.

"Stop it!" my mom shouted, desperately trying to

break us apart.

She pretty much had to lay on Nikki to stop me from throwing punches. Hopping up, I began pacing the floor while my mother inspected Nikki's face.

"What in the hell is wrong with you two?! Jules, look at her lip! Y'all know better!"

"Mom, I didn't want her here in the first place! You did!"

"Jules, stop it! She's here because she needed the help and that's what family does! I was hoping it would bring you closer together like when you were kids!"

"Tuh!" I snorted.

"Jules always been selfish!" Nikki shouted, standing, wiping blood from her lip.

"Nikki, you stop it too! What you said was a low blow and I woulda popped your ass too!" My mom finally defended me, although I was pissed that she now knew I'd caught chlamydia!

"I want you out!" I yelled.

"Fine!"

"No! Nikki, go on and stay with Stacy for a few days and after everyone calms down, we can talk this out like a family, damnit!"

KNOCK! KNOCK! KNOCK!

Before I could protest my mother's efforts, a knocking on the door drew my attention.

"Look at this shit! Probably one of her niggas with some hot shit for us!" I spazzed, hurrying to the door, ready to hand her ass over!

Swinging it open, I was surprised to see Venom's bodyguard from the club! After the fight with Nikki, I'd forgotten all about the phone call!

"You're..."

"Corey," he said, looking from me to my mother and to Nikki. "Am I interrupting?" he asked, I'm sure picking up on the fucked-up vibes.

"Actually, yes. We're having a family moment! Who are you?" my mother answered.

"Mom! Chill! This is my friends..."

"Car service. Sorry for interrupting, ma'am," he said politely, looking at my mother and back to me. "He's waiting."

"Jules, where are you going?" my mom asked.

"Hold up! I remember you! You work for Venom! And he sent you here... for *her?!*" Nikki asked, as if she couldn't believe it.

He just looked at her, but didn't respond.

"Give me ten minutes! Do you want to come in and wait?" I asked, opening the door wider.

Looking at the angry and confused women, he chuckled, shaking his head, "No thanks. I'll be safer out in the truck."

"Wait! Is Venom out there?!" Nikki asked, making a move towards the door, just as I shut it.

"Nikki, I swear to God, I'll beat your ass again if you even go near that truck!"

Giving me an evil look, she marched back over next to my mom and folded her arms across her chest.

"Jules, what is going on?!"

"Mom, I met a friend a few days ago and I'm going to hang out. That's all," I said, trying to hurry past her to go get dressed.

"But–"

"Aht aht! Stay in your lane!" I told her the same thing she told me earlier.

"Little girl, I'll–"

Her threats were drowned out as I reached my room, scrambling through my closet. I quickly threw on some skin tight jeans and a black lacey top and boots. Taking off my scarf, I combed my hair down, applied a little lip gloss and a splash of perfume. This was the fastest I'd ever gotten dressed in my life!

Rushing back downstairs, I gently moved my mom from the door as she was peeking out, and ignored Nikki, who was desperately trying to get more information.

"Are y'all two, like, a thing now?" she asked, following me outside into the yard.

"Maybe," I smirked, flipping my hair, enjoying the jealousy written all over her face.

"Humph! You know he probably only wanna fuck!"

"Who cares!? You mad he don't want you?" I teased.

"Girl please! Everybody wants me!"

"I want you, you trifling whore!" Tash said, coming up behind her, scaring the shit out of both of us because I didn't see or hear her walk up.

"What?!" Nikki said, spinning around.

In the next moment, Tash hit her so hard, she fell to the ground, knocked out cold. I mean, she gave her that Lisa Ray punch that knocked Ronnie out at the end of *The Players Club,* type of hit. A one hitter quitter!

"What the fuck did I miss?!" I asked, astounded watching Nikki snoring at my feet, before glancing up at Tash, who stood glowering down at Nikki with balled fists.

"Damn, Tash! Young metro didn't trust her?"

"What the fuck is going on tonight!? TASHA, HAVE YOU LOST YOUR MIND!?" my mother screamed, running outside.

I looked from my panicked mother, who was on her knees cradling Nikki, to Tash, waiting for an explanation.

"I caught her ass at the hotel earlier...with Riq."

"WHAT!?" me and my mom shouted at the same time.

"This has to be a mistake! She wouldn't–"

"Yes she would! Mom, I'm sick of you making excuses for her!" I said, stepping over Nikki to embrace Tash.

I considered her my family more than my cousin, anyway. I even felt partly responsible for bringing her into our lives. And Tyriq! I'm sure Tash went on his ass, but he had a second beat down coming if I ran into him! Now it made sense why Nikki seemed so shook! She knew Tash was on her ass! As I hugged my bestie tightly, I could feel her body shaking with anger and was surprised to hear her sobs.

As long as I'd known her, I'd never seen her cry. I'd cried on her shoulder countless times, but never her.

"I'm so sorry, boo," I told her, trying to fix her hair that was all over the place.

She nodded, trying to get herself together.

"Before that, I saw my raggedy ass egg donor down on third. She tried to set me up, Jules," she admitted before crying harder.

I didn't even know what to say! I thought her mom was in some fancy rehab! I felt horrible that my friend seemed to be having the day from hell.

"Come on. Stay with me," I said, grabbing her hand tightly.

"Excuse me. Jules, we really–" Corey paused, surveying the scene.

Shit! I forgot Venom was waiting for me! Well, fuck it, my friend needed someone right now. Venom would just have to catch me another time.

"Corey, I'm sorry, but as you can see, it's a little hectic over here. I'll have to see Venom another time," I confirmed.

"Wait! Oh my God! You were 'bout to go see Venom?! Jules, go. I'm fine."

"Are you crazy?! After everything that's happened, I'm not leaving you!" I exclaimed, looking at Tash like she'd lost her mind!

"Ju, I took Lucky up on his job offer," she said raising a brow, letting me know it was more to the story that she couldn't disclose right now. "So go. I'll fill you in on everything tomorrow."

When I didn't respond, she added, "I promise, I'm good. I feel much better now that I got to lay hands on her!" she said, nodding towards Nikki.

"But, what about–" my mother started to speak.

"I got her," Corey sighed, scooping Nikki up as if she weighed nothing and heading towards my house.

My mom looked at me and Tash, "Tasha, sweetie, I'm sorry that happened to you. That girl...ever since Nicole died, she's been...difficult. But that's no excuse. I'm gonna have a long talk with her... when she wakes up," she said, before giving Tash a hug, and giving me a quick kiss on the cheek.

"I'm gonna have a talk with you too," she said, glancing at Corey, who was walking out of the house, "tomorrow!"

She walked towards Corey and stopped, having a few words with him, probably giving him some sassy mom threat before heading inside to no doubt, go and baby that hoe.

"You sure you good?" I whispered, "I can cancel this. I don't know how I feel about leaving you like this."

"Bitch, go! Have fun and let the nigga bite you!"

I laughed, "Shut up, weirdo!"

"Seriously, I'm good, boo. I got all that nigga clothes in my trunk and I'm 'bout to go have a bonfire!"

Laughing loudly, I gave her a high five, just as Corey walked up.

"So what's up? You still coming?" he asked, nervously glancing back at the house.

I chuckled, knowing my mom probably put the fear of God in him and nodded my head. Tash and I hugged before we parted ways and I followed Corey to a silver Acura truck. When he opened the back door for me to climb in, I was a little disappointed to find that Venom wasn't there. Getting comfortable on the soft, gray leather seats, I waited for Corey to pull off before starting my interrogation.

"Where's Venom?" I asked.

"I'm taking you to him," he responded smartly, causing me to suck my teeth.

"I know that! But where?"

"He wants it to be a surprise."

"How did he know where I lived?"

He chuckled, "He has his ways."

Folding my arms in annoyance, I leaned up so that I could see his face in the rearview mirror, "Are y'all like, crazy psychopaths. This not no sex trade shit, is it?"

He laughed loudly, "No, we're not crazy. I could ask you that after what I just witnessed at your crib! What was that all about?" he asked.

"You won't answer any of my questions, so I'm not answering yours!" I said defiantly, sitting back.

He shrugged, continuing to drive.

I tried to ignore him, until my curiosity got the best of me again,

"How long have you worked for Venom?"

"Not that long," he responded vaguely, irritating me.

"Why are you so tight-lipped about everything?!"

"Venom is my man's, plus he pays me. You don't. So, I'm not about to sit around and spill all his coffee!"

"You mean *tea*!" I spat, folding my arms and rolling my eyes.

"Whatever, ma. You know what I meant!"

Sighing, I shut my mouth, not wanting him to part his rude ass lips again until we got to wherever it was that he was taking me. Shit, I probably should be paying attention to my surroundings anyway. I still wasn't a hundred percent sure that this wasn't some sex trade shit! I mean, he didn't outright deny it.

Slipping my hand inside of my purse, my fingers grazed across the box cutter that I'd tossed in there, just in case somebody felt like trying me. Peering out of the dark tinted window, I saw that we were on a fairly busy street and that helped me relax a bit. My mind wandered to Tash and Nikki. I couldn't believe my cousin would do something like that to someone who was so close to me. Secretly, I wondered if her ass was on drugs. She did some unstable shit at times.

Unlocking my phone, I started to text Tash, but

remembered she didn't have her phone on. When Corey pulled in back of a closed building and cut the engine, my nervousness rushed back in full force. Looking from the deserted parking lot to the dark building, a million thoughts flew through my mind. If these niggas thought they were gonna get me in that building and chop me up or sell me off to some rich Abu Dhabi nigga, they picked the wrong one!

Before Corey could turn around, I pulled out my box cutter and pressed it to his throat.

"What the fuck?!"

"Shut up! What the fuck y'all trying to pull?!"

"Yo! You on some other shit! Take the Goddamn knife off my throat!"

"Get out," I instructed him.

"Bitch, is you crazy!?"

Instead of responding, I pressed harder, until he finally unlocked the door. As he was easing out, I climbed up front and pushed him the rest of the way, quickly locking the door. I was about to pull off when Venom came storming out of the exit. His colorful eyes took in the chaotic scene before focusing on me. I wanted to gun the engine, but my body felt paralyzed, watching the amused expression on his face.

He said something to Corey, who was obviously irate, holding his neck, before walking over to the driver's side, where I still sat, unable to move. He grinned, showing his pretty white fangs, and pointed to the lock. Like a dumbass, I unlocked the door and he gently opened it. Suddenly, I felt like I could move again, but my fear was gone. Reaching out, his cool hand gripped my wrist and I allowed him to pull me from the truck.

"What you doing pulling a weapon on my mans?" he asked, his voice filled with humor.

I glanced over at Corey, who didn't find anything funny and was staring at me in a rage.

"I didn't cut him! This just looked real sketchy and I wanted to go home!" I defended myself.

"You still wanna go?" Venom inquired, squeezing my hand harder.

"No," I replied honestly.

He was looking at me like I was Christmas dinner and I was more than ready to be his meal! Smiling wider, he led me towards the building, past Corey, who was still grilling me.

"Stop it! That dull ass blade didn't even cut you! I bet you'll spill the tea next time, won't you?" I said.

Venom laughed, "Chill, Cor. She ain't even draw blood."

Without saying a word, he sucked his teeth and stormed towards the truck.

"You said *next time*. It's gonna be a next time?" he asked.

"That depends..."

"On?"

"On how you treat me tonight. You can start by telling me why you keep tryna drag me inside this damn building! You never heard of Olive Garden or Ruth Chris?" I demanded, stopping and folding my arms across my chest.

Waiting for him to respond, I stared at him, taking in his smooth, brown skin and perfect features. His skin and hair seemed to almost glisten in the moon light, mesmerizing me to the point that I had to stop myself from reaching out and running my fingers through his long, thick hair. The longer I stared, the more I noticed just how perfect he was. Not a blemish or flaw insight. Almost as if he had a filter on.

This shit is unreal, I thought.

"First of all, that shit you just named is basic. I'm tryna be original," he stated.

I pursed my lips, because I'd been to Ruth Chris before and it was nice as hell! And expensive. There was nothing basic about it, but judging from what little I knew of him, I knew he was extra as hell. From his music to his style and this damn vampire act.

"Listen, I can show you better than I can tell you. Trust me?"

"I barely know you! Why should I trust you?" I asked, defiantly.

"You saved my life, what reason would I have to lie to you or hurt you?" he inquired sincerely.

I couldn't think of a reason, so I allowed him to lead the way as we began walking again.

"I thought only the sun or a stake through the heart could kill vampires," I said, jokingly.

"And silver. Silver bullets," he responded, seriously.

I glanced at him again to see if he was joking, but he was stone-faced.

I figured the constant attempts on his life was something he didn't like to think about, so I tried to lighten the mood.

"You know, they say if you save a vampire, they owe you their life."

He laughed, "Who the hell is *they*?! You making shit up now!"

I chuckled at him pulling my card, as we stepped inside. I paused, letting my eyes adjust to the darkness inside, and looked around in shock. It was a club, I didn't know which one, but from the empty seats and spacious dancefloor, I could tell. It was empty, except for us. Looking up at him, I waited for an explanation.

"The owner owed me a favor, so I had him shut it down for the night."

I couldn't hold back the smile that forced itself onto my face.

"What if I wouldn't have come out?"

"Then I was coming to get you," he responded.

Smirking, I continued to look around until he grabbed my hand once more, leading me to an elevator, which whisked us to the top floor. A large office sat off to the left of us, but he pulled me in the opposite direction, towards a large closed door. Using a key, he pulled from his pocket, he opened it. My eyes bugged as I took in the soft, red lighting, flower petals strewn all over the floor, and the low gold table, surrounded by overstuffed, colorful, satin pillows.

I was at a loss for words as he guided me to one of the comfortable pillows, urging me to take a seat.

"Impressed?" he asked, smirking, while taking a seat across from me.

I sure in the fuck was, but knowing that he was probably used to women falling all over themselves around him, I decided to play hard to get.

Fixing my surprised face into a sneer, I replied, "It's ok. I'm more interested in the company versus the surroundings. You can pour honey on shit, but it's still shit," I spoke, folding my arms across my chest.

"Damn!" he exclaimed, before laughing. "I don't know if I should be intrigued or offended that you low key just compared me to a piece of shit."

I giggled, "I didn't call you a piece of shit...yet. Let's see how the night goes."

Before he could respond, a light tapping on the door interrupted.

"Come in," he said.

Two young teens entered, both balancing large, brass colored trays on their shoulders. Smiling happily, they spoke to Venom and then me, before placing the trays down and unveiling a Moroccan feast, including cous-cous, one of my favorites!

"Is everything good, Venom?" the young man asked, while the young girl with him stood to the side.

"Better than good," Venom responded, pulling a wad of cash from his pocket and peeling off a considerable amount for each of them.

They grinned widely before making their way from the room.

"That was generous of you," I said, referencing the hefty sum he'd just broken the youngins off with.

He shrugged, "Gotta look out for my young bulls. They ain't got too many people watching their back," he responded, scooping some of the dishes onto our plates.

I smiled because I was a strong believer in the *It takes a village* motto. Ripping apart a piece of the flat bread, he dipped it in a red sauce and held it to my mouth. Opening up, I let him feed me, and closed my eyes, savoring the rich, tangy flavor.

"Umm," I moaned, chewing the food and enjoying the smell of all the combined spices.

Opening my eyes from the food heaven I was in, I saw Venom watching me.

"Enjoying it? Or would you rather we clean up and go to Olive Garden?"

"If you touch my plate before I'm finished, I'll bite your finger!"

He laughed, holding up his hands in mock surrender, "I swear I won't go anywhere near your food. Tell me something about yourself," he said.

I shook my head, "Uhn uhn. I got questions and before I tell you one thing about me, I need answers!"

"Aight. Ask me anything. I can't promise I'll answer all of your questions, but the ones that I can answer, I will," he spoke, leaning forward and clasping his hands on the table.

"Fine. The girl that was at your show? Is she your girlfriend?"

His face got tight, and the soft, red lighting played up the anger that flashed in his eyes.

"Serina. She is," he replied flatly.

My mouth fell open in surprise and I didn't bother to close it, not caring that he could probably see the chewed-up rice inside. I was not expecting that answer! I thought for sure he would lie or have an excuse.

"So why am I here?" I demanded, starting to get angry.

"Because I don't love her anymore. She was my first real relationship, but...she changed. We both did."

I nodded, grabbing the cloth napkin from my lap and dabbing my mouth.

"So instead of breaking up, what, y'all just cheat on each other?!"

He shook his head, "Serina knows that I see other women. She's the one who suggested it."

Oh hell no!

"Nope. Uhn uhn! Listen, I don't know what kinda kinky games y'all into, but I'm too grown to play! I got enough on my plate without being dragged into your weird relationship," I said, standing.

"Jules, it's not a game. You asked me a question and I'm answering you honestly. The least you can do is let me explain the situation!"

I leaned against the wall, refusing to sit at the table with him, and folded my arms,

"Fine. Make me understand, Venom 'cause this shit is sounding crazy."

"When I realized that things between Serina and I weren't going to work, I tried to fix it, but she chose to ignore it. Finally, once I'd had enough of pretending that nothing was wrong, I broke it off. She's a very determined woman, it was actually one of the things that drew me to her in the first place. She insisted we just needed a little excitement. Something different. And she proposed the idea of bringing in another woman, not just into our bed, but into our relationship."

My eyes grew wide as I realized what he was alluding to, but I stayed quiet, silently urging him to finish.

"The first few times, I told her no–"

"You said no to a second vag at your disposal?!" I inquired, with a *yeah right* attitude.

"Look, I know with this music shit I come off as flashy and over the top, but certain shit, I prefer to keep it private. Everything ain't for everybody, you feel me?" he responded, genuinely.

Nodding, I walked back over to the table and sat back down, pulling my plate to me. This night wasn't going anything like I'd thought it would, but never the less, I was intrigued.

"Finish," I told him softly while spooning up some spicy sauce.

"One day, I come in the crib and I don't see her, but I can smell the sex in the air," he started back, and I raised my brow ready to see where this story was about to go.

"Naturally, I follow the smell, ready to kill whoever was in my house, but imagine my surprise when I open the door and see Serina, with four of her fingers shoved inside of her bestie, Lexi!"

I choked on my drink, spitting it out of my mouth and all over the table. Shaking my head, I waved him off as he leaned over to pat my back. After a coughing fit, I finally caught my breath.

"She was fucking her best friend?! Is that who she wanted to bring inside of the relationship?" I asked in disbelief.

He nodded, handing me a napkin. "Yeah. And we did. And I can't sit here and lie and say it's been bad. Me and Lexi became good friends. She understands music, she not materialistic, she a go-getter. We ended up having more in common than we both did with Serina."

"Wait...I'm trying to wrap my head around this. Sooo you and Serina *and* Lexi are in a relationship? Like, the same one?" I asked, trying to gain clarity on the ridiculousness he was telling me.

"Yeah."

"But, If you and Lexi are more compatible, why not

just kick Serina out and you and Lexi go live happily ever after?"

He shook his head, "Its not that simple. Remember I told you I like to keep some shit private? Serina knows a lot about me and my family. The only way to assure that she keeps what she knows to herself, is to at least tolerate her. It sounds harsh, but I'm keeping her alive."

"Keeping her alive? What does that mean?" I asked, already having an idea as to what he meant.

He stared at me a moment before responding, "Nothing. What's your next question?"

"My next question is if all tree of y'all are together, what in the hell am I doing here?!"

"You here because I liked what I saw and heard, and I wanted to learn more. I know my lifestyle is different from most, but I'm asking you to give me a chance and get to know me, the real me, before you tell me no."

I gawked at him, "You want me to be your one, two, three, third girlfriend?!" I questioned, holding up three fingers.

"Damn, Jules. I just said I liked you, I ain't ask you to be my girl. You move fast as hell!" he joked, laughing to himself.

"Boy bye! I know you feeling me with your stalking self!" I spat.

"You right. But I gotta tell you the rest."

"I know it's not more!" I said, getting serious real quick.

"Two more. Kember and Savalia. Kember, I met at a video shoot. I liked her energy and passion. I explained my situation to her and she was down. And no complaints from Serina or Lexi so we made it a thing," he shrugged, as if he was telling me it was going to rain later, instead of the fact that he got a whole ass Scientology cult!

"Kember? The video vixen?! Is that why her ass just suddenly stopped twerking through my TV?"

He nodded, "That's her," he chuckled. "I asked her if it was something she wanted to keep doing, she said no, so I provide for her."

Rubbing my temples with my fingers, I asked, "What about the other one? Savalia?"

"Believe it or not, she was a librarian."

I fell over laughing. I can not with this damn story! This man had taken me through so many different emotions tonight, in such a short period of time, that I was starting to feel like I was losing my mind!

"A librarian! Of course she was. Go on," I said, folding my hands in front of me.

"Kember introduced her. They already had their own connection."

"So, they have a relationship inside of the relation-ship. This is like the fucking matrix! Venom, are you serious right now?!"

His expression stayed the same as he nodded his head.

I stood, "I've heard enough. Thank you for the food, and the fuck boy tutorial, but I'm more than ready to go."

"That's cool," he stood, walking over to me. "But before we leave, tell me what makes me a fuck boy? 'Cause I kept it a hundred when I coulda bullshitted you? 'Cause I put some thought into this date rather than just taking you to some generic restaurant and then to the room I rented at some cheap ass hotel?"

"Don't you dare!" I snapped, poking him in his chest with my nail. "Don't act like I'm in the wrong 'cuz you wanna live like some weird cult leader! You pursued me, not the other way around! You pursued me, only to add me to your fucking team! Nah Coach, I'm benching this one out!"

"I didn't say you were wrong! You feel how you feel! I'm not wrong either though. I'm not lying to nobody and nobody is getting hurt. We all know what's good."

Crossing my arms, I gazed at him. He had a point. What he was doing didn't make him a bad person. Hell, he seemed to have more respect than Rich, who was only supposed to be in a relationship with one person!

"You're right. Sorry if I made you feel some type of way; it wasn't my intentions. I'm working on not being so judgmental. But still, I have to say, I don't think this is for me."

"Here you go, moving too fast again. I just want you to get to know me and let me get to know you," he said, placing his cool, large hands against the sides of my neck, applying a light pressure.

I can't lie and say that little maneuver didn't have my panties juicy. This man was crazy, and this situation is crazy, and if I allowed myself to become too involved, he'd no doubt have me out here looking crazy. But my gut was urging me to do something unsafe and unfamiliar. To be a carefree black girl just once! But my head was telling me to run. Guess who won?

"Fine. We can get to know each other. Slowly."

A gradual smile spread across his face, his sharp fangs blindingly white against his smooth brown skin.

"Perfect," he said, still impossibly close to me.

"Perfect," I repeated, not able to contain the sly grin that spread over my face.

"Can I ask you one last question?" I said, easing back before we got too close too soon.

He grinned, reaching up to gather some loose dreads that had fallen from his long ponytail, putting his cut up, tattooed arms on display.

"It's not going to be your last question, but go ahead."

I smirked, because he thought he knew me already, even though he was right.

"You said you can't let Serina go because she knows too much of your business. So why keep adding women? Aren't you worried about the rest spilling the beans?"

"They all sign contracts before we make anything official. Serina is the only one I think would be silly enough to break her contract. Plus, she's the only one I don't trust."

I simply nodded, wondering what else happened between him and Serina to make him not trust her. He was leaving something out, but I decided to let it go...for now. I wasn't his woman; we were just getting to know each other, so every little detail wasn't my business.

"You wanna finish eating, or go see what the night has in store for us?"

I wanted to remind him that I had to work in the morning, but I was throwing caution to the wind.

"When in Transylvania," I said, nodding towards the door.

He laughed, opening it for me.

"What you got planned?" I asked, glancing over my shoulder at him as we headed back towards the elevator.

"Honestly, this was as far as I planned. I figured we

could just play it by ear."

Inside of the elevator, I just had to ask, "What's so secretive that everyone has to sign contracts? You in the mob?"

He was quiet for so long that I didn't think he was going to answer me. The elevator dinged and the door slid open. We stepped out and he was still quiet, until he suddenly stopped walking.

"It's real, Jules."

"What's real?" I asked, scrunching my brows, confused.

"This," he said, gesturing to himself. "Me. I'ma real vampire. It's not a gimmick, or something I made up. It's real."

"I see..."

Shit! My ass would decide to be carefree and run into a fucking mental patient! His ass probably sit around all day doing lean and bath salts! The one time I decide to let my hair down!

Glancing towards the nearest exit, I took off, running as fast as my legs would carry me. Bursting through the door, into the frigid night air, I hauled ass across the parking lot, thankful that Corey wasn't out here. The low temperature wasn't having an effect on me, due to my soaring adrenaline.

As I turned onto a main street, the wind whipped my hair, causing a cherry colored veil to obstruct my vision when I turned to see if he was behind me. Turning my head back around, I ran smack into a wall.

"OW!" I yelled out as I started to fall, but I stopped before I could hit the ground.

Well, someone stopped me. I was being held by

Venom, as he steadied me on my feet. Disoriented, I looked around, and when I didn't see a wall, I realized I must have run right into Venom.

"How did you–"

"I already told you."

"Venom...that can't be real! Do you know how crazy you sound?!"

"I know. But you asked me what the contract was for. I been telling you my business all night, so I figured I might as well be truthful."

Staring at him, I realized that he really believed he was a vampire! Why the sexy ones always crazy?!

"For the sake of argument, let's say you are a real... *vampire*," I whispered, looking around. Even though the streets were practically deserted, with only one car passing every few minutes or so. "How do I know that you're not just plotting on your next meal?"

He grinned, "Believe me, I wanna eat you, but not how you think," he said, running a hand down his close-cut beard.

Can you catch crazy? I thought to myself as I actually stood here thinking about getting head from a self-proclaimed vampire.

"I'm not crazy," he said, sounding like every crazy person I'd ever met. "Bear with me. Let me show you a part of my world. If you still don't believe me by sunrise, or if you change your mind about us getting to know each other, I'll let you go, and I'll never bother you again. My word," he promised, holding up his right hand.

"Deal?" he asked, holding out his left hand.

Against my better judgment, I placed my hand in his, "Deal."

6

VENOM

I DON'T KNOW why I was giving up all the tapes on myself, and I don't know why I was risking taking her to this place, where, if she turned out to not be who I think she is, could endanger my entire world. What I did know, is I wanted to be closer to her and if this was the only way, then fuck it, I was about to risk it all.

"You sure you want to go here?" Corey asked from the front seat, for the hundredth time, causing Jules to fidget next to me, nervously.

I should've brought Sypher instead, but I had him on another mission at the moment.

"Corey..." I spoke in a warning tone, before turning my attention to the beauty next to me.

Even scared out of her mind, her deep, brown eyes shone with curiosity, while her full lips rested in a little pout, making her look like a sexy kitten.

"You good?" I asked, placing my arm around her shoulders, resting my fingers on her chest, above her large, soft looking breasts.

"As I'm gonna be."

"We here," Corey announced, pulling on a regular looking Philly street of large row homes.

Jules leaned up, looking around, her eyes bouncing from house to house.

"You want me to wait?" Corey asked, as I opened the door.

"Yeah, we shouldn't be too long," I told him as I helped Jules out.

"Hold up. Cor, you got a pen or a marker or something?"

He dug around in the console before handing me a pen out of the window.

"What you doing?!" Jules asked, leaning away from me as I tried to write on her throat.

"I'm putting a V on you so nobody bothers you," I informed her.

"I don't like that shit, Venom," she told me.

She was sexy as hell when she bossed up, and I couldn't wait to officially make her mine, but first, she needed to understand that there is always a method to my madness.

"I know you don't, but where we going ain't sunshine and lollipops. Shit is dark. These motherfuckers need to know you with me, for your own safety."

She peered at me for a moment, until she saw just how serious I was, and she finally tilted her head back, giving me access to her throat, which I desperately wanted to sink my teeth into. Ignoring my hunger, I carefully drew a dark 'V' at the base of her neck. Once I was ok with my marking, I handed him the pen back and grabbed Jules' hand.

"You ready?" I asked her.

She nodded, so we began walking until we came to the house directly in the center. Doing my special knock, I waited, until the cover over the peephole slid to the side. The door opened and I was greeted.

"Venom! What brings you tonight?" the young-looking man asked, before stepping to the side to let us enter.

"Just came to play," I told him.

"I see," he said, his eyes glancing over at Jules, who was gripping the fuck out of my hand.

His pupils began to cloud over in crimson, as he practically salivated. Jules gasped, and damn near broke my fingers.

"The fuck is wrong with you?!" I snapped, giving him a shove with my free hand.

He shook his hunger off, and when he looked at me again, his eyes were their normal brown shade.

"My fault, bro! They playing the blood lust games in here tonight and the smell is driving me crazy! I apologize, sis. Didn't mean to scare you. Any friend of Venom's is a friend of mine."

"S-sure," Jules mumbled, still unsure.

As we walked further inside, the base of the music became louder.

"Wait," Jules tugged me, and I stopped waiting to see what she had to say.

"This whole row of houses...it's just a front?" she asked, peering down the long club.

I grinned, "Yeah. Pretty cool, huh?"

"Yea. I would've never guessed."

"That's the point, sweetheart."

We both looked around, and I wondered what she was thinking, watching the mix of vampires and their humans partaking in different games. One girl danced, sandwiched between two vampires as they took turns lightly biting her. Homie at the door wasn't lying when he said the smell was driving him crazy. I was fighting to keep myself in check as the smell of blood wafted through the air.

"Let's get a drink," I suggested, thinking it would take the edge off of my hunger.

"Jules," I said, when she didn't answer me.

Following her line of eyesight, where she was stuck staring, I watched one of the female vamps, sitting on her human's lap. Just a glance and they looked like two lovers whispering, giggling and kissing, but a deeper look showed her inconspicuously jacking him off while biting on his tongue and lips. She must have felt us watching, because she quickly looked over, blood dripping down her chin. Her eyes were filled with blood lust as they reflected the low lighting of the club.

In a flash, she was out of his lap and directly in front of us.

"Who's your *friend,* Venom?" she asked, licking her bloody lips with her pierced tongue. I could hear the fresh blood in her voice, making it deeper than normal.

Her silky, Hershey colored skin, glowed with her fresh intake of blood, as she pushed a few strands of her shiny, black faux hawk from her face.

"Potion, this is Jules. Jules, this is Potion," I said,

making the quick introduction, but Jules stayed silent, probably shocked to see what I told her was real.

"Jules," she spoke, circling her, "She's pretty, can she play?" Potion asked, seductively, running her fingers through Jules' hair, causing her to jump back.

"Hell no, I can't play!" Jules answered for herself before I could.

The game of seduction that Potion was playing, quickly morphed into rage, as she glared icily at Jules.

"You disrespectful little bitch! If you weren't with Venom–"

"But she is! And if one hair on her head is harmed tonight, I'mma come for you! Now get back to your own game and stop testing me like you don't know who I am!"

Focusing her anger on me, she let out a low hiss, before slithering back over to the man she left damn near unconscious in his seat. Throwing her head back, she looked over at us before baring her fangs and roughly piercing her human's throat. She went back to jacking him off as she bit him, and he shook in pleasure.

"Oh my God. It's real," Jules spoke to herself.

"Drink, let's get a drink!" I demanded, leading her to the bar.

As we approached, two vamps got up, and we took their seats. Immediately, the bartender came and greeted us.

"We got A positive, B positive, O and tonight we got some rare RH negative! What'll it be?" he asked.

"That RH humanely sourced?" I inquired.

"All our blood is donated and tested! Good to go!"

"Cool. Let me get a glass of that RH with a little gin," I said.

"Got it! And for you?" he asked, looking to Jules.

"Um, just bottled water."

"Coming right up," he said, leaving to go get the drinks.

In a flash, he was back, carefully sitting the skull-shaped glass in front of me, so as not to spill any of the dark red liquid inside. He then handed Jules a bottle of Waiakea volcanic water, and placed a glass filled with ice in front of her. After handing him a twenty, I took a swallow of my drink and sighed because it was watered down. Hopefully, it'd be enough to take the edge off, or I was gonna have to make this a short night, so I could go home and feed.

"You're really a vampire. Vampires really exist," she said, gawking at me with wide eyes as I threw the rest of my drink back.

I nodded, "I am. This is the reason for the contracts. If something like this was to become public knowledge, it'd be bad for all parties involved."

She nodded, sipping her water. She finally believed me; now maybe we could get somewhere.

"We can go now, if you want," I told her, sitting my empty glass on the counter.

"You think we could stay a little longer? What's going on over there?" she pointed further down, towards a large crowd in front of a stage.

I looked at her surprised, "You want to stay in a secret vampire club and watch a show?"

She smiled, "Kinda."

"It's your night," I told her, grabbing her hand and maneuvering us through the thick crowd until we had a close view of the stage.

Women danced naked in cages on each side, while Millennium, a well-known vamp in the community, sat in a chair in the middle of the stage, while his human danced seductively in front of him, doing acrobatic tricks on the greased-up pole. We all watched as she hypnotized, not only Millennium, with her moves but the rest of us as well. Her slim, flexible limbs slid down the pole and into an effortless split.

Leaning onto her stomach, she crawled along the floor until she was in front of Millennium. Using her hands, she crawled up his body and stopped at his thighs. He handed her a dagger, which she slowly drug down her chest, making a small cut as tiny specs of blood began to form. While holding Jules' hand, I felt her pulse quicken, causing me to glance at her as she watched intently along with the rest of the crowd.

Pulling her closer to me, she looked up at me and blushed before smiling shyly. I positioned her in front of me and wrapped my arms around her shoulders, as we continued to watch, quietly. It was strange because just minutes ago, the bass was booming and now it was so mute that we could probably hear a pin drop. The woman on stage had now crawled into his lap and offered her chest to his face. While running his hands down her back, which faced us, he slowly licked up her chest.

I watched as his eyes turned bloodshot and his fangs began to extend, causing his face to morph into an almost animal appearance. Jules gasped and backed closer to me, which now had her back pressed firmly against my erection that I'd been trying to hide from her. She paused, but didn't move away. Instead, it seemed as though she leaned more into me as she leaned back and placed her warm, soft hands, on my arms.

I inhaled her scent, which was sweet and warm but because she was excited, I could also detect the smell of her blood and her arousal. It was deep and musky and combined with the sweetness of her skin; it was like a heady aphrodisiac. Sweat beads formed on my forehead as I mentally struggled to control myself. Meanwhile, on stage, his fangs had become fully extended, and the woman tilted her head back so far that her long, brown hair almost grazed the floor.

Finally, he sunk his teeth into her throat with a loud crunch. She moaned loudly as the slurping sounds floated through the air. As his drinking became rougher and more frequent, her moans turned to screams.

"Is she about to...?" Jules leaned her head back to whisper.

"She's about to cum, baby," I replied in her ear.

Sure enough, within seconds, she flooded his lap. Using his own blood, he sealed her small wound, but before she could come down from the high of having her blood snatched from her veins, he pulled out his dick and pulled her down on him. Her moans and whimpers started again as the sounds of smacking flesh could be heard. The metal chair he was sitting in, scraped loudly across the floor as he stood, carrying his "*victim.*" She wrapped her legs tightly around his waist, attempting to keep up with his strokes, but she was no match for his supernatural pace.

"Oh my God!" Jules whispered, placing a hand over her mouth.

"Are you okay?" I asked, concerned that this might be too much for her.

"I'm sorry. Can we go now?"

"Of course," I told her, quickly adjusting myself so my erection wouldn't be visible, and taking her hand.

As I led her through the crowd, I became anxious that I'd fucked up, showing her too much at once. I shouldn't have brought her here, especially on game night. What the fuck was I thinking? I probably scarred her for life. After saying my goodbyes to a few vamps that I fucked with, we made our way outside. Jules was hushed, seemingly in deep thought.

"Jules, my bad. I didn't mean to offend—"

I was cut off from my apology as she grabbed the collar of my Versace shirt and pulled me down to her, pressing her soft lips against mines, kissing me, catching me completely off guard. But shit, I wasn't complaining, I could ask questions later! Taking control and deepening our kiss, I sucked her tongue inside my mouth, trying to catch her soul. Gripping her ass, I pressed her body tightly against mine while making love to her tongue.

She moaned into my mouth, while trying to get closer. When she grabbed my dick through my jeans, I forced myself to stop before it went too far, and I couldn't stop.

"Damn!" I chuckled, catching my breath.

"I know! I'm sorry! I just...I've never seen anything like that before! I guess I got a little excited."

"Believe me, you don't have to be sorry! I'm glad I didn't scare you away. I didn't, right?"

She shook her head, biting her juicy bottom lip, "No.

You didn't. Give me the contract," she demanded, stepping closer to me.

She was playing a dangerous game with me, like I wouldn't devour her right on the street.

"It's a little more to it than that. We need to sit down with my lawyer and negotiate what each of us expects. You got a little excitement rush at the moment. It's normal."

She cocked her head to the side and placed her hands on her hips, "There is nothing normal about the way I feel right now!"

Grinning, I gripped her ass up and pulled her to me

"There's nothing more I'd rather do right now than have you sign that contract and take you home and mark you all up," I told her, leaning closer to her face. "But I'd feel more comfortable talking to you about it when you come down from the high of it all."

She pouted, "At least you're not trying to take advantage of me, I guess."

"It'll be plenty of time for me to take advantage of you later," I told her, rubbing her thick ass through her jeans.

POP!

POP!

POP!

Gunfire exploded in our direction. Thinking quickly, I pushed Jules to the ground.

"Ahhh!" she screamed, covering her head.

Corey screeched up to the curb to shield me with the truck, while he returned fire. Bullets whizzed past my head from behind. I turned to see Potion, Millennium, and a few other vamps shooting at the black car filled with Rogue vampires. A bullet shattered their back windshield and they hauled ass down the street.

I patted myself to make sure I wasn't hit and then grabbed Jules from the ground. Opening the door, I got her inside and inspected her. She was shaken up, but she wasn't hit.

"What the fuck, Venom?!" Potion's voice rang out behind me.

Spinning around, I faced her and the other vamps who'd come out to cover me.

"The Rouges," I said.

"No shit! We figured that! How'd they know you were here is the question!" she said, tucking her gun back inside of her leather thigh boot.

"They probably followed me. Put the word out; I want all of the Rogues brought to me, alive!"

They nodded and Millennium spoke, "Venom, you should lay low until–"

"Nah! That's what they want! I ain't hiding from a motherfuckin' thing!" I snapped.

They stood in silence, not daring to question me, until finally, Potion spoke. "I don't know about y'all, but this shit just killed my blood high! I'm going back in to snack on my human. Venom, I'll let you know what I can find out."

I nodded, "I appreciate y'all covering me," I said, giving each of them a handshake, before they left one by one.

"Corey, good looking! If you hadn't covered me..."

"You know I always got you," he said, but seemed distracted.

I nodded, "Let's take Jules home and go meet up with Sypher. I'm tired of these bastards popping up!"

Inside of my truck, it was eerily quiet. Corey was mute and didn't even have his music playing. Jules stared out of the window. I was pissed that these fuckers had made it their mission to end my life, but I was even more pissed that they fucked up a good night!

"Hey," I spoke lowly to her.

She faced me, and I felt like shit seeing the dried tear stains stripping her face. I felt even worse when fresh tears fell from her eyes.

"Ma, it's ok. You good, I'm good. Nobody got hurt," I said, trying to console her as I wiped the tears from her cheeks.

"This time," she whispered.

"Every time! I'mma make sure you're always good and–"

"Venom! There's a hit out on you! How long you think it's gonna take before they finally catch you?!" she yelled.

I looked at her in surprise and glanced at the rearview mirror to see Corey's eyes watching me in confusion.

"Jules, what you know about a hit?" I asked.

She sighed heavily, "There's this guy at my job. He saw the pictures me and Tash posted from the night of your show. I guess he was trying to warn me to stay away, but I lowkey thought maybe he was just hating because he'd been trying to talk to me for awhile and I wasn't feeling him like that. But he told me that there's a bounty on your head," she informed me, sniffling her tears.

I clenched my jaw, trying not to let my anger show. "Yeah? What's his name?" I asked calmly.

She looked at me, thinking about it before shaking

her head, "I don't want to be involved in this. And I don't think he had anything to do with tonight or the other night. I don't want innocent people getting hurt because of me."

"Jules, I only asked you his name. You know I can find out on my own If I really want to," I reminded her.

She sighed, "Stefan. His name is Stefan."

"Thank you."

"You're... you're not gonna kill him, are you?"

"You really want me to answer that?"

"Yes! Tell me the truth."

"Jules, I might. There's no reason he would know something like that unless he's connected to somebody in the know. I just want to ask him some questions, and hopefully, for him, he answers correctly." I shrugged.

Her mouth dropped open, but she didn't say anything else. Once I got tired of her silent treatment, I snatched her up and sat her on my lap, forcing her to look at me.

"I hate to see you sad, but if you ever ask me a question, I'mma keep it one hundred."

She nodded, "I understand. I don't like it, but I can respect it."

Smiling, because I was satisfied with her response, I kissed her again, anxious to feel her thick lips. During the kiss, I caught a whiff of blood and pulled back, furrowing my brow.

"What?" she asked, confused.

Moving her shirt, gently from her shoulder, I noticed a small cut, probably from when she hit the ground. I could feel the blood lust rising and I squeezed my eyes shut. Running my finger across the cut, I examined the droplets of blood before putting it in my mouth. The mini sample I tasted, had me on cloud nine. My fangs extended on their own, but I stopped myself from diving into her.

Surprisingly, she didn't seem afraid, instead, reaching out to gently touch my face. "I still can't believe this is real," she whispered.

"It's real," I told her, biting my finger and using my blood to seal her little scrape.

We both watched as new skin instantly appeared. She touched it before looking up at me.

"Besides getting shot at, did you enjoy your night?"

She laughed lightly, "I actually did."

"You still want to sign that contract?" I asked, fingering her crimson-colored hair.

"I might," she smiled. "When do we sit down and talk about it?"

"I'll call you tomorrow night. Do me a favor, stay away from bull that gave you that info, aight?"

"I will," she assured me.

When the truck stopped, I looked over. We were at Jules' spot. After thoroughly checking our surroundings, I got out and reached out a hand to help her out. I'd never get over the feeling of her soft skin against mine, and I hoped that once she had time to settle down and sleep on it, that she wouldn't change her mind about the contract.

"So... this is it, huh?" she asked, watching me with her large, almond-shaped eyes.

"Just for now," I assured her, as we strolled, hand in hand, towards her door.

The sun was just beginning to rise, swirling the dark sky with hues of purple. It was quiet, except for the wind blowing some leaves down the street. I looked around as she pulled out her keys and opened the door. Giving her a tight hug, I quickly pecked her on the cheek, not wanting to get stirred up again. Not sure if I'd be able to control myself.

"I'll call you tomorrow night. Remember what I said," I reminded her.

"I will," she said.

Finally, I released her so she could go inside, and I jogged back to the truck.

"What's up? You been acting funny since the shooting," I questioned Corey as soon as I got in.

"I don't think that they followed us. You know I'm on point about watching for other cars," he said.

I nodded, knowing that he was right. "So what then? Somebody let them know where I was?"

"I think so. About twenty minutes before they showed up, Serina called me. Nagging me about where you were. I told her you were at the vamp spot," he sighed.

I knew that bitch was foul! On me, if I find out she got something to do with all this shit that's going on, she won't live to see her next sunset.

"I see," I gritted, pulling out my phone.

"My fault, man. I didn't think–"

"You good, Cor. You was just following instructions," I told him while dialing Sypher.

I wanted the girls to know that they could always reach me, so they had both Corey and Sypher's numbers for emergencies.

"Yo!" Sypher answered as I put him on speaker.

"What's good? Anything move?" I asked.

"Nah. Her car ain't moved, and nobody came in or out of the crib," he informed me.

I had him sitting on my crib, but more so keeping an eye on Serina's sneaky ass.

"We on our way, so just stay put for a minute. Good looking," I told him before hanging up.

Corey breathed a sigh of relief, "Bet! At least we know it's not her."

"How? 'Cuz she didn't leave the house?! You know her lazy ass barely leaves! She the type to make a call and have somebody else do the footwork," I chuckled, angrily.

"Did she even say what she called for?" I inquired.

"Nah. She sounded pissed. I just figured she got into it with one of the other girls again. Or she knew you were out with ol girl, Edward Scissor hands."

I laughed loudly, thinking about Jules.

"You thinking about bringing her in, heavy?"

I nodded, "Hopefully. If she don't wake up and change her mind."

"What you think about what dude told her about a hit?"

"You found out where she works, right?"

"Of course. Walmart. 'Bout ten minutes from her crib."

"Word? We'll handle that tomorrow. Find out what time he go in. But first, I'mma handle the snake in my crib."

He caught my eyes in the mirror, "V, make sure she really on some slimeball shit before you move. Killing humans, that ain't you. Especially one that you loved at one point."

He was right; I'd never killed a human. I'd killed other vamps when I'd had to. But with humans, my presence alone was enough to make mothafuckas either wanna get down or lay down. My blood was usually donated from fine ass, willing, human women. But like my nigga Pac said, *I ain't no killa but don't push me.* And Serina was pushing me to my limit!

"Right," I said, lowly, hoping he would pick up on my cue, that I was no longer interested in this conversation.

He did, and the rest of our short drive was silent, how I wanted it. When we pulled up, I spotted Sypher, parked inconspicuously, across from my home. Hopping out, I gave him the signal that he could leave. Nodding, he slowly pulled off.

"Tomorrow," I reminded Corey, before giving him a handshake.

He nodded and parked the truck before getting out to switch cars and head home. Jogging up my steps, I opened the door, only to find Savalia and Kember doing some yoga shit inside of the living room. They were both in that down doggy position, and I had to admit, it was a nice view. Chuckling to myself, I watched them stretch before Savalia looked over her shoulder and smiled at me.

"Hey, bae!" she squealed, jumping to her feet, practically skipping over to where I leaned against the door frame.

"What's up, Val? How was your night?" I asked, wrapping my arms around her slim body in a hug and kissing her cheek.

"You missed it! Me and Kember went to the new art studio they opened over on Broad."

Raising a brow, I looked to Kember, surprised she went to go view art, knowing that wasn't her thing. She smirked, while stretching her arms above her head, putting her full curves on display through the thin gray pajamas she wore. Taking a seat on the sofa, with Savalia plopping down right beside me, I watched as she continued her stretches.

When she was done, she seductively sashayed towards me, gently taking a seat on my lap.

"It was boring, but whatever makes Val happy," she shrugged.

"It was not boring!" Savalia protested.

Kember waved her off and focused on me. "How was your night? Where you been? Did you have a show!? You know I wanted to go to one!" she pouted, bombarding me with questions.

"Nah, no show tonight. I, uh, was out with someone," I told her.

She narrowed her eyes, looking me up and down before grinning, "Who is she? Is she cute?" she asked, causing Val to suck her teeth and cross her arms.

"I mean, not that I'm interested! I'm asking for you," she tried to clean up her words.

I laughed at her as she maneuvered around on my lap so that her long legs were draped over Val's.

"Yeah. Yeah, she bad. I'm thinking about bringing her in."

I watched both of their eyes widen in surprise.

"Seriously?! I hope she's nice," Val said.

"Fuck if she nice! Is she gonna be cool with the set-up, 'cuz God knows I can't deal with another Serina!" Kember spat, rolling her eyes.

"I explained everything to her; we'll see if she's still

down in a few days. But lemme ask you something real quick. Y'all notice anything funny bout Serina lately?"

"You mean more than usual? Tuh!" Kember replied.

"She seems agitated lately. More than usual," Val answered.

"Why you asking? What's up with her?"

"Nothing! Just keep your eyes on her for me."

"Sure. You wanna come play?" Kember asked, standing and pulling Val to her feet.

My dick involuntarily jumped, but my mind was focused.

"Not tonight. Raincheck," I told her, "but y'all have fun though."

"You know we will," Kember said, winking at me, before heading upstairs with Val in tow.

Smiling, I shook my head, half wishing I could go with them.

"Damn," I muttered to myself.

I stood getting my thoughts together, before going upstairs. Walking past the first room, I heard the soft moans of the two lovers wafting through the door, but I stayed on my mission, finding my way to Serina's room. Of course, it was empty. Her ass was probably in my shit! Heading to my bedroom, I pushed open the door and was met with the angry glare from Serina, sitting cross-legged in the center of my bed.

"Where the fuck have you been?!" she yelled, jumping up from the bed.

"Don't you ever question me! I ask the fucking questions! The fuck you been up to?"

"Huh? I've been here! Waiting for you!"

"What did you call Corey for?" I asked, walking up on her.

"I-I just wanted to know where you were. Wh–"

"Give me ya phone."

"For what?!"

"GIVE ME THE FUCKIN' PHONE!"

Quickly, she scrambled to the bed and snatched up her phone, handing it over to me before throwing her hands on her hips. Typing in her code, I went to her call log. It was empty except for the call she made to Corey. Glancing up at her as she watched me nervously, I went to her texts. Empty. I went through her emails and social media accounts while I was at it.

"Happy?" she asked as I handed the phone back to her.

"Nah. Why is your call log and texts empty, Serina?" I asked.

"What? Because my phone is set to automatically delete!"

"Your call log too?" I inquired, removing my chain and walking past her to place it on the dresser.

"Yes! Now, where were you?"

"Out!"

"Out where? With a bitch!?"

"Nah. With my new girlfriend. Now get the fuck out. I told your hard-headed ass I don't like nobody in my space!"

"Wait, what!? You didn't run that past me!"

My fangs extended and I turned around with the quickness and had her ass gripped up in less than a second.

"I don't have to run shit past you! You getting way

ahead of yourself! Now get the fuck out!" I demanded, giving no fucks about the tears welling up in her eyes.

"And if I find out you a snake, I'mma chop your head off, you understand?" I asked, still gripping her up by the collar of the silky blue nightshirt she wore.

When she nodded, I let her go, and she hurried from my room. I was definitely going to keep a close eye on her.

7

NIKKI

"Ow! Damn, can you be careful?!" I snapped on Stacy, as she pressed the ice wrapped in a rag to the side of my swollen face.

She stopped and sighed, "I'm only tryna help, Nikki. I still can't believe they jumped you! I mean, your own cousin?" she paused, shaking her head. "Shits crazy!"

"I know! But those bitches always been jealous of me," I lied, too embarrassed to tell her the truth.

"Ow!" I yelled again, snatching the ice from her and gently pressing it to my swollen face.

I was lucky my fucking jaw wasn't broken. I'd slept with a bunch of men that claimed to be taken, but this was the first time one of their girls had caught up to me. What the hell would you wanna fight the other woman for? She don't have no commitment to you. The man does! Fight his ass! Ok, so maybe I was slightly in the wrong, only because Tash and my cousin were close as hell, but I got tired of hearing that bitch brag about how faithful her dude was.

That's why when I saw him at a pregame party, I decided to test his faithfulness. And like I thought, a nigga is only as faithful as the blood flow to his dick! All I had to do was get a few drinks in him and follow him to the bathroom and just like that, his dick was in my mouth. I was going to leave it at that one time, but the dick was good and he was generous with his money.

He tried to break it off plenty of times, to the point where he would work my nerves always crying about how much he loved Tash and how wrong we were. But his love wasn't strong enough to resist this pussy. No man was that strong-willed!

"What the hell did they jump you for?" Stacy asked.

"I already told you! They jealous!" I snapped, talking out of the side of my face that wasn't swollen.

"Uhm hmm," she said as if she didn't believe me, standing with her hands on her hips. "Look, I love you Nikki, but you can't stay here."

My jaw dropped, causing me to wince because it was so swollen. "What?! Why not? Look at my face!"

"I see your face. I can't miss it! And that's just it! It's always some drama with you! I know them girls didn't jump you just 'cuz they jealous! You not telling me something and I already have an idea what it is! I just don't want the drama, Nik. Me and Mark are in a good place–"

"That's what this is about?! You putting me out on the streets because you don't want me around your nigga?! I thought we was better than that, Stacy!" I frowned at her.

"We are! But bitch, you got twenty something problems and we in our thirties! I don't have the time! And nobody is putting you on the street! I know you got a bunch of guys you can stay with!"

Folding my arms across my chest, I gave her the evil eye. I had niggas, but most of them lived with their girls. I had a little money saved up, so I could get a hotel room if I wanted, but I didn't want to spend my own money.

"Can I borrow a few dollars to get a room then, since you throwing me out?" I asked with puppy dog eyes.

She huffed, "Fine, Nikki." Before marching down the hall and disappearing inside of her bedroom.

I sighed, pissed that she wasn't willing to let me stay with her. With friends like her, who needs enemies! Just then, I heard keys jingling at the door. Quickly, I tossed my braids to one side, trying to cover my face and forced some tears down my cheeks, just as Stacy's boyfriend entered the apartment.

"H-hi Mark," I spoke lowly.

"Hey, Nikki. Where's.... What the fuck happened to you?!" he asked, making his way over to where I sat on the couch.

"I got jumped," I answered in my most pitiful voice. "And my best friend is kicking me out," I pouted, slightly spreading my legs.

My jeans were skin tight, so I wasn't surprised when he glanced down at my fat pussy print.

"What you mean she kicking you out?" he asked, gently touching my injured face.

Slowly, I licked my lips and looked at him through my wet lashes, "Just what I said! Nobody gives a fuck about me!" I cried, pulling him closer.

I didn't flinch when his hand accidentally brushed my breast, but he didn't move it away either.

"Let me holla at her real quick," he said, rubbing my hair with the hand that wasn't casually massaging the tops of my exposed skin.

"Mark!" Stacy screeched from behind him.

He removed his hand and jumped out of my face so quick it caught me by surprise.

"What's up, baby? I was asking Nikki why her face looks like Martin's when he fought Hitman. You kicking her out?"

Stacy sucked her teeth, glancing from him to me, "This don't concern you so stay out of it! Besides, only one of our names is on the lease and it ain't yours! Nikki is fine; she has places to go. Here," she said, handing me a few twenties.

They were rolled up, but it felt light as hell and I knew it was only about a hundred dollars.

"Aye, that better not be my re-up money, Stacy! Your name on the lease but I pay the fuckin' rent!" Mark hollered. "I don't see why you just don't let her stay on the couch for a couple weeks."

"Yea! Seriously, Stacy, I can just–"

"Bye Nikki!" she said, grabbing my duffle bag and heading towards the door.

Huffing, I marched towards her, "Thanks, *friend*. I won't forget your generosity!" I told her, snatching my bag and walking out.

"Anytime boo," she smiled before closing the door in my face.

"Bitch!" I grumbled, listening to her and Mark argue through the door.

"You don't know her like I do! I bet my life she got caught fuckin' somebody man! And don't think I didn't peep how close y'all was on that damn sofa!"

"Nah, babe. It ain't like that. She not even my type!"

Sucking my teeth, I walked off, throwing my bag over my shoulder. Going down the steps, I turned my head, so that people coming up couldn't see my face. Outside of the building, I counted the money she gave me, and sure enough, it was only a hundred. Where in the fuck did she expect me to sleep with only a hundred?! I swear she could be so selfish sometimes!

Suddenly, it dawned on me where I might be able to stay for free. Pulling out my phone, I unblocked his number and hit him up. I was starting to get nervous that he wouldn't answer, but finally, on the fourth ring, he picked up.

"The fuck you want, bitch? You better be calling to tell me you went and got checked out!"

"As a matter of fact, I did! And I didn't have shit! So, blame another bitch!" I shouted, hurrying away from the entrance because an old couple was walking past me, staring at me like I was crazy.

"I wasn't fucking nobody else but you and her! You crazy if you think I don't know ya shit spicy!" he spazzed.

"Oh, and I guess it's no way your pure little princess coulda gave it to you, huh?"

"Fuck outta here, Nikki! I know you gave me the shit! What the fuck you want anyway?"

"I need a place to stay for a minute," I sighed.

"What? Why? Did you tell Jules about us!?" he panicked.

I laughed, "Nigga no! And in case you haven't noticed,

Jules ain't worried about you. She out with Venom as we speak," I smirked, happy to burst his bubble.

"Venom!? When the fuck did that happen?!"

"Um, I think at his show. He was all up on me, and her thirsty ass just had to have the attention! Now they like. A thing. You haven't been watching her Instagram?"

"She blocked me. Where you at?"

"In front of Stacy's building."

"Aight. Give me fifteen," he said, hanging up.

I smiled to myself, glad that I'd gotten under his skin. Rich annoyed the fuck out of me, but he was easy to toy with. I definitely did give him chlamydia, which he passed to my cousin. It wasn't on purpose, just one of those things, you know? I went and got checked out around the same time as Jules, and secretly took my antibiotics. I would never tell Rich that though. He had a habit of losing his temper with me and I'd rather him take that crazy shit out on Jules!

My smile faded as I thought about her and Venom and I quickly went to her insta to see if she'd posted anything tonight. She had one post from about an hour ago. It was a picture of a man's hand, that I assume was Venom from the skull ring and iced out bracelets, holding a skull-shaped glass. She'd captioned it, *first dates*. Jealousy seeped through my veins as I fought the urge to throw my phone.

Why did everybody wanna wife this bitch?! She was boring as hell. I just didn't get it. If I was a dude, I'd want a woman who was fun and exciting. A boss bitch that wore her sexiness like a badge of honor. A bitch like... well, a bitch like me! Angrily, I exited out of my phone, ignoring the missed calls from my Aunt.

She seemed to be the only person that gave a fuck about me. My own mother went and got herself killed, running the streets. I learned early on, that the world was a cold, heartless place and in order to survive, I had to become just like it. Sighing, I folded my arms across my chest to block the wind chill and headed to my car to wait for Rich.

I never wanted to start with him. He was cute and getting to a little bag, but he was my cousin's man at the time, and I wasn't *that* heartless. He and Jules had been dating for about six months, and it was a regular thing for him to spend the night now and then. I'd come in late one night from partying, and everyone was sleeping, so I thought.

Stripping down in the bathroom, I hopped in the shower. When I pulled back the curtain, Rich was standing in the bathroom, in nothing but his boxers.

"Oh my God!" I exclaimed, *placing my hands over my wet chest, while trying to conceal my bottom half with the shower curtain.* *"What the fuck are you doing in here?"* I whispered.

He grinned, his eyes roaming any and every bare spot he could find on my body, before he finally answered my question.

"I came to give you the dick that you can't stop thinking about."

My eyes widened in surprise, and I frowned my face in confusion before laughing out loud, *"Boy! You got me fucked up! Nobody is thinking about that dick except my cousin, you know, your girlfriend in the next room?! Now get the fuck out!"* *I told him, reaching for my towel that hung on the door, and wrapping it tightly around myself before stepping out.*

"Nah, you got me fucked up. I wanna see what all the fuss

is about. Erybody know Nikki," he said, snatching my arm and pulling me closer to him.

"Are you dumb?!" I demanded, snatching my arm away. "You my cousin's man! You think I'm not gonna tell her what you tried?!"

He laughed, "You think she'll believe you over me? She knows, just like the rest of the city what you good at and what you good for. You a whore. What? Now you wanna have some morals? Fuck outta here!" he spat, viciously yanking my towel from my body.

My eyes watered, knowing that he was right. My cousin barely tolerated me, and I knew what everybody thought of me. If I was to go wake her up right now and tell her what happened, she'd almost certainly think it was my fault. I let him fuck me that night, just to get him out of my face and I promised myself I wouldn't let it happen again, but afterwards, I started to notice more and more how Jules walked around, barely acknowledging me, nose in the air.

She thought she was so much better than me, but I had that secret over her, which made me able to deal with her smugness. When he approached me again, I didn't put up a fight. In fact, I enjoyed that shit!

"Fuck her," I mumbled to myself, just as I spotted Rich's Impala pulling into the parking lot.

He spotted me and pulled beside me. Stepping out, I made sure my braids covered the battered side of my face, before I slid inside of his car.

WHAP!

His hand quickly shot out, smacking me in my face, causing my head to hit the window.

"Ow!" I yelped, covering my face.

"Bitch! I know you gave me that shit! You..." he paused, laughing. "The fuck happened to your face?"

I sucked my teeth, "It don't matter. I need somewhere to stay for a couple days."

He paused, lighting his black and mild cigar, "Yeah. You can stay. Not for free, but you can stay."

I glanced at him because I know he didn't think I was gon' pay him. One thing I didn't do, was give men money! I don't have no fucking kids and I wasn't about to play mommy to no grown ass men.

"If I had money, I wouldn't need a place to stay, Rich."

"You'se a lying ass. I know your tricking ass got money. That's not what I want. You can pay another way," he told me. "I want you to help me get Jules back."

I rolled my eyes and started to tell him where the fuck he could go, but he cut me off.

"You gon' fuck that nigga Venom and make sure she knows about it. If that shit don't work, then I'mma take his fuckin' head off. Either way, she'll come crying back to me."

I smiled brightly, not caring about anything he said past me sliding this pussy on Venom.

"Yesss! Now this is a plan I can get behind!" I exclaimed, rubbing my hands together, excitedly.

He looked at me in disgust and shook his head, "I shoulda known your hoe ass would be hype 'bout laying on your back. Get out. Follow me to the crib."

I didn't give a fuck about his personal opinion of me. It wasn't as if he was an angel in this situation. Smirking, I stepped out and hopped inside of my own vehicle, looking at my face in the mirror before starting it up. Finally, things were looking up!

8

_____

VENOM

"You sure he workin' today?" Sypher asked me, checking his watch.

I leaned on the counter, pretending to be interested in the jewelry, but really, keeping an eye on the auto department. I'd brought Sypher with me instead of Corey, opting to switch them out, leaving Corey to keep an eye on Serina. I was waiting on bull Jules mentioned to show up. He was supposed to show up at 4. It was five minutes past and I was starting to get anxious.

"Yeah," I responded simply, adjusting my sunglasses and making sure my hair was tucked securely inside of the dark hoodie I wore.

I'd disguised myself so I wouldn't be noticed since homie seemed to know me, but I didn't know who he was. Glancing over again, I noticed a different employee standing near the tires.

"Syph, go check his name tag."

He nodded before dipping off.

"Ahem, did you need any help?" a young girl appeared behind the counter.

She smiled brightly at me and batted her lashes.

"I'm good, shorty. Just looking," I said while glancing back and forth between her and Sypher.

"You seem really familiar. Do I know you?" she asked, squinting at me and taking in my form as I stood up from the counter.

"Nah, I don't think so," I replied, turning to walk away and saw Sypher throw up the sign that it was him.

Nodding, I headed outside to wait for Sypher to bring him out. Out back, where we'd parked, I leaned against the truck and pulled out my vape pen with the blood cartridge and pulled from it, exhaling the red, odorless smoke. The feeling was an instant high, spiking my adrenaline. Tossing it in my pocket, I cracked my neck and impatiently waited. Hearing the door to the auto department open, I became alert, listening to the foot-steps and voices, as I leaned against the other side of the truck, facing away from the door.

"I appreciate you taking a look at the tires for me, bro," I heard Sypher capping.

"It's cool. I'mma just look on the inside of it and copy the numbers so we can get you some new ones."

As they approached the truck, I walked from behind it, facing him, while Sypher pulled out his gun. Stefan looked at me in surprise.

"Venom!" he yelled, surprised.

"You know somebody that got money on my head, nigga?" I inquired, but I paused, something wasn't right.

Suddenly, he leapt onto the truck and jumped up on top of the building.

"Oh shit!" Sypher exclaimed.

"Mother fucker!" I yelled, in shock that he was a Rogue vamp!

Running past Sypher, I climbed quickly up the wall to the top of the building, spotting Stefan scurrying down the side. Seeing me, he let go and jumped from his halfway mark, to the street below. Jumping from the building to the nearby treetops, I followed him from above before jumping down and landing in front of him, catching him off guard. He swung, but I easily dodged it before throwing a punch of my own, which connected with his jaw, causing him to fly backwards.

I stomped him on his chest, the sounds of his ribs shattering was like music to my ears. I'd finally gotten my hands on one of the Rogues! How fortunate was I, that he also happened to be a goofy tryna block me from Jules?

"Nigga! I should kill your ass right now!" I snapped, lifting him with one hand by his throat and tossing him into a brick wall.

His back hit the wall with a loud shudder. Gripping his collar, I snatched him up from the pile of trash cans he'd fallen over. He shoulda fell inside them motherfuckers, ol trash ass nigga!

"V!"

When I heard Sypher shout my name, I glanced at him briefly, and just that quick, Stefan had come out his shirt and disappeared down the block. I looked at the shirt I still held, gripped between my hands and shouted.

"FUCK!"

I stood as Sypher made his way over to me, trying to

block me from onlookers, that I hadn't noticed my fight attracted. Glancing around, I noticed more people beginning to gather and record with their phones.

"I had 'em, Syph! A fuckin' Rogue was in my grasp! Fuck!" I yelled, flailing his shirt around.

"I know, but come on before you end up on World Star," he responded.

Pulling my hoodie further over my head, I lowered my face and hopped inside of the passenger side of the truck while he jogged around to the driver's side and jumped behind the wheel, opting to back down the street so the people with their phones out couldn't get a look at our plates. I was still pissed that he'd literally slipped through my fingers, so I lashed out, punching the dashboard until the woodgrain began splintering.

"Calm down, man! At least you can put a face to the Rogue organization now!"

"Fuck that! I ain't got time to be playing Sherlock in these streets! I had his bitch ass!"

"And you'll have him again! Stop fuckin' up the truck!"

Sighing, I sat back, examining my busted knuckles that were quickly healing and thought about the odds of running into a Rogue at fuckin' Walmart! My mind switched to Jules. It wasn't safe for her to go back there now and I hoped she hadn't changed her mind about the contract.

"Yo, take me to Jules' spot. I need to make sure she not going to work."

"Damn! I forgot about that! I don't think she gonna be too pleased that she can't work. She strikes me as one of them me too independent types."

I chuckled because he had a point, but she was a challenge that I didn't mind accepting. When we pulled up on her street, the last bit of sun had completely set. One of the things I liked about winter on the East coast was how fast the sun went down. I could already feel the small amount of energy I'd expended during the fight, returning to me.

"Park right here," I said, motioning to a spot a little ways down from her house.

Pulling out my phone, I dialed her and was surprised when it went to voicemail. I called again only to get the same result. I knew she couldn't still be sleep after checking the time. It was quarter to five. My anger emerged when I saw her step out of her door, and look around cautiously, before making her way to her truck, dressed in her work uniform.

Clenching my jaw, I ignored Sypher, who looked like he wanted to say he told me so. Slipping out of the truck, I swiftly appeared at her car and leaned against it.

"Oh!" she yelled, surprised, placing a hand on her chest. "Venom! I–"

"You what? I asked you not to go in today. You agreed. So what's up?" I inquired, staring at her.

"I-They called. Some people called out. I was just going to do a short shift," she explained nervously.

I nodded, "So, fuck me and what I asked you to do, huh?"

"No, but, listen, Venom. I'm not some immortal, or a silver spoon kid! I got real life problems. Bills, a sick mom, bills! I know it's probably not much to you, but I need my job! And save that 'how much you make, I'll pay you for today' bullshit, if that's what you was gonna say!"

she spat, tears welling in her eyes, threatening to spill, as she tried to move me from her door.

Not budging, I pulled her to me shaking my head, "Jules. It's not safe for you there. I just left," I told her, watching her eyes widen. "And fuck paying you for the day. Let me help you find something that you can use your degree in! Fuck all the petty shit! You trust me?" I asked, lifting her tear-stained face so she couldn't avoid my eyes.

She slowly nodded, but that wasn't enough for me.

"Nah. Lemme hear you say it, so we don't have to have this conversation again. Do you trust me?" I asked more sternly.

"I trust you," she said.

Grinning, I wiped her face and nodded towards her house, "Your mom in there now?"

"Yea. She's already sick, and some stuff went down with my cousin last night. Now, she can't get in touch with her and I think that's making her sicker. She won't even get out of bed!" she cried.

I hugged her tightly, allowing her to get her fear and anxiety out before grabbing her hand. Leading her back to her house, I patiently waited as she unlocked the door. Inside, I looked around her home. It was clean, which was a plus. It was nothing fancy, but it was cozy and large. Removing my sunglasses and hood, I shook out my dreads and watched as she picked up a fat, black cat.

"This is Egypt," she said.

Smiling, I rubbed her ears, and she purred. Jules watched shocked.

"I can't believe she let you pet her. She hates everybody with her mean ass," she giggled.

I chuckled, "Most pussies purr when I touch 'em," I joked.

Her mouth dropped, "You make everything so nasty!" she said.

"You don't even know the half," I informed her, eyeing her curves through the tight khaki pants she wore. Biting her lip, she shook her head and blushed.

"Where your mom at?" I asked, ready to meet the woman that created the beauty standing in front of me.

"Upstairs. Come on," she said, placing the cat gently to the floor.

She scampered towards the kitchen as we headed upstairs. She stopped in front of a door and knocked gently.

"Ma, you dressed?" she asked.

"Yea, come on in," a weak voice replied.

I glanced at myself in the hallway mirror that hung on her wall and was disappointed that I was rocking this gray sweat suit, instead of my nice gear.

"I thought you were going to–" she paused, noticing me entering behind her daughter. "Who's this?" she asked, sitting up in her bed a bit and adjusting the pink robe she wore.

"This is, uh..."

"Venom, her boyfriend," I spoke up, reaching out a hand for her mother to shake, while holding in my laughter at the shocked expressions on both of their faces.

"What?!" her mother asked surprised, placing her weak hand in mine.

"You're the reason she finally been getting out of the

house?! Humph, I like you already!" she said, causing me to laugh, while Jules sucked her teeth.

I shrugged, "Enjoy life or die trying."

"Ok!" her mom agreed.

"Oh my God! I'mma go change while y'all talk," Jules informed me, waving us both off.

"You that singer that all these young girls are going crazy for, huh? You know any Luther Vandross?"

I laughed genuinely, "No ma'am, I'm a rapper."

She looked me up and down, "You involved in any gangs? Drugs?" she questioned.

I shook my head, opting to leave out the multiple attempts on my life, "Nah. I'm just trying to live a peaceful life," I responded.

When she looked at me as if I was lying, I changed the subject, "Tell me about you? Jules said you're not in the best of spirits," I asked, focusing on a glass of water on her nightstand.

"Jules is always worried about something. I keep telling her she's too young to be so stressed," she replied, smoothing her blanket.

I could tell she didn't want to talk about her health, probably because it was worse than what Jules thought. I could smell death not to far off, and it saddened me to think that she might not have long left. Her sassy nature reminded me of my own stepmother.

"My stepmom watches these crime shows all of the time," I told her, pointing to the television.

She chuckled, focusing her attention back on the TV, giving me time to bite my finger and squeeze a drop of my blood into her water. I put just enough to help heal her body without overtaking her cells.

"It's the best way to figure out how to get away with murder, if someone were to, oh say, fuck with your child."

Chuckling, I held up my hands in defense, "Thinly veiled threat received, but I promise Jules is in good hands," I assured her.

"Um hmm, she better be! I may not be strong enough to beat you, but everybody can get laid down by some bullets."

"I promise you can save your bullets. I got her, and you too," I said, handing her the glass of cool water, which she drank down.

Just then, Jules entered the room, and my eyes and dick damn near popped out. She wore a tan colored one-piece thing that was almost the same color as her skin. Brown furry boots stopped at her knees, and she'd brushed her crimson colored hair up into a neat bun, with the toddler hair waved all around her edges.

Her bright red lips drew my attention as I had the urge to mess up the carefully placed lipstick.

"Damn," I mumbled, forgetting her mom was right there.

"I didn't know where we were going, and I didn't want to be underdressed. Is it too much?" she asked.

"No! It's perfect. You're perfect," I told her, standing from my seat on the soft chair next to her mother's bed.

"Thank you," she smiled, and then focused on her mom.

"You ok? Do you need anything before I go?" she asked, leaning over to give her a kiss on the cheek and giving me a perfect view of her round ass.

"No, go have fun. I'm fine. For some reason I got a little energy boost," she smiled. "It was nice to meet you,

Venom. Remember what I said," she told me, raising an eyebrow.

"It's burned into my memory," I said.

"Good! Now go have fun at the skating rink or whatever you kids do," she joked, waving us off.

I chuckled while Jules shook her head. We left out, and I apparently couldn't keep my hands to myself once we were outside. She giggled, playfully slapping my hands away from her ass.

"I haven't signed anything so keep your hands to yourself!" she joked, sticking out her tongue.

"With you looking like that, I'm ready to risk it all and say fuck that contract," I told her in all seriousness.

She paused, "Really?" she asked, looking up at me and raising a brow.

I knew it was stupid of me to forgo a contract, but I wanted her so bad, that I was willing to make a dumbass decision.

"Yeah," I answered.

She stared at me for a moment, before she shook her head, "Those contracts are for your protection. I wouldn't feel right. Let me at least look it over first."

Breathing a silent sigh of relief, I smiled from ear to ear, happy that she was concerned with my protection. It just made me want her more.

"Bet! Let's go," I said, picking her up and tossing her in the air before catching her again, causing her to scream in laughter, as I jogged to the car.

"Damn! What happened?" she asked, nodding towards the dashboard, once we were settled inside.

"Your boyfriend had a hissy fit," Syph responded, chuckling as he pulled off.

I shot him a look, and he shut up, while Jules looked to me for an explanation.

"Nothing," I shrugged. "Just a little accident. Everything is cool," I explained nonchalantly.

She looked at me as if she didn't believe me, before sitting back and relaxing against the leather.

"We going to see Walt," I informed Sypher who nodded and switched lanes.

"Who's Walt?" she asked, as I scooped her up and sat her on my lap.

"My lawyer," I said, eyeing a small red tendril that was curled up at the back of her neck.

Fighting the urge to move it and sink my fangs into her skin, I looked away, out of the window.

"Can I ask you a question?" she inquired, turning sideways on my lap, causing my dick to strain against my sweats.

"What's good?" I said, sliding her closer on my lap.

"Did you tell the other girls about me?"

"I told Savalia and Kember. Serina was trippin' like Ella, so I didn't tell her shit, and I didn't mention it to Lexi yet, but I think she has an idea."

"Oh okay."

"Okay, what? What's bothering you? Now is the time to figure everything out," I told her.

"It's just... I guess my main problem is... I don't feel like the drama. I've been locked up and had to report to anger management. I've grown since then, but I have a feeling Serina might take me back there. If I have to constantly fight, what makes you different from my ex?"

"I feel your point, but don't ever compare me to another nigga. I can handle Serina, so you won't have to.

If she gets out of line, she can leave. Honestly, she been treading on thin ice for awhile now. And you don't have to fight over me. If she say or do something out of the way, let me know, and I'll handle it. I'mma be jealous if you giving her all your energy instead of me," I said.

She laughed lightly, "Is that so? What about me? I'm definitely starting to catch a few tiny feelings for you. What if I'm jealous watching you with other women?"

"A few tiny?!" I repeated, frowning my face up.

She laughed again, "Something like that."

"Aight then. If you barely feel anything, then other women shouldn't bother you."

"Don't play with me, Venom," she said, her face inches from mine, close enough for me to see the crazy in her pupils.

"You stop playing with me! Talking about some tiny ass feelings. I know you feeling a nigga or you wouldn't be willing to go through with this. And I'm definitely feeling you. Probably more than you think. Communication is key. If I ever do anything to make you uncomfortable or jealous, tell me, and I'll fix it. Just always keep it a hundred with me and I'll do the same with you."

"Agreed," she said, leaning into me.

9

JULES

BITCH, YOU REALLY GOING THRU WITH IT?!!
YASSSSSS!!

I discreetly checked the incoming text from Tash, and placed my phone back on my lap, giving my attention to the lawyer who sat in the middle of the long conference table. Venom sat at one end while I sat at the other. Nervously, I fidgeted with the ballpoint pen in front of me, while Walt went over the contract and the legal repercussions that would follow if any part was violated.

Shit, honestly, I was already in violation because part of it that I was in no way, outright or deceptively to reveal Venom's true identity as a non-human entity. Welp, that was a wrap when I called Tash this morning and told her everything that had happened. Damn, I had to tell somebody! A real vampire wanted me to join his cult, or his *situation,* as Venom would rather it be called.

If I did decide to tell, I highly doubted that anyone would believe me anyway. The only reason Tash believed me is because she's half crazy herself. That, and she's known me forever and knows I wouldn't lie about something like this. Besides, I swore her to secrecy, and I know she won't run her mouth.

"Have I explained everything sufficiently enough?" he asked, looking to Venom and then me.

"Of course. Can you give us a few minutes to go over everything in private?" Venom asked.

"Sure," he said standing, adjusting his navy-blue suit jacket. "Just buzz when you're ready for me to finish."

Venom nodded, watching him exit the room. My already high-strung nerves got even shakier as he rolled back in his chair and stood. Thank God for sweat pants! Only he could make it look like a three-piece suit, not standing out from the corporate setting at all.

When he hopped up on the table, taking a seat directly in front of me, I was mesmerized stealing glances at the large imprint of his dick traveling down the side of his leg.

What the hell am I about to get myself into? I wondered, while squeezing my thighs together.

When I finally looked up into his animal-like eyes, he smirked, letting me know that he'd been watching me, lusting over him. Embarrassed, I focused on the thick paperwork in front of me. Phrases like, *at Venom's request,* and *bound by blood,* swirled on the paper in front of me, increasing my nervousness. Was I really going to go through with this? I was really starting to like him, and the fact that he'd won my mom over spoke volumes!

She didn't care for any other men I'd introduced to

her. But was I really ready to sign something like this? I'd been doing a good job putting on this carefree persona, but I didn't know if I could handle the other women. I wasn't used to sharing and wasn't sure if I was ready to start.

"What's wrong?" Venom asked, causing me to shift my eyes from the contract to him.

I sighed, placing my pen down, "Venom, this is a lot. I thought I could handle this, but..." I let my voice trail off.

"It's cool," he said, placing his cool hands on my face. "I want you to be a hundred percent sure. The last thing I want to do is force you to do anything that you not comfortable with."

I could clearly see the disappointment on his face, which he tried to mask.

"You said we can negotiate, right?" I asked.

"Anything you want."

"Ok, right here, on page 8, it says that we'd be bound by blood. Does that mean you're gonna turn me into a vampire or something?"

He chuckled, "No. It's how I get my sustenance. Some vampires take blood forcefully, that's never been my thing. I'd rather get it from a willing participant-"

I nodded, "Like your women," I finished for him and he nodded.

"Ok. I have a request."

He motioned for me to go ahead.

"I want to be the last one. No women after me," I told him, closing the contract. "And I can't live in the house. I can visit and stay for awhile, but I need to be able to keep an eye on my mom."

He smiled, showing off his white fangs, "I'll have

Walter add in the clauses. But I got a feeling your mom will be ok," he grinned, handing me my pen.

I paused for a moment, before signing my name. I still wasn't sure, but I could leave anytime I wanted to, and the second I felt like this was too much, I would. Gathering up the papers, Venom walked to the other side of the table and pressed a button I hadn't noticed before. In seconds, the door opened, and Walter walked back inside of the room.

"Everything alright?" he inquired, looking from Venom to me.

Venom nodded, handling him the contract, "There's a few things we need to add; I'll text everything to you."

"Alright. Well, I'll just file this away," he said, astoundingly professional, considering the situation.

Venom waited until he left before turning his attention back to me.

"What now?" I asked, still nervously fidgeting in my chair. "Do I meet the others now?"

He pulled me from my seat, looking me over, seductively before answering,

"Nah. You can meet them later. Right now, is about me and you," he responded, pulling me closer to his body and licking up my neck before placing his lips on mine.

I don't know what got into me at the moment, but I knew what I wanted inside of me right then and there! Feverishly, I pressed myself against him and parted my lips allowing his tongue to invade my mouth.

"Let's go," he demanded, pulling away, leaving me breathless.

We both hurried from the large office, anxious to consummate our contract. On the elevator, I watched him, his smooth movements that looked so fluid. His slim, but muscular arm flexed as he quickly pressed the button. Biting my lip, I stared at the blessing in the gray sweats.

"If you keep looking at me like that, you gonna have a problem," he spoke seriously.

"I want all the smoke," I replied, closing in on the few feet between us, continuing our kiss from the conference room.

"Fuck it," he mumbled, pressing the emergency button, stopping the elevator.

Dropping my purse to the floor, I leaned my head back and moaned like a cat in heat, while he kissed my neck and simultaneously slid my coat off my body and tossed it to the ground. He paused, looking me in my eyes, while his hand paused on the zipper at the back of my neck.

"You sure you ready for this? This is a whole different monster," he said, grabbing my hand and placing on his stiff dick that was constantly thickening and growing against my hand.

Squeezing what I could fit in my hand gently, I nodded, and in no time, he had me unzipped and damn near naked, except for my bra and panties. He lifted me and I instinctively wrapped my thick thighs around his waist before he snatched the thong from my body, causing me to gasp. Instantly, the sweet, musky smell of my saturated pussy filled the small space.

Ripping my bra straps with his teeth, my titties jumped free and landed in his mouth. I squeezed my eyes shut, letting the sensation from his tongue and teeth wash over me. I'd never been so ready for dick in my entire life! Impatiently, I ground my crotch against his, not giving a fuck that I was leaving a wet puddle on his grays. His member strained for release inside of his pants, and god, I wanted to free him like Harriet did the slaves!

Tightening my thighs around him, I used my muscles to slide his pants down. He chuckled, his breath tickling my hot skin, as I dry humped him through his boxer briefs, that I wasn't able to get off. He bit the top of my breast, lightly, sending what felt like a small shock, down my body.

"Oh my God," I whined. "Venom, please!"

"Please what?" he growled close to my ear.

Everything he did, seemed to have a heightened, sexual effect over my body. I opened my mouth, but no sound came out as he balanced me with one hand, and pulled his dick out with the other. It was shockingly cool, as he rubbed the thick, marble-like member against my wet, hot folds. If he kept pressing on my swollen clit, I was bound to cum before he even entered me.

Sweat beads broke out across my forehead and chest as I gyrated my hips, determined to get him inside of me, but he kept evading it.

"Answer me. Please, what?"

"Fuck me! Please fuck me!" I yelled.

In a flash, my back hit the cool, metal wall and I could feel Venom positioning himself. Slowly, he lowered me, and I clawed at his shoulders as I felt myself stretching to accommodate his girth. I tensed, feeling him deeper inside of me. He was too big, and I was in pain trying to take him.

"Shit," I mumbled as he slid another inch inside.

"Relax, baby. Breathe through it," he coached.

"I'm trying," I said through gritted teeth, struggling to relax my muscles.

As I did, he slid completely inside of me, catching me off guard.

"Ahhhh!" I yelled, as he began overtaking my body.

His deep kiss muffled my screams while he pounded away. Once I got used to his size, I started to enjoy it as he scraped and beat on spots I didn't know I had. His skilled strokes were quickly bringing me to orgasm. I was drenched, and the slippery noises echoed inside the elevator, along with our heavy breathing and moans.

"Fuck, Venom! Yes!" I screeched shakily, as my entire body began to throb with pre-orgasmic magic.

"Who you belong to, Jules?" he demanded, switching his style, now giving me long, slow strokes. "Who pussy is this?"

"Ummmm! Uh! You! Yours!" I screamed out as I came hard.

"This juicy motherfucker all mine?" He continued his questions.

"Yes, Venom!" I moaned, feeling high off my own ecstasy.

He lifted me higher, almost completely off his dick, leaving in the tip, before letting me fall back down on it. He continued bouncing me like I was a rag doll and my body responded by releasing juices all over him.

"Ahhh yes! Fuck me, Venom!" I cried out as he grabbed my ass to speed up his pace.

He was stroking faster and faster until he almost became a blur. Multiple orgasms were inching closer to release. He slowed a bit and stared at me. His normally colorful eyes, were clouding over in a dark shade of crimson red.

"Let me taste you," he said, his voice deeper and raspier than normal.

I knew from the look in his eyes what he meant, but I tensed in fear. He must have felt my resistance.

"You're mine, right?" he questioned again, still stroking my insides.

"Y-yes," I said, gently leaning my head back.

His fangs began slowly extending, causing his face to look animalistic. Without warning, he plunged the knife-like teeth into the side of my neck. A burning sensation coursed through me as my skin was broken open and my blood pulsed out. He let out a low growl as he slurped the fluid from my throat. As he bit deeper, I moaned from the intense sensations that slowly tiptoed down my spine and gathered at my base.

Taking deep breaths, I tried to gain some control, but I was too overcome with the foreign feelings that had me ready to lose it.

"I'm gonna cum again," I mumbled, all my energy starting to form in the pit of my stomach.

"Cum for me," he said, biting deeper.

On command, I came harder than I'd ever cum before.

"YESSSSSSSS!" I screamed, wrapping one hand in his dreads and using the other to dig my nails in his back.

When I finally came down, I was drained. I started to feel weak. Real weak.

"Venom," I whispered, hoarsely, patting his back while he still sucked hungrily on my neck.

He gave a little growl before abruptly pulling himself away.

"Fuck!" he shouted, his mouth and chin smeared with my blood.

He came deep inside of me, sandwiching me between the hard metal of the wall and his rigid body. My body tingled as I felt myself beginning to lose consciousness. I felt him press his lips to my neck again, and I knew I wouldn't survive another bite right now, but it felt so good I was ready to die trying.

Instead of biting me, I felt my skin warming, and my wound closed. Slowly, he licked my neck, cleaning any excess blood that spilled. Gingerly, he pulled out of me, our combined fluids running down my thighs. Cradling me bridal style in his arms, he sat down on the floor with me in his lap.

Feeling like I was in between life and death, I whispered, "Am I going to die?"

"No," he said, smoothing a few strands of hair that had fallen loose away from my face. "I took too much, but you'll be fine. That's my fault. I wasn't expecting you to taste so...it won't happen again," he assured me.

It was the last thing I remembered before sleep overtook me.

10

SERINA

"WHAT IS TAKING SO LONG?! How much longer do you expect me to keep living like this?! How much more information do you need?!" I hollered into my phone.

"As long as it fucking takes! He's the first and only son of the Court! You can't possibly be stupid enough to think a couple drive-bys would kill him!" The voice on the other end argued.

"But–"

"No buts! Give me some fucking information I can use or the whole deal is off!"

Furious, I hung up and deleted the call history. Venom was far from stupid, and it was only a matter of time before he figured out I was the one behind all of the shootings. At this point, it was either him or me. I hated that he'd even put me in this position! If he'd just turned me, one of the million times I'd asked, none of this would have happened.

I felt betrayed, giving my all to him, supporting that stupid ass rap career, and even giving him the option of other women. You know what they say, 'Give a nigga an inch and he'll take a mile.' As his woman, I should've been entitled to the power that comes from being a vamp. Shit, if he'd just turn me, I'd leave. That's all I ever wanted. I brooded, sitting alone in the dark, inside of my room.

I could hear the other girls laughing and giggling downstairs, and that pissed me off even more. Here I was, miserable as hell, trapped in this weird, loveless relationship, and these bitches were having the time of their lives! Nope! I was putting a stop to it! Hopping off my bed, I flung the door open and stomped downstairs. I was surprised to see my best friend, Lexi, down here fraternizing with these hoes. Damn! Did nobody understand the concept of loyalty anymore!? I paused at the bottom of the stairs and folded my arms across my chest, looking at Lexi.

"Well, isn't this a cute little sister wives' moment," I spoke sarcastically, slinging my hair over my shoulder, giving each of them an icy glare.

The smell hit me late, but I finally noticed the light haze of smoke as Lexi passed a blunt to Kember. Savalia's punk ass stood to leave, because she didn't want no smoke with me, but Kember pulled her back onto her lap.

"Val, you ain't gotta go nowhere just because this miserable bitch is tripping!" she said, waving her hand in my direction before taking a puff.

My eyes widened, "Excuse me?! You little ghetto–"

"Serina! Stop. We're just hanging out. Why don't you come chill and relax for once? Kem, tell her the story about Young Thug that you was just telling us," Lexi said, trying to diffuse the situation.

Kember rolled her eyes before beginning, "I was doing a scene for his video–"

"Hoe, please! I am not interested in your ran thru pussy tales! What you all fail to realize, is I'm the head bitch in charge around here! If it wasn't for me, none of you bitches would be here! That includes you too, Lexi! I'mma need all y'all to respect my position or–"

"Ha!" Kember laughed loudly, interrupting my speech. "Girl, you swear this flavor of love or some shit! You not New York, bitch! And be glad it's not set up like that, 'cuz your ass would've got your walking papers a long fucking time ago! Venom don't even like you or trust you! Now take your miserable, no dick getting, thirsty ass back upstairs!"

Rage coursed through my body, knowing she was telling the truth. Walking over to her, I hawk spit in her face like the industry trash that she was.

"Whoa!" Lexi exclaimed, jumping up, running in front of me.

Kember hopped up, knocking Savalia from her lap, and pushing Lexi out of the way. She punched me in my face, dazing me, but I threw a punch back. We were tumbling around, with her sneaking hits while Lexi and Savalia struggled to pull us apart. I had a tight grip on her hair, but Lexi finally pried my hands off and grabbed my arms.

As she did, Kember took the opportunity to punch

me, before Savalia grabbed her. I yelped as the hit stung my face.

"You let that bitch hit me!" I yelled at Lexi.

"Serina, calm down! I was trying to break it up!"

"I hit you a bunch of times! You only mad about that one?" Kember laughed from across the room, with Savalia still holding her.

"That's it! I'm pulling rank! As soon as Venom walks in this house, I'm putting my foot down! We've been more than charitable, but the free ride is over!" I spat.

"He don't want you! What don't you understand?" Kember bellowed, struggling to get back to me.

"We'll see," I said, folding my arms.

Lexi shook her head.

"What? What you shaking your head for? You supposed to be my best friend! You're supposed to back me up!" I shouted, turning my anger towards her.

"I am your friend but right is right and wrong is wrong! Some of the shit you been up to lately... You dead wrong," she spat, giving me a knowing look.

Sucking my teeth, I waved her off and turned to head back upstairs to see what this jealous bitch did to my face, but stopped in my tracks when I heard the lock turning. Quickly, I smoothed my hair and put on a fake smile, but it dropped, as Venom walked in, carrying...the bitch from his show!

He had the nerve to actually cradle her chunky ass gently! Oh hell no!

"VENOM! What the fuck is this?!" I questioned, frowning my face at the woman.

Ignoring me, he spoke to everyone else, as they each walked up and kissed him on the cheek. Rolling my eyes,

I placed a hand on my hip, shocked that he was really stunting on me for these bitches.

"Is this her, V?" Savalia's ditzy ass asked.

"Yea. This is Jules. She's a little out of it right now, but she'll be good in a few hours. I'mma go make her comfortable and I'll be back down to chop it up," he said, nonchalantly, as if I hadn't forbidden him to bring this girl into our home!

"Really, Venom?!" I questioned, as he walked past me.

"Yup," he said, simply.

"But... there's no more rooms! Where do you expect her to sleep?" I continued, trying my best to get him to see that this wasn't a good idea.

"She gonna be staying in my room."

My eyes widened in disbelief.

"Uh uh uh!" Kember chuckled, plopping down on the couch and crossing her legs.

I cut my eyes at her before hurrying to follow Venom up the stairs. He always caught an attitude with me when I went in his room, and here he was, with a bitch we barely knew, and he was allowing her to sleep in his bed!

"Venom! We need to talk! I'm not having this!"

He laughed and kept walking towards his room. Watching him carefully take off her cheap shoes and coat, made me sick to my stomach. He yanked down his covers before laying her in the bed, softly. Tears sprung to my eyes, because I remembered when he used to be so careful with me. Now I could barely even get a kind word from him.

Once he made sure his new toy was tucked in, he took off his jewelry and kicked off his sneakers. He paused at the door, since I was blocking it. He sighed, "What's the problem now, Serina?" he asked, exasperated.

"Venom, we need to talk. This is serious! I take a lot of shit from you, but this is too far! Do you know I'm really considering packing my shit and leaving?" I lied.

"Serina, I don't have time for your mind games tonight. If you want to go, then GO! I'm sick of this shit with you!"

"But I love you! I can't imagine life without you!" I said, working up some tears.

"It's too late for all that lovey dovey shit. Besides, I'm never gonna turn you. That's what you waiting around for, right?"

"Whattt? No! Wow, you think so lowly of me. That shit hurts! I've got feelings too! What makes her so much better than me?" I questioned, pointing at the bitch in his bed.

He shrugged, "She genuine. You fake. Simple as that. Move."

My mouth dropped open, but I didn't want to push him too far, so I stepped to the side and let him pass. Ohhh, I wish I had a stake, 'cuz I'd stab him in his fuckin sleep! He closed his door, and I followed him back downstairs, pouting behind him. The first thing I noticed was the smug look on Kember's face. Rolling my eyes, I opted to sit on the other side of the room.

"She's gorgeous Venom!" she exclaimed, while I made a low gagging sound. "You sure she cool with all of this? Some of us aren't so friendly," she said, cutting her beady eyes at me.

"She said she is, but I know she's not. I'm just hoping

she will get used to it, which is why tomorrow, I want to have her formally meet you all."

"Ohh, maybe we can do a brunch!" Savalia chimed in.

"Ohh yay! And can we give each other pedicures too?" I asked, sarcastically, mocking her excitement.

I stopped when Venom gave me a death look.

"A brunch sounds cool Val. Thanks. Lexi, what's wrong? Why you so quiet?"

I glanced at her, and she nervously looked at me before finger combing her curly, red hair. "I'm fine. Just thinking about some things I need to order for the boutique," she replied.

I breathed a sigh of relief. Lexi overhead a part of my phone conversation one day, and she was smart enough to put two and two together, so I was thankful that she didn't rat me out. It still didn't absolve her from fraternizing with these wack hoes in here though.

"You need funds for anything?" he asked.

"No, Venom! I told you time and time again, I got it. But thanks for the offer," her stupid ass responded.

"Uh, V, you didn't ask me if I needed any funds," I spoke in a sweet voice.

He raised a brow, "You got a business?"

"No, I–"

"Starting school? Got a job and need an interview outfit?"

"No! I wanna go shopping and–"

"What happened to the ten stacks I put in your account the beginning of the month?"

"I had an emergency pop up!" I defended, embarrassed that he was questioning me like I was some type of leech or something.

"She sure did. Wigs and labels!" Kember laughed. "Bitch, I saw your little Facebook story!"

"Venom, I swear to God! I'm so over this! Put this bitch in her place or I will!" I snapped, jumping to my feet.

Kember hopped up, ready for another round, "Please try! God, I want you to try!" she shouted, clapping her hands.

Picking up a large vase, I threw it at her head, but Venom easily blocked it, and suddenly appeared in my face.

"On everything, I'm trying my best not to put hands on you, but you really 'bout to make me fuck you up, Serina!" he shouted, his icy hands gripping my throat.

I struggled to breathe as he continued, "I'mma put some more money in your account, because tomorrow, I want you gone! Pack tonight!" he growled, finally letting me go.

I fell to my chair and cried, waiting for someone to come comfort me. When no one did, I huffed, hopping up and running upstairs. If he thought I was leaving, he should think again! No way in hell was I gonna roll before becoming a vampire! He had me fucked up! After splashing some water on my face, I calmed down and was able to come up with a plan.

The next morning, I woke up with a smile on my face. Opening my curtains, I allowed the sun to shine inside, brightening the room. Brushing my teeth inside my bathroom, I examined my face in the mirror. There was a tiny cut under my eye and minimal swelling. Nothing my Mac couldn't fix. I had bruises on my neck from Venom gripping me up, but that too could be covered. Soon, he'd be begging for forgiveness.

Throwing on some Gucci jeans, a matching tee, and my Prada boots, I stepped out into the hallway. Quietly opening Venom's door, my stomach turned sour, seeing him sleeping peacefully, cuddled up with his fluffy new toy. Closing the door, I swallowed my anger and headed downstairs. Hearing banging from the kitchen, I sauntered in that direction. Savalia was up, preparing to make this fucking brunch she was so gung ho for. Ingredients, like milk, eggs, butter, grits, fruits, shrimp, and salmon were out on the counter, while she whisked something in a large blue bowl.

When she noticed me, she stopped, and nervously glanced around.

"Hi, Val!" I chirped, cheerfully, causing her eyes to buck.

She always had such a deer caught in headlights expression on her face, that made me want to slap the shit out of her, but, as agonizing as it was, I kept the fake smile plastered on my face.

"Um, good morning, Serina. Listen, I don't want any trouble. I'm just—"

I held up a hand, cutting her off, "Why would you think I wanted trouble?" I asked, innocently. "Listen, I apologize for last night. I was feeling a little crampy and I took it out on you guys. So, to make up for it, I decided to help you out with the brunch!"

"Really?! I knew you couldn't be that mean! That's why when Kember said you were a raggedy, miserable bitch, I told her something had to be wrong! Are you feeling better now? Want me to make you some tea?"

I stood there, biting the inside of my jaw, while forcing a smile, "No. I'm ok, now. I'll just set up while you cook," I told her, opening the refrigerator, and grabbing a bottle of champagne.

I set the table with the fine china, folded napkins, even cut up some fruit and made a little salad. Finally, I stacked the champagne flutes in a pyramid. Grabbing the champagne from the ice bucket, I said, "I'm gonna have a bit of this now."

Savalia smiled, turning her attention back to the shrimp and grits she had on the stove, while I popped the cork. Pouring a tiny bit in my glass, I made sure Savalia was still focused on the stove, before opening the cabinet under the sink and grabbing out the rat poison. I dumped half of the bottle inside of the champagne and swirled it around so it'd disappear, then I placed it back in the ice bucket.

Humming Cardi's *Be careful with me*, I took a sip of my own unpoisoned glass and took a seat. Soft footsteps approached, and Kember appeared, looking like she hadn't bothered to wash the crust from her eyes. She gave me a stank face before padding her bare feet over to Savalia.

"Hey, bae! You got it smelling good as hell in here!" she said, kissing her cheek, before grabbing a piece of bacon.

I rolled my eyes because I didn't understand why these dyke hoes wouldn't just move out and get their own shit! Surely the excitement of being with a vampire should've wore off by now, right? As if she could feel my disdain, Kember turned towards me.

"I hope she didn't cook anything, 'cuz I don't put it past her to try and poison us all!"

Damn near choking on my beverage; I coughed uncontrollably.

"Kember, cut it out. It's a new day. Serina apologized and she's been very helpful. We should all try and get along. Love always trumps hate."

I stared at her, trying not to laugh at her bullshit I have a dream speech. I couldn't believe people like her actually existed! She was too easy to win over. Hopefully, her little pep talk would convince her ghetto ass girlfriend.

Kember sighed, "Fine. Only for you Val. But Serina, if you–"

"I've turned over a new leaf. Everything you guys said to me last night made me think about the type of person I've become, and... I just want to be happy again. No hard feelings," I said.

Savalia smiled brightly, while Kember still looked as if she didn't fully trust me, but eventually, she nodded.

Two down, one to go, I thought to myself, popping a piece of pineapple into my mouth.

"Where's the guest of honor?" I inquired.

Kember shrugged, "I heard some movement coming from Venom's room, and you know he's never up this early, so it must be her."

As if on cue, footsteps headed in our direction. The new bitch appeared, fresh-faced with her hair neatly brushed up into a bun. This was my first time getting a really good look at her because the first time I saw her was in a dimly lit, smoky club. She wasn't bad looking like I originally thought, but still, she wasn't me.

We all stared at one another until Savalia broke the ice.

"Hi! It's so good to meet you! Jules, right? Venom told us a lot about you!" she said cheerfully, walking up and hugging her.

The new girl looked slightly taken aback, but she hugged Savalia back.

"Um, thanks. This is all…"

"Weird, right?" I spoke up.

"Um, kinda. It's very different from what I'm used to, I guess."

"Understandably. I'm Kember, it's nice to meet you."

"I know you. You was killing it in that Migos video," she laughed.

"You saw! Girl, they flashed me on and off so quick I didn't think anyone could tell it was me!" Kember chuckled.

Oh great, these bitches are bonding.

"This is my girlfriend, Val. She did all this amazing cooking. She thought having this little shindig would get you acquainted with all of us. I'm sure you already got acquainted with Venom," Kember joked.

Jules looked a little uncomfortable while I seethed, knowing that she'd fucked Venom, and I hadn't got any dick in months!

"Too soon, Kember. She doesn't know us like that yet. I'm Serina by the way."

She looked at me for a second, before narrowing her eyes, "I remember you from the club…"

When I didn't respond, she placed a hand on her hip, "Are we gonna have a problem?" she asked, raising a brow.

Venom sure did have a thing for cleaning up the ghetto. Sheesh.

"Girl, no! I'm over that. We're all good."

She dropped her guard a little bit as I slid her the bowl of fruit. "Peace offering?" I said.

Taking a seat, she picked a cherry and gave me a weak smile.

"This is really nice of you! Everything looks delicious," she said as Val began uncovering numerous brass trays.

"I bet it does, you big bitch," I mumbled under my breath.

"What you say?" she asked, cocking her head to the side.

"I said, Yes it does! I dig this! Anyway, where the hell is Lexi?" I said, changing the subject.

"She said she had some errands to run at her shop, but she would be back in time for the brunch," Kember informed me, helping Val with the buffet styled meal.

"Huh? Since when are you and Lexi so close?" I asked.

"Serina, Lexi has always been cool with us. She just pretended not to be whenever you came around. She was trying to spare your feelings. But...since we're all cool now, that doesn't matter, right?" Kember tested me, watching my face for any reaction.

"That's right," I smiled through gritted teeth.

"So, uh, should we wake Venom up?" Jules asked.

"No! It's not safe for us to physically try and wake him, because he could mistakenly kill us while he's sleep. It's best to let him wake on his own," Savalia informed her, although I wish she would've just let her try.

"Ooh! Wow! Ok then. So, what does everyone do? Kember, do you still do videos?"

She shook her head, "Nah. I got tired of dealing with

that industry. Besides, Venom takes care of me nicely. I saved a lot of the money he's given me, and he's going to show me how to invest some of it."

I snorted, "So you pretty much have free room and board with your girlfriend, while getting occasional dick from Venom," I spat.

I tried my damnedest to hold it in, but it just poured out, like diarrhea of the mouth. Shit!

"My bad! I'm working on me. I'm not perfect, but I didn't mean that. Stupid, stupid," I said, patting myself in the head.

Jules looked shocked, while Kember looked like she wanted to cuss me out.

"Its ok, Serina. One step at a time." Val gave me her, oh so sought after, fortune cookie wisdom.

"Let's make a toast!" I exclaimed, first pouring orange juice into the flutes, before filling them up with my special champagne.

Handing each of them a glass, I smiled genuinely for once.

"Mimosas!" Val squealed.

Kember smiled, grabbing some fruit and placing it in Val's glass.

I made a face at their little moment, before clearing my throat.

"To Jules! Welcome to our small but loving family. Here's hoping for many years, till death do us part!" I cheered.

I pretended to gulp, while watching everyone. Savalia chugged hers, but Kember paused, "Jules wait! Try it with the fruit!" she said, touching her wrist.

NO, NO, NO!! ALL YOU BITCHES DRINK! I screamed in my head.

Glancing at Savalia, I noticed a funny look on her face. She glanced at me and grabbed her throat. Quickly, dumping my glass behind me, I held up the empty one, "Everybody drink up!" I said cheerfully.

As they raised their glasses once more, Savalia hit the ground.

"OH MY GOD!" Kember shouted, dropping her glass and rushing to her side as she convulsed on the floor.

"Shit! I'll call 911!" Jules said, sitting her drink down and running from the room to get her phone.

"VAL! VAL! WHAT'S WRONG?! WHAT'S HAPPEN-ING?!" Kember cried, while Savalia began to foam at the mouth.

Her eyes looked to me, and she grabbed her throat before they rolled back in her head.

"Maybe it's a seizure!"

"What! She's never seized before! Val please!" Kember cried, cradling her shaking body.

Suddenly, she stopped moving. Savalia was gone.

11

TASH

"No, yea. Girl, of course I understand! I'm just worried about you. That shit sounds strange, especially since you said she was fine just seconds before," I said to Jules, while lying in bed with my phone on speaker.

"I know! The entire thing has me a little shook. And Venom doesn't want to talk about it. I just... I think I might've bitten off more than I can chew."

"Is that vampire lingo? Look at you, sounding like a creature of the night already!" I joked, trying to lift her spirits.

She chuckled lightly, "See. I can't with you. Anyway, how's the Bahamas?"

"It's ok. If you've seen one island, you've seen them all," I lied so she wouldn't feel bad about missing the trip.

"Girl bye, with your fraudin' ass! I know that shit is beautiful! Have fun...but be careful with Lucky. I know what went down with Riq and Nikki really hurt you, but don't jump right into another possibly fucked up situation. Take your time," she warned.

Sighing, I walked to the balcony of my suite, and looked out over the never-ending blue, green waters, and breathed in the warm, salty air. I was in paradise, but my heart was broken into a million pieces, leaving me tortured. I couldn't believe the man that claimed to love me to death, would throw away all of our dreams for a piece of pussy that's for everybody! Well, fuck him! I'm in the fucking Bahamas, with a boss, no less. We'll see who has the last laugh!

"Thanks boo, but I'm good. I'm not looking for anything serious with Lucky. A little fun and a bigger bag is the goal," I told her. "Now stop calling me and go tend to your brooding vampire."

"Yea, I guess I should. Alright, girl, wish me luck. Love you."

"Godspeed, sis! Love you more," I said, before ending the call.

A light knocking on the door caught my attention and I pulled my white, silky robe tighter around my body.

"Room service," a smooth voice, with an island accent spoke.

We'd just arrived last night, and I declined to eat because I was so jet-lagged, but I hadn't gotten around to ordering anything yet. Opening the door, I gave a confused smile to the handsome toffee complected man with short, sandy-colored dreads.

"I'm sorry. I think you have the wrong room. I didn't order anything," I explained, tucking my hair behind my ear.

He smiled politely, "Your companion, Lucky, he ordered. He also left a message for you to be dressed and ready to go by one o'clock. He apologizes for being unavailable this morning," he informed me, rolling the cart inside of my room, as I stepped to the side.

"Oh," I said, surprised. "That was nice of him."

My stomach growled as I watched him uncover numerous dishes, some familiar, some not, but everything smelled amazing! I couldn't believe a few days ago, my world had come crashing down, and now I was on a beautiful island, being served like a Queen! In the words of Drake, I want this shit forever, man! I planned on getting close enough to Lucky, to study his moves, because I wanted this life permanently.

"Thank you so much," I said, digging inside of my purse and handing him a five-dollar bill.

"Oh no, miss. I've already been greatly tipped! Please enjoy and don't hesitate to call the front desk if you need anything at all!" he smiled, before leaving me alone with the smorgasbord of food.

Picking the omelet, that was colorful with a slew of chopped vegetables, and a bowl of fruit, I plopped down on the large, soft bed, digging in. I'd been to Jamaica with Riq, and Hawaii with Jules for a girl's trip, but I've never stayed in a five-star resort and been treated like diplomatic royalty! This was some new shit here!

Once I got my fill, I pushed the cart outside of my door, and since it was a quarter of twelve, I decided to start getting ready for Lucky. Disrobing, I strutted to the bathroom, pausing to look at my body in the mirrored bathroom door. My tall frame was slender, but I still had curves, thanks to the squats I regularly did. My smooth dark skin was blemish free. I should've modeled, but I didn't have the patience for the struggle in the beginning. I needed my bag, ASAP!

Inside of the glass, futuristic bathroom, I brushed my teeth in the invisible sink and washed my face, before pulling my twenty-six inches of loose wavy bundles up into a giant bun, pissed that I'd forgotten my damn shower cap. Turning on the water, I watched in amazement as the wall slid open, revealing smoked glass and six sprinklers. Water burst from them, before the overhead waterfall turned on.

Spotting some coconut body wash, I grabbed it, along with a fresh rag, and stepped under the waterfall. The perfect temperature of the water relaxed me and washed over me, and I quickly remembered my hair and moved my head to the side.

"I should've got some braids," I mumbled to myself, squeezing the wash into the palm of my hands, and lathering up.

My mind drifted to Riq, and the last conversation we'd had before I blocked his ass.

"*Come on, Tash! We can work through this.*"

"*No, the fuck we can't! How could you, and of all people, with Nikki!? What? You got some sick kick out of making me look stupid?!*" I screamed, holding back tears.

"*Baby, no! I fucked up once—*"

"*Once?! Once is enough! I won't give you the chance to make it twice!*"

"*Listen! I fucked up once, at Jahmer's party. I was fucked up and I made a mistake with her. But she taped the shit and every time I tried to flee her, she said she would show you the tape. I wanted to tell you, but I knew you'd react like...like this!*"

Throwing away my shit, ignoring me. But burning down the house... you overreacting!"

"Nigga, you tryna get me booked?! I didn't burn down shit!" I lied, not knowing if he was taping the conversation.

"But whatever happened, you deserved that shit! Mother-fucker, that party was damn near a year ago! You been fucking that bitch for a year?! Swear to God, I'm gonna get checked out and if I got anything, if even one pubic hair is singed, I'mma kill you and your whole fucking family! Have fun sleeping on your mom's couch, you dusty, dirty ass!" I raged before hanging up and blocking him and his mom's number and collapsing into tears.

Shaking my head, I rinsed off and stepped out, finishing my shower. Wrapping one of the giant, fluffy towels around my body, I pulled my hair from the bun to assess the damage I'd done in the shower. It wasn't too bad, but I needed to flat iron my leave out. While plugging it up in the bathroom, I heard my phone ringing. The special ringtone I'd given my grandmother blared in the room. I hurried out so I wouldn't miss her call.

"Hey, mom mom!" I answered.

"Hi, baby! I told you to call me as soon as you landed! Had me worried sick!" she scolded.

"My bad, Granny. It was late when I got here and I was so tired," I explained.

"I figured as much. That boy been parked in front of my house all night. Calling me because he can't get in touch with you. He's a damn pest!"

I sucked my teeth, "Don't pay him no mind! And don't answer his calls. I'mma deal with him as soon as I get back home! He knows I don't play about you!"

"He ain't bothering me. If he wanna sleep in his car

outside of my house, that's fine. I'mma pray for him, but if he gets too out of hand, I'll personally send him to the Lord," she said, and I could hear her loading bullets in her gun.

Screaming in laughter, I said, "I'm sure that ain't necessary, mom mom! I don't need you getting locked up behind my mess!"

"Uhn hun, take your own advice, 'cuz I know you burnt that house down! That boy called crying talking about his birth certificate and stuff was in there."

"Welp, I guess he an illegal immigrant now! He better be lucky it was just his paperwork and not his black ass!"

"I don't know who raised you, Left eye, but I'mma put you in charm school when you get back."

We laughed a bit, and it made me feel better to hear my Granny's voice. After we said our I love you's, I finished getting dressed. The end result was a sexy, tropical look. I'd decided on a yellow wrap dress that looked bomb against my chocolate skin and flattered my curves nicely. I paired it with some new strappy sandals I ordered from Fashion Nova, that had turquoise stones embedded in them, enhancing my fresh pedi.

I didn't need much makeup, except to fill my sparse ass eyebrows and a little lip gloss. My long, black hair hung loose and wavy. Spinning around for the mirror, I felt satisfied with the look. I didn't know what Lucky had planned, but I figured this fit was multi-purpose. I even had on my cute little blue bikini underneath it, just in case.

Grabbing my phone to check the time, I saw it was one fifteen. Just as I was about to call Lucky, someone knocked on the door. Swinging it open, I threw a hand on my hip and looked at Lucky, who looked good in his all-white. He was a big guy, who resembled Fat Joe with a full beard, but the real Fat Joe, 'cuz once he lost his weight, he was just Thick Joe. He had mob boss vibes, and from the stories I've heard, might not be too far off from the truth.

"You're late," I sneered, as he walked past me, smelling like expensive cologne.

He circled me like a shark sniffing out blood, looking me up and down as I spun, smirking at him.

"Damn. If me being late means you gonna look like this, I'm never gonna be on time!"

Shaking my head, I chuckled, "That's not professional," I told him, flinging my hair behind my shoulder and grabbing my purse.

"Oh, you gon' be like that? I guess you don't want to know why I'm late. It's cool, I'll holla at you later," he said, walking past me to exit the room.

My mouth dropped. I know he wasn't leaving after I spent all this time getting dressed!

"Really Lucky?!" I said, grabbing his arm. "Ok, why are you late?"

He grinned, reaching into the pocket of his white, linen, button-down shirt. Producing a tennis bracelet, littered with diamonds, he dangled it in front of my face. The bright, high, sun beamed into the room, causing the gems to twinkle like stars.

"I saw this and thought it would look good on your sexy ass," he said, fastening it around my wrist.

"Oh my gawd!" I whispered, excitedly, holding my arm up, watching the rainbow prism from the clear diamonds reflect on my skin.

Without thinking, I grabbed him in a tight hug,

careful not to get my lip gloss on his white clothing. Surprisingly, he didn't feel soft, like I'd imagined. His massive body was solid. When he pressed me against him tighter, I snapped back to reality, and gently pushed away.

"Thank you, Lucky. I don't want you to think I'm unappreciative when I ask this...but, do you give all of your employees diamond tennis bracelets?"

He scoffed, "Didn't you watch me give Venom a chain?"

I made a face, 'cuz he knew that wasn't what I was talking about, but I decided to drop it because my arm wanted me to be great.

"Um hmm. Anyway, where are we going?"

"You ask too many questions. Come on."

Sighing, I followed him out of the room, closing the door behind me. This was gonna be an interesting day. Outside, the weather was warm and breezy, and the sounds of some islanders lightly playing steel drums, only added to the tropical atmosphere. We walked past groups of tourists, towards a white Jeep Wrangler. The roof and doors were off, giving it the perfect island vehicle.

I smiled widely, already thinking of photo opps for Snapchat!

"You like it?" he asked, helping me into the passenger side, but actually taking a grope of my ass.

"This jawn fire!" I said excitedly, causing him to laugh.

Immediately, I whipped out my phone and started snapping away, making sure to casually get my wrist in the shot.

"Where you from?" he asked, once I was done stunting.

"Chester. It's right outside of Philly."

"I know that, and I know where Chester is. My nigga Meek was locked up there. I mean, your people's. Where they from? You look like these motherfuckers," he said, nodding his head towards the streets that were crowded with Bahamians.

"Oh! As far as I know, I'm black. Not Caribbean black, just regular black," I shrugged. "I don't know who or what my father is, and my mother is a crackhead sooo, who knows," I spoke, getting quiet.

"My fault. I didn't mean for you to rehash some old shit; I was just curious."

"It's cool," I said, looking out into the streets, and silently annoyed with myself for telling him my business.

I was a little uncomfortable, because I didn't want him or anyone else to look at me with pity. The silence around us roared so loud, that I started to ask him to take me back to the room, but my ringing phone stopped me. I huffed, checking the caller ID and seeing Riq's sister.

"Hello," I answered, kicking myself for posting that snap chat.

I knew that was why she decided to call now.

"Hey, Tash. How you been holding up?" she asked with fake sympathy.

Me and Trisha were cool, but she always took Riq's side when we argued. His sister and mother babied him so much it was sickening. Now she was calling me with this fake shit. If Vivica Fox taught me anything, it's that two can play that game.

"I've been ok. Just holed up in my Granny's house. Girl, I don't even want to leave the house. I'm barely eating. I'm praying for strength and wisdom during this difficult time," I said, sure she could hear the wind blowing through the phone.

Lucky cut his eyes at me in confusion, and I smiled, placing a finger to my lips to let him know to be quiet.

"Oh really? Well, explain the snap you just posted! You on vacation while my brother is suffering!? I thought you were better than that!"

"Bitch, fuck outta here! That nigga suffering because he can't keep his little dick out of sloppy holes! And I sure the fuck am on vacation! I needed it after dealing with your brother! Now go get the nigga from in front of my grandmother's house, and put him on your Mama's tit, where he belongs!"

"You dirty bitch! I got something for your ass when you get back to the city!"

"Welp, catch me then. Right now, I gotta get back to my fun in the sun! Smooches!" I giggled, hanging up, and blocking her ass too.

Placing my phone back inside my purse, I looked over at Lucky, who'd stopped driving and was staring at me.

"What?" I asked innocently.

He burst into laughter, "Yoo, you shot the fuck out! That's how you talk to people and you expect to work for me? Nah, babe. I pride myself on professionalism."

"Professionaallissmm!" I yelled in my Soulja boy voice.

"Boy bye!" I laughed. "I've heard stories about you that's far from professional!"

He chuckled, nodding his head, "Whatever they say I did, I did that shit. I was gonna ask what made you change your mind about taking this trip with me, but that phone call just gave me a clue."

"Yup," I sighed. "Niggas ain't shit. What's new?" I asked sarcastically.

"I can't hate on that man. Shit, I ain't even mad at him. His fuck up, is my come up."

I giggled, "Mmm hmm, you coming up on a bomb ass assistant," I said, playfully poking his arm.

"We'll see," he said, not taking his eyes off of the road.

When I saw a sign that said *Blue Lagoon*, my eyes bucked, "Are we going to see the dolphins?" I inquired.

I'd been googling stuff that I wanted to do while I was here and seeing the dolphins was one of them!

"We can do better than that. We gonna go talk to them niggas."

I laughed, "You mean we're going swimming with them! Wait, can you swim?" I asked, seriously.

"Oh, cause I'm fat I can't swim?" he asked.

"No! I mean...I meant," I stumbled, trying to get my foot out of my mouth.

He laughed, "Chill, I'm just fuckin' with you. Yeah, my fat ass can swim. Ain't too much I can't do," he said, placing his hand on my thigh.

"And I'm sure you can, but I won't be finding out," I smirked, moving his hand.

He shook his head and I giggled. Lucky was attractive, big boy and all, and he for sure had swag and oozed power, but I was serious about getting these coins, and I wasn't gonna be his hoe to get it. I was determined to make him respect me and see me as somebody he could get money with.

We parked, and walked the rest of the way, where we were greeted. The men obviously were familiar with Lucky, as I'm sure we cut a long line. We were escorted across a small private beach, and I made sure to take pictures of the beautiful blue water and white sand. We were led to who I assumed was the instructor. He and Lucky shook hands, before he smiled at me and held his hand out for me to shake.

He gave us a brief history of the island and the dolphins and sea lions, before handing us each a piece of fish.

"Who wants to feed them first?" he asked, rubbing his hands together looking from Lucky to me.

"He does!" I answered quickly.

"You ain't shit," he chuckled.

The instructor walked halfway into the water and clapped his hands. In seconds we could see at least five dolphins swim up. Some jumped up out of the water, while others did that thing where they stand on their tail and laugh at you. I laughed, edging closer.

"You guys have your swimsuits?" he hollered over to us.

Lucky looked towards me, "We can always go naked if you don't have one with you," he grinned.

Smirking at him, I dropped my purse to the sand and untied my sandals. Lucky watched with interest, as I started unwrapping my dress, purposely taking my time. When I finally got it off, I carefully folded it and placed it neatly on top of my purse.

"That's a good look," he mumbled, staring at me from head to toe like I was the snack, dinner and dessert.

"Thank you," I said, adjusting the strapless top.

He unbuttoned his shirt, revealing lots of scars and tattoos, and folded it, placing it near my pile. I noticed the gun he had tucked inside of his pants, but I didn't say anything about it, as he removed it and placed it under his shirt in the sand. Taking off his pants, he sported colorful trunks underneath. He was a big guy and I was shocked to see that he was actually muscular.

"What you looking at?" he asked, catching me staring at him as he removed his heavy looking chains.

I smirked, "Nothing much. What about my hair?" I asked more to myself than him, but his smart ass responded anyway.

"Take that shit off and let's go."

"First of all, this ain't a wig! It's a sew in, and the hair is expensive as hell! It ain't no taking it off!" I spat, throwing a hand on my hip, while he laughed.

"It's not that serious. I'll buy you more. You probably don't need the shit no way."

Sucking my teeth, I quickly braided my hair into two pigtails and followed him to the water, where the instructor was patiently waiting. We fed the cute little sea creatures and petted them before actually swimming. I laughed hard as hell when Bubba, one of the dolphins, sprayed Lucky in the face with water, and he reached for his gun, forgetting it wasn't on him.

I was still laughing once we were finished and heading back to the car.

"You really thought that shit was funny," he said, once again, helping me inside.

Wiping tears from my eyes, I tried to catch my breath, "I can't believe you would have shot that cute little dolphin! He was only playing with you!"

"Fuck that nigga! He was showing the fuck off. He better thank Poseidon, or whoever the hell he pray to, that I didn't have that gun on me! Nigga woulda been seafood salad!" he said, seriously.

I stared at him with wide eyes before bursting into another fit of laughter.

"Oh, you think it's a joke? I'm taking your ass back to the hotel!" he grinned.

"Lucky, no!" I said in between my screams of laughter. "I'm sorry. I'mma stop," I said, holding in my giggles.

Turning my head, I stared out the opposite side of the Jeep trying to get myself together. When I had it under control, I looked at Lucky, who was staring at me. I know my face looked crazy, from trying my hardest not to laugh at him.

Shaking his head, he chuckled, "Goofy ass broad."

"I'm goofy, but you the one trying to have a shoot out with a dolphin?!" I exclaimed.

"Shut up," he finally laughed. You hungry?"

I nodded my head, "Yes."

We drove in peaceful silence, as I enjoyed the beautiful scenery zipping past in a colorful haze. Finally, we pulled up to a place called *The Bahamian Club*, and drove in front for the Jeep to be valet parked. As I stepped out, Lucky came around and looped his arm through mine, after tipping the valet. I noticed people watching us, as if we were celebrities, and it was definitely something I could get used to.

Inside, we had to walk through a casino to get to the restaurant. I was hoping we'd come back and gamble a bit before we went back to the hotel. Bypassing the people waiting, we were led straight to the back, to a private table. Lucky pulled out my chair, and I smoothed my dress before sitting so that it wouldn't wrinkle. The soft lighting bounced off of the gold and glass designed tables, and the sound of water running added to the ambiance.

'Once we ordered, the specialty conch soup for me and steak for Lucky, he leaned back in his seat.

"You gon tell me what's bothering you?"

I looked at him in surprise, shocked that he was able to read me so well, after only knowing me for a short period of time. Also, I needed to perfect my game face, because I really thought I was hiding everything good enough that he wouldn't notice.

"I was just wishing that my girl Jules and Venom could've made it. She really needs a vacation," I admitted.

"Yeah, I had some people I wanted Venom to meet before his tour starts."

My eyes widened, "Tour? When is he going on tour?" I inquired, wondering if Jules knew he was leaving.

"Three weeks from now. I'm waiting on his verse for another of my artist's singles, just to get him properly introduced to the world, then it's tour time."

"Oh!" I said, making a mental note to ask Jules about it.

"What's up with him and your girl? They serious?" he asked, taking a swig of his imported beer.

Now, I didn't know how close Venom and Lucky were, so I wasn't sure if he was privy to personal information, but I knew that Jules had sworn me to secrecy about damn near everything, so I decided to play down their relationship. If Venom wanted Lucky to know his business, he could tell him. I did not want to deal with an angry vampire, and I definitely didn't want to deal with Jules crazy ass!

"Nah. From what I know, they just chilling. Nothing serious," I lied, taking a sip of water to mask the fabrications rolling off of my tongue.

He shrugged, "Aight. So what else is bothering you?" he asked, sitting up and folding his hands on the table.

I chuckled nervously, "You a psychic or something?"

He shook his head, "No. I'm trained to read body language. Most conversations are only forty percent verbal; the other sixty is nonverbal. Where I'm from, knowing how to tell if someone's word matches their actions could mean life or death," he spoke, seriously.

It seemed as if a hundred memories flashed through his eyes in that moment, and I wanted to ask him more about his background, but we were interrupted by our cheerful waiter dropping off our lunch. The sweet, spicy smell of my soup and the buttery rolls temporarily hypnotizing me.

"Umm, this smells amazing!" I said.

Lucky, who'd already started cutting into his medium rare steak, looked up at me, forking a piece into his mouth.

"You want me to kill him?" he asked, nonchalantly, chewing his meat.

I choked on my damn soup! He caught me off guard, and the way he asked, as if he was asking me to pass him the steak sauce!

"Boy, what?!" I exclaimed, trying to laugh it off.

"Don't call me boy. I'm a man. And you heard what I said. Say the word, and he'll be dead before we touch down," he told me, spearing a piece of his lemon asparagus.

"Lucky, no!" I whispered.

"You still got feelings for him?" he asked.

"No. I mean, yeah, kind of. I mean, we were together for a long time, and that shit doesn't just fade overnight," I said, playing with my soup.

"Would I ever take him back? Hell no! But that doesn't mean I want him dead. Do you kill your exes?" I asked, trying to lighten the mood.

"Some of 'em. Some I just get deported."

"Deported?! Deported where?!" I asked, not knowing if I should run or laugh.

"Shit, Africa, Puerto Rico, wherever the hell they ancestors came from!"

Ok, now I was laughing! His ass was a fool!

"Hmmm, is that why you were asking me about my ethnicity earlier? You think you just gonna ship me off if I start getting on your nerves?!"

He chuckled, "Nah, I was genuinely curious. Besides, you already worked my nerves multiple times and I ain't sent you nowhere, yet."

My mouth dropped, while he laughed at my expense.

"Pick up your jaw before I put some of this steak in it. I know yo ass hungry; tryna be cute ordering soup and shit."

I laughed, "Excuse me for being cultured. I wanted to try an island specialty! I can get steak anywhere!" I scoffed, waving off his plate.

He smiled, "Not like this. Try it," he said, cutting a small piece and holding it out on his fork.

It did look good, and he was right, I wasn't going to get full from this soup, even though it was delicious. So, I leaned up and opened my mouth as he gently placed the steak inside. It damn near melted on my tongue and I instantly regretted not ordering it.

"Uhmm, can I have some more?" I asked, covering my mouth with my hand.

"Hell nah!" he laughed, moving his plate. "Drink your soup!"

I sucked my teeth, "Should have known you wasn't gonna share no food," I mumbled, crossing my arms.

He stared at me, "You got jokes. See how funny it is when your ass hungry later."

"I'll just order room service on you," I said defiantly, sticking out my tongue.

The rest of our lunch was fun and surprisingly, eye-opening. Lucky opened up a lot, answering most of my questions and confirming what I, and the rest of the world thought, he was crazy as hell. I did have to admit, he was charming, generous and most importantly, honest. He managed to take my mind off of missing my bestie, and my dirty ex. Afterwards, he paid and left a hefty tip.

"Can we gamble?" I asked, returning from the restroom.

"I only gamble when the odds are in my favor, but you feel free. I got some calls to make," he informed me, handing me a wad of cash, wrapped in a Balenciaga band.

"I don't need this much!" I said, not really wanting to gamble with his money, especially if he wasn't going to play.

"It's only seven hundred. I don't keep a lot of cash on me," he insisted, handing it back.

"*Only* seven hundred?! This is my rent!" I exclaimed.

He laughed, "Go head and play. See if you get lucky."

"Ok," I said, hesitantly taking the cash.

He walked towards the smoking area, lighting a cigar and pulling out his phone. After I cashed it in for chips and effectively dodged old men, who clearly thought that I was looking for a sugar daddy, I headed straight to the blackjack table.

"Pretty lady, you feeling lucky today?" the dealer asked as I approached.

I glanced through the crowd, over at Lucky, who was busy on his phone, and grinned.

"Yes. I am feeling lucky," I said, confidently, smoothing my dress before taking a seat at the table.

Placing all of my chips on the table, I said a quick prayer and smiled at the dealer, who raised a brow. He flipped over my first card, a queen of spades.

"Stay!" someone shouted behind me.

I shook my head, playing with fate, "Hit me."

The dealer looked at me as if I was crazy. So, did everyone else around me. I had nothing to lose. If I lost, I'd just go back to my gorgeous five-star hotel. But if I won...

"Hit me," I said again.

Slowly, he turned over my card. An ace! I screamed, jumping up from my seat. A half an hour later, I was five thousand dollars richer. Deciding to quit while I was ahead, I gathered my winnings and cashed out.

"How'd you make out?" Lucky asked, as I switched towards him.

Digging inside of my purse, I pulled out my own wad of money and reveled in the surprised expression he wore. Licking my fingers, because I was extra, I counted through the money, handing him seven hundred of it.

"Here's your money back. I'm exactly forty three hundred dollars richer," I grinned.

He smiled broadly, "That's what's up! You gonna buy some bundles and red bottoms or something?" he asked, tucking his phone into his pocket while trying to hand me back the seven hundred.

"No!" I said, taking the knot and shoving it into his pocket. "I need to find something to invest in. I know I can multiply this!" I said, waving the money. "Can you help me find something to put this in?" I asked.

He stared at me, shocked, while I looked at him in confusion.

"What?" I asked.

"You really serious?" he admonished.

"Yes! That's what I've been trying to tell you! I got a grandmother to take care of! She took care of me her whole life; I owe her. Without her..." I shook my head. "And anyway, I don't want to be wiping ass for the rest of my life. Something has to pop off!"

"I didn't know you were this serious. Usually, women expect me to fund their dreams. This is new to me. I'mma put you on. What you know about keeping books and keeping your mouth shut?" he asked.

"Lucky, for real!? Oh my God thank you! I'm a genius at bookkeeping and I swear I can keep a secret! Loyalty over everything! I didn't see nothing; I don't know nothing!" I exclaimed.

He laughed at my enthusiasm. "You good, Tash. You officially apart of the team," he informed me as we waited outside for valet to bring the Jeep.

"I'm not even gonna try to sleep with you no more," he added.

For some reason, I felt slightly disappointed. I was starting to feel him, and a tiny part of me wanted to end up in his bed. But if I had to choose between Lucky and the bag, I picked the bag. The Jeep pulled up, and we got in. I was feeling good after winning money and getting a new job, but something I couldn't put my finger on, nagged at me.

"I'mma take you back to the hotel while I handle some business. You wanna do something to celebrate tonight?" he asked.

"Yeah, of course!" I said.

After he dropped me off, I decided to put on a different swimsuit and go lounge outside at the resort. It was only six o'clock, so the sun was still bright in the sky as I strutted around, finally taking a seat at the outside bar area. After I ordered a Long Island, I found a lounge chair and got comfortable, the sun heating my oiled skin on the outside and my Long Island warming me from the inside.

I decided to call Jules and tell her my good news.

"Hey, girl," she answered, sounding better than she had earlier.

"Hey, boo! You sound happy," I said.

"Yeah. Me and Venom had a long talk and I feel better. So does he. He thought I was going to leave because of everything that happened. We're in a better space, other than this fake ass bitch, Serina. I don't trust her ass and I'm waiting for her to try me!"

I laughed, "Don't worry 'bout that bitch. Shit, it sounds like Venom feeling you heavy! She probably won't even be around much longer. Hey, did you know he's going on tour soon?" I asked, sipping my drink.

"Yeah. Not for a few weeks though. He asked me to come with him."

I grinned, "You should go!" I told her.

"Maybe. Anyway, what's going on with you? When you coming back? I miss you!" she fake cried.

"Bitch, please! You not thinking about me! Over there getting vampire pipe!" I joked. "Nah, Lucky gave me a job for real!"

"Yasssss! You his assistant?"

"Nope! I'm going to be keeping his books for multiple businesses."

"Bitch, you never kept no damn books!" she said.

I laughed, "So what! How hard can it be?"

"Your fraud ass better learn quick! How's Lucky anyway?"

"Surprisingly, cool as ever! I mean, he's crazy as fuck, but in a sweet way."

There was a long period of silence, so I glanced at the phone to make sure I didn't accidentally hang up.

"Hello?" I asked.

"I'm here. Tash, don't do anything you'll regret. I know you and you sound like you got a little crush over there."

"Its strictly business," I told her looking out at the pool. "But I need another drink, so let me get settled and I'll call you back," I said, needing to get off of the phone with her.

"Uhm hmm. Make sure you call me back. Have fun. Not too much."

"Bye, girl!" I said, disconnecting the call.

I could already tell she was about to kill my vibe. I

swam a few laps in the pool, before ordering more drinks. Five Long Islands later, I was officially wasted and trying to remember what floor I was on.

"Miss, do you need some help?" the waiter from this morning asked as I leaned against the wall, waiting for the elevator.

"Everybody on this island is so...helpful!" I giggled, drunk as Ned the wino.

He chuckled, "We like to make everyone's stay as pleasant as possible. Let me escort you to your room."

I nodded, "Ok. I'm staying in this hotel."

"Yes. I know this."

"That's right!" I laughed, "Wait. Lucky. Is he here?"

"Yes. He's been back for about an hour."

"What's his room number?" I asked.

"He's on the top floor. Only room up there, but you need a special key to get the elevator to go there."

"Well, can I have it?"

"I'm sorry. I can't–"

"What?! I thought you had to help me!"

"I'm trying, but–"

"Listen, I'm an integral part of his company, and I want. No, I demand to speak with him!" I insisted, slurring my words.

The man sighed, "One moment please," he said, pulling out a phone.

I watched as he walked away, making a call. Finally, he returned, producing a key, which he stuck into a small slot on the elevator that I hadn't noticed before. Still polite as ever, he gestured for me to get on.

Clumsily, I stumbled on and bowed to the man,

"Thank you, kind sir," I spoke in an outrageously horrible British accent.

He chuckled as the doors silently closed. Crazy thing, the closer I got to the top floor, I could smell Lucky's cologne. With each floor, the sandalwood scent became stronger and stronger. Finally, the elevator stopped, and the doors slid open, allowing me to walk straight inside of his suite.

I looked around in awe at his temporary living quarters. Everything was all white, reminding me of what I thought a *Bad Boy* party would have looked like back in the nineties. I giant crystal ceiling fan made a whirring noise in the otherwise silent room. His balcony was open, and the slight breeze that blew in caused the thin, soft material of the curtains to billow and sway seductively.

As I stepped further inside, I noticed he had a few separate rooms inside his suite. The movement of the elevator descending back down caused me to jump, then giggle at my own silliness.

"Tash, I'm back here," he shouted.

After taking off my shoes so I wouldn't get the plush, white carpet dirty, I walked barefoot across the room, enjoying the feel of the softness against my feet. I followed his voice to the last room, which happened to be an office.

"Wow, you even work on vacation," I spoke from the doorway.

His back was to me as he typed away on a laptop.

He laughed, "I'm trying to close out this one account. This is actually your job! You should be doing this shit," he said, turning around.

He paused, staring at my bikini-clad, oiled up body, as

I casually posed against the door frame, jutting my chest out. He studied me for what seemed like forever, before he spoke.

"I'm confused," he said, standing, finally tearing his eyes from my body to look in my face.

I raised an eyebrow for him to continue.

"You told me you wanted a strictly professional relationship. But here you are, half-naked standing in my suite."

I smiled as he made his way closer.

"What's confusing about it?" I asked, turning and walking from the room, giving him a good view of my firm, little ass in the process.

I could hear his footsteps following behind me. "We're on an island, shouldn't I be in a bathing suit?" I stopped, peering inside of his bedroom at his particularly large bed.

"That still doesn't explain why you're in my room."

Walking inside of his bedroom, I spun to face him. "I thought you could read body language?" I asked, before reaching behind me and untying my top, allowing it to fall to the floor at my feet.

He smiled, "I'm 'bout to thumb through all your pages," he said, lifting me off my feet and throwing me onto his soft bed.

I giggled as I bounced around. He quickly undressed and made his way over to me, grabbing my legs and roughly pulling me to the edge. He untied the strings on my bottoms and snatched them off. Spreading my legs, he stared at my pussy lustfully.

"I'm a big nigga 'cuz I like to eat," he said, before diving his face into my already moist peach.

Propping myself up on my elbows, I watched as his tongue expertly maneuvered around my clit, causing me to throw my head back in pleasure. His large hands gripped my thighs, pulling me closer and I thought, this had to be what little animals felt when they were being swallowed whole by a giant anaconda. Slowly, he was devouring my entire pussy, and the feeling was incredible!

"Oh shit! Eat this motherfucker, Lucky!" I yelled, as my clit throbbed under the pressure of his tongue.

He said something, but it came out garbled since his mouth was busy at the moment.

"UH UH UH!" I screamed, sounding like Young Dolph or Gucci Man or whatever.

I was cumming, and I was cumming hard. All of the stress in my body rushed out forcefully, leaving me relaxed and limp.

"Nah, don't fall back now. Put your big girl panties on and ride this dick," he said, hovering over me, my juices glistening in his thick beard.

He laid back on the bed and lifted me on top of him. I moaned when I felt his hardness slide against my wet middle. Placing my hands on his chest, I eased down his body, anxious and curious to see what he was working with. My face now inches from his dick, I grinned. He was long, thick and rock hard. Teasing him with my tongue, I slowly ran the tip around his shaft, while using my soft hands to massage his balls. I did this for a few minutes until his toes began to curl.

Taking him into my mouth, I deep throated as much as I could, stopping once he hit my tonsils.

"Hmmmm," I hummed around his dick, feeling him grab the back of my head.

When he started intertwining his fingers in my hair, forcing me down further, I backed up, his member slipping from my mouth with a wet pop. Climbing back up his body, I positioned him at my opening and carefully slid down his pole, relishing the feeling of being stretched as he filled me up to the hilt.

"Oh shit!" we both breathed out in unison, as I slowly began to ride.

Placing both of my feet on either side of him, I picked up the pace, riding him like a professional jockey. The sound of wet skin on skin grew louder throughout the room. When he roughly grabbed my hips and began slamming me down harder, I lost control, calling this nigga everything from daddy to big poppa, as I came again.

Rolling me over quickly, he pushed me flat down on my stomach, while gripping my hair tightly so that my head was pulled back. He pounded into me with so much force that I found myself unsuccessfully trying to crawl away.

"Don't run. You wanted this dick and you gonna take all of it!" he said, hammering me as if he worked out every day and I know his big ass didn't.

"Fuck, Lucky! Right there! Don't stop!" I screeched, feeling him chiseling away at my g-spot.

At that moment I gave no fucks about my neck beginning to cramp, or the fact that he was heavy as fuck and I was starting to lose my breath, or that he was pulling my hair so hard I could feel my tracks loosening. Fuck it! I was gonna be one broke neck, suffocated, baldhead hoe, about to cum for the fourth time!

"AHHHH!" I yelled, as new sensations racked my body.

He paused briefly, "Oh, you a squirter," he said in my ear, finally releasing my hair.

I didn't have the energy to respond, as he lifted my legs in a wheelbarrow position, causing my chest and face to press deeper into his soft sheets that smelt like his cologne. This new angle felt crazy, and now I really was struggling to get away. I didn't think my body could handle another orgasm so soon after the last one, but if he kept this stroke up, it was bound to happen.

"What the fuck did I just tell you?!" he demanded, yanking me back further on his dick.

"Lucky, please! I can't!" I whimpered.

"Fuck that!" he grunted, crouching behind me and turning me so that we were in a sideways position.

He continued pounding, but now he'd stuck one of his thick fingers up my ass. Using his finger and his dick to seesaw me, my body started convulsing, and tears and sweat rolled down my face, dampening the sheets.

"OH MY GOD!" I murmured, feeling my body go awff!

"FUCK!" he shouted, squeezing one of my nipples.

That ministration caused me to cum once more. A long, drawn-out explosion, that had my body twitching and a ringing in my ears. Pushing himself inside of me as deeply as he could, I felt him unload his warm jizz, coating my walls. After what felt like forever, he collapsed on top of me and I turned my head towards the window, so I could breathe. We both lay there, panting heavily, struggling for air.

"Goddamn! I'm giving you a raise," he said, in-between breaths.

I chuckled, "I don't even know how much I make yet," I informed him, fighting the fatigue that was washing over me.

"Whatever you thought, double that shit!"

I giggled, letting sleep take over, feeling him beginning to soften inside of me. I had a feeling life with Lucky was about to get really interesting.

12

JULES

STANDING IN MY HOME, I was shocked to see my mom moving around with so much energy! She was vacuuming and had *Earth, Wind and Fire* blasting so loud that she hadn't even noticed me come inside with grocery bags. I watched her for a moment, chuckling to myself, because this brought back memories of her waking me up, early Saturday mornings to do chores.

"Mom!" I shouted over the noise.

Taking notice of me, she smiled, turning off the vacuum cleaner and lowering the volume on her stereo that was pretty much an antique. I smiled widely, noticing the healthy glow of her skin. She'd added a few curls to her hair, and even put on her favorite maroon colored lipstick. I hadn't seen my mom look this healthy and happy in a long time.

"Hi, Ju!" she smiled, making her way over to me, grabbing one of the bags from my hands.

"Mom...you look..." I stopped, still in partial shock.

"I look good, right?" she said, flinging her hair, "I feel even better! Like I'm thirty again."

"You look great! What's going on? Did they change your meds or–?"

"Child, I haven't taken that medicine in days! I forgot to take it one morning, but noticed how much energy I had. You know how they say sometimes meds can make you feel sicker? I think that might've been the case," she spoke to me over her shoulder as I followed her to the kitchen.

I wanted to be upset with her for forgoing that medicine, but I couldn't deny her healthy looks and youthful energy. I thought about the last time I saw her, a few days ago, when I'd introduced her to Venom, and stopped in my tracks, wondering if he had anything to do with her sudden vigor for life. I'd spoken to her over the phone every day, and she'd assured me that she felt fine, but to see it in person brought me happiness I couldn't describe.

Quickly, I wiped the tears of joy that threatened to spill down my cheeks, before my mom noticed.

"Hmph, I see I'mma have to start doing my own shopping," she said unpacking the bags and frowning her face at the healthy food I'd bought.

"Alright, mom! Don't get carried away! You still need to eat healthy and stick to a good diet plan," I chastised, shaking my head.

"Yeah, yeah," she waved me off. "Anyway, how are you and Venom?" she asked.

At the mention of his name, a small smile formed on my lips and of course, my mom noticed.

"Only time I smiled when somebody mentioned a man's name was when I was in love," she said, giving me her full attention.

"Mom! It's way too soon for that! I really like him. A lot. He's sweet and he actually cares about other people, probably more than himself, but, love?" I said, placing the almond milk inside of the refrigerator.

"You gave up those cookies yet?"

"Mom!" I exclaimed, spinning around to face her.

"Girl, please! Don't mom me! He's a good-looking man; you're a beautiful girl. You love, opps, I mean *like* him," she said sarcastically. "I'm not blind, Jules."

I sighed, "Its, it's complicated."

"How so?"

As cool and understanding as my mother was, there was no way in hell I was going to tell her that I was in a polygamist relationship with a damn real-life vampire! She'd think I was on drugs!

"Well, you know I told you about his friend that recently passed. He's been withdrawn and distant. I mean, we spoke about it, and it's gotten a little better, but I don't know how to comfort him. It's hard. And then he'll be leaving for his first big tour in a few weeks. There's just so much going on that I don't see how we can be serious," I revealed the parts that I could.

"I'm sure you being there is comforting enough. People grieve differently. Just give him enough space to allow him to do it how he needs to, but be there. Now, as far as this tour, I don't have any experience with that, but did he invite you?"

"Yeah, he invited me to go, but it's for three months! I can't leave you that long!"

"What!? I don't ever want you to put your happiness on hold for me! Besides, I'm fine! And what's that face phone stuff you and Tash always doing? We can do that. He wants you to go and I think you should."

"But–"

"But nothing! Everything will be fine. Now, if you just don't want to go, that's fine too, but don't use me as an excuse. You tell that man the truth."

I sucked my teeth, "I just don't know, mom. Have you heard from Nikki?" I asked, changing the subject.

Her eyes saddened as she shook her head, "No. She won't answer any calls, or return my messages."

Instantly, I became angry. Nikki was so selfish! My mom was one of the few people that genuinely cared about her and she was ignoring her.

"Mom, Nikki is grown, and I don't think you should be stressing yourself out about her! She's a big girl, and she puts herself in these predicaments! It's not your job to rescue her!"

She sighed, taking a seat at the kitchen table and balling her hands in front of her. "Nikki is my responsibility, Jules. She's my daughter."

I dropped the eggs I was holding and spun around in shock.

"W-what did you just say?"

She tapped the table for me to sit and I almost tripped over my cat, who'd scurried into the kitchen after hearing the crash. Pulling out a chair, I sat down, staring at my mother.

"I was only fourteen when I got pregnant with Nikki. I

was still a baby. When I told your grandmother, she kicked me out. She was embarrassed. Back in those days, the worst thing you could do was embarrass your family. A pregnant fourteen-year-old would surely humiliate the family name," she said, her eyes welling up with tears.

I grabbed her hand, trying to take in the story that poured from her lips. "Grandma kicked you out? At fourteen?!"

"Yes. I never wanted you to look at your grandmother in a bad light, so I always made sure you had a good relationship with her. She always felt remorse about how she handled that situation, and I forgave her."

We were both in tears now, while the cat looked at us as if we were crazy.

"How did Aunt Nicole end up with her?" I asked, grabbing some paper towels for our wet faces.

"Nicole had just turned twenty and she was dealing with a married man that no one knew about. He was some well to-do politician, and he'd put her up in a nice apartment. When our mother told her about the situation, she took me in. She wanted me to finish school so when I gave birth to Nikki, I signed my rights over to Nicole, and the family all agreed to never speak on it. When I was 18, I met your father, and we married a year later. That's when I had you."

I nodded my head, "I remember after Daddy died in the accident, and Aunt Nicole was murdered, Nikki came to stay with us," I recalled.

"Yeah," she sighed. "And by that time she was already an out of control teenager. I tried," she stopped, her voice cracking.

I squeezed her hand tighter.

"I tried to steer her in the right direction, but she took Nicole's death hard."

"Mom, I'll find her. Please don't worry. Nikki is a lot of things, but she's a survivor. I'm sure she's somewhere working on somebody else's nerves. I'll find her," I assured my mother.

"It feels so good to finally admit all of this out loud, but I feel like I'm betraying my sister."

"Mom, Aunt Nicole stepped up and did what she did because she loved you. If anything, I'm sure she's probably glad that you finally unburdened yourself of this secret. You were just a kid," I comforted her, thinking back to when I was fourteen.

There's no way I would've been able to take care of a baby when I could barely take care of myself. I could only imagine my Mom's pain. Damn! So, Nikki was my sister. Hearing the story made me feel a little more sympathetic to her situation, but she was still a hoe that I didn't trust. Nevertheless, I needed to find her and try to make amends for my mother's sake.

This was a lot to take in, and I needed some air. Hell, I needed a drink! I needed Tash, but she wouldn't be back home until tomorrow, and I didn't want to keep calling her and bothering her with my shit while she was on vacation. Wiping my face, I stood and hugged my mom, who was still quietly weeping.

"Mom, stop. It's ok. I'll find her, alright?"

"I hate to put my burden on you."

"You're not a burden! You've done nothing but help me my entire life and...Nikki is my.... sister. Don't worry," I told her, finding it hard to say the word *sister* out loud.

I left, sliding into the Phantom that Venom let me

drive to go run errands. I looked at my phone, my finger hovering over Nikki's name, but I couldn't bring myself to call her yet. I was still pissed about what she did to Tash, not to mention, I had my own suspicions about her and Rich. Sighing, I tossed the phone on the passenger seat and headed to Venom's.

Pulling up, I spotted all of the usual vehicles, along with a shiny, black Lincoln truck. Parking, I grabbed my Chic Fil-a bag, because I refused to eat any food in the house. What happened to Savalia wasn't sitting right with me, and even though I had no proof, my gut told me what happened to her wasn't just a freak accident. Walking past the unfamiliar truck, I wondered whose it was and who was in the house.

I started to ring the bell, but then remembered I had my own set of keys. As I walked in, I saw Serina standing near Venom's office. When she noticed me, she hurried over, taking the keys to the Phantom from my hand.

"Finally! I've been waiting for you to get back so I could use the car! I've got to get an outfit for Savalia's funeral tomorrow," she said.

"You could've drove your Benz," I said, looking at her as if she had two heads.

"Tuh! That old thing!? Why should I, when I can drive the Phantom. We need to be respectful of each other's time!" she said, flipping her hair and walking past me.

It took everything in me not to grab her by her bundles and beat the shit out of her. I wished Venom would have kicked her ass out like he planned, but after what happened to Val, I knew he just didn't have the energy to deal with Serina and her drama. She left out, letting the door slam behind her.

"I hope you never come back, bitch," I mumbled to myself.

As I walked closer to Venom's office, I could hear the hushed voices behind the large, gray-stoned door, and I wondered if Serina was over here trying to spy. Kember had told me she had a few suspicions about Serina and her motives, but now I was starting to see some shit for myself. Ringing the small bell on the side of the door, I planned on telling Venom exactly what I'd just witnessed.

The heavy door swung open, and I couldn't help but smile, looking up into Venom's handsome face. He smiled, pulling me close, before I could say a word, kissing me, and easing his tongue inside of my Polynesian sauce flavored mouth. The deeper he kissed me, the wetter my panties got, and I marvel at the effect he had over me whenever we were close. It was almost electrical.

I dropped my bag of food and was ready to rip his pants off until someone behind him cleared their throat, breaking us from our moment. Embarrassed, I leaned to the side to see who else was inside. A man, with the exact same eyes as Venom, leaned against the desk. I glanced between him and Venom. They could've been twins, except the man was clearly older, though not by much, and huskier.

He was dapper, sporting an expensive looking, dark, three-piece suit. Next, I noticed an elegant woman, sitting on the soft leather chair, watching me. Her eyes were dark, with a hint of violet. Her bone structure was immaculate, and she reminded me of old Hollywood. Like a Billie Holiday, or Lena Horne in their hay day. The tight navy dress and fur shawl she wore only added to the glamour.

Suddenly, I felt plain in my hoodie and snow boots. "I didn't mean to interrupt, I just–"

Lightly, he touched my face with his cool fingers, "We were almost finished, but since you're here, let me introduce you. This is Xavier and Talia," he said, taking my hand and leading me over to them. "My father and stepmother."

I squeezed his hand tighter, digging my nails into his skin for not giving me a heads up. I would've made myself more presentable had I known I would be meeting his parents. I probably looked like a whole charity case to them.

"Um, hi. Nice to meet you both," I smiled, while giving Venom a side eye.

His father took my free hand and kissed it, nodding at me but not saying anything. Talia stood, giving me the once over. Finally she looked to Venom, "You can release her Venom. We won't bite," she said, laughing at her own joke.

He let go of my hand and allowed Talia to pull me closer to her.

"Do you have a name, sweetheart?" she asked, her purple eyes boring into mine.

"Of course! Where are my manners? I'm Jules."

"Don't worry, dear. I'm sure we caught you off guard. Jules, what a pretty name."

"Thank you," I replied.

I could hear Venom and his father having a hushed conversation behind us.

"Take back the ring, Venom! You need my protection

now more than ever!" I heard his father say.

"So, what are your intentions with my son, Jules?" Talia asked, bringing my attention back to her.

"My intentions?" I repeated, glancing at Venom, who was in a heated conversation with his dad.

"Uh huh. What are you expecting from this arrangement?"

"Um, I... Honestly, I don't know. This is one of the strangest experiences I've ever had. All I know is I feel amazing when I'm around him and I think he feels the same about me," I admitted.

Talia looked at me for a moment, before she smiled, showing her sharp, white fangs.

"I like you. You're...refreshing. Some of the women he's dealt with before... so fake and phony. I believe you really care about my son."

"I do. More than I expected actually," I said.

She chuckled, "It does sneak up on us, doesn't it? Anyway, Venom really cares for you. I can tell. So maybe you can help," she said, looping her arm through mine, while patting my hand and leading us further across the room, away from Venom and Xavier.

"Uh, help how?" I asked, glancing back at Venom, who was still having words with his father.

"Venom is in danger, which means you could be in danger. Venom is... hot-headed and proud, so he will no longer except our help. There was already one death here; we don't need another. I'm sure you're familiar with the Rogues?"

I nodded, remembering the conversation I had with Venom after he was shot at the second time.

"You think the Rogues had something to do with Val's death?" I asked.

"Maybe not directly. But I'm almost positive that somehow this will lead back to them. I'm asking you to keep your eyes open for me. And if you can, convince Venom to come back to the Court."

"Um, Talia, I will keep my eyes open, but I don't want to do anything behind Venom's back. If you want him back in the Court, maybe we should have an open discussion about it," I told her.

She stared at me for a long moment before letting my hands go.

"Hmm. Maybe," she said simply, before turning her attention back to her husband and son.

"Xavier, let Venom think about it. Let's go," she said.

I stood there thinking that his mother now hated me. I watched Xavier shove a ring into Venom's hand, which he put in his pocket at his father's disapproval. Xavier threw his hands up and shook his head, while Talia stood on her tip toes to kiss Venom on the cheek.

"We only want what's best, Venom," she told him, wiping her dark, red lipstick from his cheek. "Oh, and I like her," she said, glancing at me. "If you are to turn someone, I wouldn't mind if it was her," she smiled.

In a flash, they disappeared, leaving only me and Venom in the office.

"Well, that was...intense," I said, picking up the bag I dropped and placing it on his desk.

He chuckled, "I love them both, but they can be overbearing. What did Talia say to you?"

"She asked me to keep an eye out. They think you and possibly all of us could be in danger. She also asked me to try and convince you to go back to the Court. Do you think you'd be safer?"

"I was still getting shot at when I was in the Court! What's the difference?"

I didn't know how to answer that, so instead, I asked, "How are you holding up?"

He shrugged, "Honestly?" I nodded.

"I'm fucking pissed! I'm pissed, and I'm not gonna be satisfied until somebody pays."

I could feel the rage pouring from his body, and his eyes glowed red. A shadow played on his face, giving him an animalistic look. Snatching my food from his desk, I backed up. Not because I necessarily thought he'd purposely harm me, but he had told me when he unleashes his rage, it can sometimes be hard to control, and I didn't want to be on the receiving end of his anger.

"My fault," he said, shaking it off.

Slowly, his eyes changed back to their normal swirls of color, and his handsome face was no longer contorted. Suddenly, he appeared directly in my face, startling me.

"You know my anger's not directed at you, right?" he asked, running his fingers across my neck.

I nodded, "I know. I guess it's just still surprising to watch you morph like that."

"That's strange, cuz I morph when I bust a nut too, but you never said anything about it," he smirked.

"Well, that's because, um... I... shut up, Venom!"

He laughed as I walked past him. Grabbing my jacket, he easily yanked me back. "Where you going?"

"To eat my food in peace!" I giggled, moving his hand from my ass. "And then probably check on Kember. I think she's taking this the hardest."

"She is. Savalia's family is very conservative. They didn't approve of her living with me, and they definitely wouldn't approve of a lesbian relationship. Kember can't truly express how she feels because of it and it's getting to her. I think I'm going to have a personal memorial for her, here at the house. Just for us. For Kember," he sighed, solemnly.

I shook my head, "Her parents had no idea she was gay?"

"I think they had their suspicions, but chose to ignore it. But I'm not gonna go for them making Kember feel left out either! Fuck that!"

I nodded, feeling sad for Kember. Imagine loving someone, and when they die, you're excluded, as if you never mattered.

"How's your mom?" he asked.

"The best I've seen her in years! I meant to ask; did you have anything to do with that?"

He shook his head, giving me a surprised look.

"Nah! But I'm happy ma is doing better."

I looked at him for a moment, trying to read him.

"The lies you tell!" I said, throwing a fry at him, which he ducked.

"You'll never guess what I found out though. My cousin Nikki, well, she's actually my sister!"

"Seriously?!"

"Yes. My mom dropped a bombshell on me. And the bad thing is Nikki's missing. I told my mom I'd try to find her."

Venom's face changed and I could tell something was wrong.

"What?" I asked.

"Listen, I wasn't gonna say anything, 'cuz I didn't want to make you feel no type of way, but Nikki ain't missing."

"Huh? What do you mean?"

He pulled his phone from his phone and waved me over. He was on his Instagram page, pulling up his DMs.

"Here," he said handing me his phone.

I looked, and sure enough, Nikki was in his inbox daily for the past three days, wanting to meet up, talking raunchy, and even sent a picture of her dry pussy! I could hear the blood rushing in my ears. I was pissed!

"I never responded and–"

I held up my hand to stop him, "I know you didn't, because you not stupid," I said, cutting my eyes at him. "This is about her. I told her to stay away from you. And not only that, she's been ignoring my mother's calls but got time to do all of this?!" I yelled.

"Yo, you scaring me," Venom said.

"Boy! Shut up! You better had ignored her too!" I said, pointing a finger at him.

"On me, I did!" he said, holding up his hands in defense.

"Block her!" I yelled, pushing his phone back into his hands.

He quickly did as I asked.

"Every time I try and give that bitch a chance, she does some fuck shit!" I shouted.

"Aight, look. Calm down. You probably hungry. I get pissed like that when I'm hungry too, baby."

"Venom! It's not funny!" I yelled, but couldn't help but to laugh a little. "I swear I don't like you anymore."

He smiled, "Yeah right. Go ahead and eat and go holla

at Kember. I'm working on something I want to show you later. After you calm down."

"Fine," I said, leaving out but still pissed.

I was slightly calmer after my chicken sandwich, so I pushed Nikki and her shenanigans to the back of my mind as I headed upstairs to check on Kember, who hadn't left her room. Now that I thought about it, I should've gotten her something to eat as well, since I knew she probably hadn't even left her room to eat today. If she was hungry, I'd just go pick her up something.

SZA blasted through her door as I knocked and waited. When I didn't hear any movement, I knocked again, this time louder.

"Kember!" I called out.

Still no response. Worried that she might have done something to herself, I tried the knob. Luckily, it was unlocked. The shades were closed, giving the room a dark atmosphere. Turning down the music, I looked at Kember, who was laying in the rumpled bed, staring into space.

"Kember, sweetie?" I said quietly, making a seat for myself at the foot of her bed.

When she still wouldn't speak, I rubbed her leg and continued.

"I didn't know Val long, but what I did pick up was that she was a kind-hearted person, with a beautiful spirit. She left a void that would be almost impossible to fill, but maybe you don't have to. Maybe she left something for you to always remember. When life gets hard, remember Val and try to find the light at the end of the tunnel. I'm not very good, helping people deal with grief. I never know what to say. Everything comes out all messed up, but if you need to talk, or just a shoulder to cry on, I can help," I told her, standing to leave, not knowing what else to say.

As I stood, Kember grabbed my wrist, and I sat back down. Her watery eyes began to overflow and I plucked a tissue from her nightstand and wiped her face.

"I don't know what to do," she whispered, "I'm so confused. Like, why her? Val wouldn't even hurt a fly. So why her?!"

I didn't know how to answer that, so I said, "Kem, I promise, we're gonna find out what happened! And if anything foul went down–"

"You think it's something shady too!?" she asked, sitting up.

"I don't know, and I don't want to accuse anyone just yet. But–"

"I know that bitch did something to Val and the second I find out for sure, I'mma kill that hoe!"

"We don't know yet. I don't understand why she would be gunning for Val. If anything, I would think she would be coming for me since technically I'm the new kid on the block."

Kember shook her head, "That bitch is evil. Jules, I think she might have killed the only good thing in my life, and I can't prove it!" she wailed, snot and tears pouring from her face.

I handed her a clean tissue and hugged her. "I know we can't replace her, but you still have me and Venom and Lexi."

I made sure not to mention her family since Venom had told me that they disowned her when she decided to pursue a career in the music industry. Apparently, they were super religious and believed that she had joined the Illuminati and sold her soul to the devil. It sounded like some straight bullshit to me to disown a child for following their dream! It made me grateful that I had the mother I did.

"Do you know I can sing?" she asked.

"Like sing sing, or I sound good in the shower sing?" I asked, attempting to lighten the mood.

She chuckled, "I can sang! Val always said I should've been a singer instead of a dancer."

"Let me hear something then," I said, cutting her music completely off.

Sitting up, she cleared her throat and began humming. I recognized the tune. It was Whitney Houston's *I will always love you.* As she started to sing, my eyes bucked at how clear and crisp her notes were. She sounded exactly like Whitney! I sat there listening, remembering scenes from *The Bodyguard.* When she hit the high note at the end, I jumped to my feet.

"Yasss!" I shouted, clapping.

Homegirl had just taken me to church, gave the benediction, and passed the basket for tithes!

"Are you insane?! Why are you not giving Beyoncé a run for her money?!" I questioned.

"That's what I initially wanted to do. But they gave me the run-around. Niggas only wanted some ass, and even after they got it, the best I could do was get to be a video model. Now everyone knows me as a video hoe. I'll look stupid tryna come out with an album."

"Kember, does Venom know you can sing?"

"No."

"You know he would look out for you! Why don't you

tell him?"

"Oh my God, you sound just like Val! I don't want to look stupid! People are gonna think I fucked my way to the top."

"Who cares!? Let them think what they want! Nobody can deny your talent! I took a few PR classes. I can even prep you on how to do interviews and answer difficult questions!" I explained.

"Really?" she asked, still sounding uncertain.

"Yes. And I'm telling Venom that he's been living with Whitney Houston this whole time!"

"Let me just think about it. I've still got to get through this funeral tomorrow," she said, sighing.

We talked more, damn near until the sunset when Lexi came in.

"Hi, Jules. How you doing, Kember? I brought you something to eat," she said, holding up a Checker's bag.

"Thanks, Lexi. I was just about to ask Jules if she could take me to get something to eat," Kember said, as I scooted over to make room for Lexi.

"Yeah, I think we need to go shopping. The kitchen is damn near empty except for some canned goods," Lexi said.

I shot Kember a knowing look, figuring that she'd probably thrown everything away.

"Lexi, if you knew something about...A friend that wasn't right...you'd tell us...right?" Kember asked, unwrapping her bacon cheeseburger.

"What?! Of course, I would," Lexi responded.

"I'm going to let you two talk," I informed them, standing and stretching.

I decided to hit the shower. I needed to wash the

stress of the day off. Venom had gotten me a bunch of clothes to wear while I was here, so I wouldn't have to drudge my clothes back and forth between his house and mines. After I was done, I put on one of the pajama sets he'd gotten me, which consisted of a silk, peach colored cami top with little matching shorts.

I couldn't help but notice how peaceful it was when Serina wasn't home. Hearing music from the basement studio, I assumed Venom was down there. I chuckled to myself, thinking about how much this really looked like I was descending into the vampire's lair, with the stone walls and winding staircase. In the studio, Venom sat behind some type of keyboard, controlling the bass and instruments of the music. Sometimes he'd move a lever, and the bass would boom loudly, other times, other instruments would take over.

I just stood watching him until he finally asked, "What you think about this beat?"

I was surprised he knew I was here since his back was to me, but quickly remembered that he wasn't human.

"I like it, but it sounds sad," I replied.

"It's supposed to," he said. Come here."

Padding across the hardwood floor, I stood next to him until he pulled me onto his lap.

"Listen to this," he said, pressing another button.

His voice sounded clear from the speakers, expertly riding the beat. It was cool watching him in his element. He was serious and I could tell he was serious about his craft. I listened to the lyrics, which were about pain and loss. Different from his usual party, sex and violent raps. He was obviously expressing his grief over Val, although he never mentioned her name directly in the lyrics.

"I love this, V. You should have someone sing on the hook," I said, thinking about Kember.

I was itching to say something about her voice, but I promised her I wouldn't, so I shut my mouth.

"Yeah. Yeah, that would be dope!" Venom responded.

"Ok, enough sad shit. What you think about this?" he asked, switching songs.

This one was upbeat and filled with bass, causing me to twerk on his lap.

"Ayye!" I said, dancing harder as the rhythm changed.

"That's how you feel?" he chuckled, leaning back, allowing me to do my thing.

Feeling him begin to harden under me, I kept up with the beat but changed my dance to mimic riding a dick. I could tell that he was enjoying it when he placed his large, cool hands on my thighs, guiding me further back until I could feel him through his jeans, rubbing against my clit. My body was beginning to heat up, and I took control, spinning around to face him.

"I can't tell the difference between the silk and your skin," he said, running his hands over my body, while staring me in the eyes.

"Let me help you," I said, standing and slowly removing my pajamas, leaving them in a pile at my feet.

He licked his lips, staring at my body as I carefully sat back down on his lap.

"Better?" I asked.

"Almost," he said, standing.

Wrapping my legs around his waist so I wouldn't fall, I braced myself as he laid me on the soft, butter leather sofa. Biting my lip in anticipation, I watched excitedly as he undressed. His cut-up torso covered in tattoos made me sit up. I reached out to touch him, but he pushed me back. Next, he kicked off his Timbs and unzipped his jeans.

His imprint strained to be released, and I was so happy when he finally slid down his jeans and Versace briefs. His dick sprang up and out, rock hard, against his stomach. His veins pulsed and rippled through his member, giving it an angry appearance. I licked my lips, watching the pre-cum glistening on the head. I reached out to touch him again, and this time, he let me.

Using both hands, I wrapped them around his shaft and slowly massaged making a motion like I was grinding pepper. I loved the feel of his hardness wrapped in the cool, satiny feel of his skin. After a few minutes of the massage, I slowly eased the tip inside my mouth. There was no way I was going to fit his entire massive size in my mouth, so I used both hands at the base, and worked my tongue and lips around the rest.

Spit ran from my mouth, giving extra lubrication to my hands as they slid with ease around him. He groaned, a deep, guttural sound, before pushing me off. My jaw was sore, but I hid it well, allowing him to push me back. He crouched down, pulling me towards him by my waist. I jumped slightly, feeling his tongue lick straight up my middle, from my ass to my clit.

"Uhmmm," I moaned, as he slurped my sensitive bud into his mouth.

I was already soaked, so he easily slid two fingers inside of me. He curved them and simultaneously sucked the soul from my pussy. The pressure from the inside out caused me to cum harder than I ever had before.

"Ahhh! Oh shit, Venom!" I yelled, my thighs clenching around his head.

He pushed them back apart and kept going. I tried to wriggle away, but he had an iron grip on my waist. Finally, he pulled back, kissing and nibbling on my thighs. I gasped when I felt his teeth sink into my skin. The pulling sensation of him sucking my blood was causing me to hang on the verge of another orgasm. Reaching down, I grabbed his dreads, desperately trying to pull him back up to my pussy.

He chuckled, not budging, still drinking from me. My body began to shake uncontrollably, and he finally stopped. I felt the familiar tingling as he used his own blood to close the bite mark. Instead of diving back into my pussy, he moved up, running his tongue over my nipples. Arching my back, I could feel beads of sweat forming on my forehead and slowly sliding down my temples. I ran my hands through his hair and down his chiseled back as he switched from one nipple to the other, methodically teasing me.

When he looked up, I crushed my lips against his, tasting my juices and blood mingled on his tongue making an intoxicating cocktail. As we kissed, our tongues wrestled for control. My tongue scraped against his fangs, and he hurried to suck the droplets of blood. Unexpectedly, he slid inside of me, and I let out a muffled scream since my mouth was still held, hostage. He slid in and out of my body, hitting every single last one of my spots along the way. My nails scraped his back as he pounded me deeper. I bit down on his neck because it was the only thing I could do to keep me from screaming out and alerting the entire house to our activities.

I didn't draw blood, but it seemed to excite him because he growled deeply and began moving inside of my body at an impossible speed.

"Venom! Yesss!" I cried as my body convulsed with back to back orgasms.

When I pried my eyes open, I thought I was hallucinating when I noticed Lexi watching us. My body tensed up.

"What's wrong?" Venom asked me breathlessly.

When I didn't respond, he looked over his shoulder, spotting Lexi.

"Can I join?" she asked, already slipping her nightshirt off.

Venom looked to me to see if I was ok with it. Honestly, I didn't know how I felt about it. Would I be able to stomach watching him with another woman? I'd never been with a woman before, so I didn't know how to act, and seeing her flat stomach and damn near perfect body had me suddenly self-conscious about mine.

But I signed up for this shit, so I needed to at least try. Slowly, I nodded my head.

"You sure?" he whispered.

Once again, I nodded. Smiling, she walked over and knelt down until she was eye level with me.

"You're so beautiful. I've been waiting for this since you joined the family," she spoke before kissing me.

Her tongue tasted fruity, like she'd just ate a watermelon Jolly Rancher and as Venom resumed with slower strokes, I sucked the sugar from her tongue. She moved to my neck and then breasts, planting kisses everywhere while Venom's hands roamed my thighs. My body was almost on overload from the contrasting touches. Some rough, some soft and the constant rubbing on my g-spot from Venom, caused my body to spaz.

I was barely over my orgasm when her lips moved down to my stomach, and then my clit. I was in so much ecstasy that I didn't notice she'd positioned her pussy over my face until she lowered it. We were now in a sixty-nine position, her expertly toying with my clit and me clumsily sucking on hers, while Venom continued stroking me.

Using my fingers, like Venom had done on me earlier, I eased them in and out of her wet hole causing her to moan and ride my face with more vigor. I actually felt proud of myself when she came, gushing all over my fingers and lips.

"Ummm," she moaned, creating a humming vibration over my bud, causing me to cum again.

Venom slowly pulled out, leaving me feeling empty, and tapped Lexi. She got up and turned around. I slid back some to make room. He entered her roughly from behind, and her face became a mask of pleasure. I instantly became jealous and fought the urge to slap the hell out of her. Reaching over her, he gently pushed me back further, until Lexi could put her face in my pussy.

She got to work, and I relaxed slightly, closing my eyes as she slowly lapped at me. I opened them when I felt his cool fingers on my face. We stared at each other as he fucked Lexi and she was slowly bringing me to another climax. Gripping my throat, he pulled me up and leaned over at the same time, kissing me deeply. Gently, he bit my lip, just as she softly clamped down on my clit making for an explosive orgasm. I moaned my pleasure inside of his mouth.

Lexi moved her head to scream out. She was cumming too, from his rough strokes. Afterwards, he pulled out of her and plopped down on the sofa. She got on her knees in front of him and began using her hands to jerk him off. As she did that, I leaned over, taking him in my mouth again, sucking him roughly. His hand tangled in my hair, and he moaned before he exploded. I swallowed as much as I could, and whatever I missed, Lexi caught.

Afterwards, we dressed, and Lexi headed back upstairs. I was feeling a little uncomfortable, but I couldn't deny that it was the best sexual experience I'd had.

"You ok?" he asked, when I refused to look at him.

"I'm fine," I lied.

"No, you not. Talk to me," he said, blocking the stairs.

"That was...it was weird," I admitted.

"You didn't like it?"

"I mean, physically yeah. But watching you... never mind. It's stupid. I knew what I was getting involved with when I signed the contract. It's not your fault," I said, attempting to move past him, but he blocked me again.

"You didn't like seeing me with another woman? Is that what it is?"

"Of course that's it, Venom! Did you think that would be fun for me?" I yelled, feeling tears forming in my eyes.

"I'm sorry. It never bothered any of them, so I didn't think–"

"I'm not them! I tried, I really did, but–" Tears fell down my face and he wiped them.

"Whatever you about to say, don't. You don't ever have

to do anything like that again, and you won't ever have to see it. I promise."

"Venom, I know you mean well, and I don't expect you to change your entire life for me, but I'm not built for this. Seeing you with her..." choking up, I shook my head. "I think after the funeral I should go back to my house for awhile."

"Jules–"

"It's not your fault, Venom. I just can't be something I'm not. Not even for you," I said, quickly ducking under his arm and running up the stairs.

I ran straight into Serina, who wore a pleased smirk.

"Aww, you're leaving us so soon?" she fake pouted.

I had it! Giving her a quick, powerful blow, I knocked her out cold. Venom appeared at the top of the stairs, taking in the scene. I said nothing as I headed towards Kember's room to see if I could bunk with her tonight. I wasn't mad at Venom. I was mad at myself. I'd caught feelings for him too quickly. Running around thinking I was that chick from *Twilight*. I should've known better. Feeling like an idiot, I quietly cried myself to sleep.

13

NIKKI

"Pass the lube. Bitch went dry again," I heard a voice say from behind me.

Tears ran from my eyes as I concentrated on giving head to the man in front of me. I wanted all of them to just hurry up and cum. Things had certainly taken a left turn for me since I'd been staying with Rich. Nigga was more psychotic than I'd ever imagined. He'd taken my car keys and refused to let me leave until I could get to Venom, which was proving to be damn near impossible since he ignored every message I'd sent him.

Another dilemma was that he was making me pay to stay here. He had random niggas coming through to fuck. The kicker was they were paying him, and I wasn't seeing a dime of the money. Finally, the man that I was sucking off came in my mouth. Turning my head, I spit the foul-tasting semen onto the old mattress that Rich had set up on the floor in his kitchen.

The nameless man behind me was pounding away, but I couldn't feel shit, because I'd been fucking all day. I was sore, tired and hungry so I was ecstatic when he began to grunt, signaling that he was almost done. I sighed with relief when I felt the warm semen spill inside of me. When he got up, I grabbed the roll of paper towels and cleaned myself as best as I could.

"Two hundred for each of y'all," Rich said, sitting at the kitchen table, watching my depravity.

The men were getting dressed, pulling their pants back up.

"Come on, man! Two hundred?! She wasn't even wet! I could barely feel anything!" the one who was behind me complained.

"Nigga, I told you what it was before you even got here! Give me my fuckin' bread!" Rich snapped, standing.

They each handed him two hundred without any further arguments. Once they left out through the back door, I spoke.

"Rich, please. I'm tired. Can I have the rest of the night off?" I said, my voice hoarse.

He sparked up his weed, and I frowned my face, because he'd mixed it with wet and the smell was horrible. Walking across the kitchen, he opened the refrigerator and grabbed a bottled water, tossing it to me.

"Stay hydrated. It's more niggas coming tonight," he spoke callously.

"I can't!" I said, tears running down my face.

"Until you do what I asked you to do, you'll do what the fuck I tell you to!"

"He blocked me! How am I supposed to get to him? If you'd give me my car keys, I could–"

"Either you stupid or you think I'm stupid! Which one is it?" he snapped, stepping closer.

I shut my mouth because I didn't want him to hit me again.

"Come here," he said, gesturing for me to sit at the table.

Naked, I stood, opening the water and guzzling it. Pulling my phone from his pocket, he typed in my code.

"Make a fake page," he said, watching my movements so I wouldn't alert anyone.

Sighing, I scrolled past all of the missed calls from my Aunt and my best friend, my tears spilling onto the screen. I swear, if I could do things differently, I would have. Starting with telling Jules about the first time Rich raped me. Going to my Instagram, I paused.

"He unblocked me!" I said, going to my messages.

"Oh my God! He wants to meet tonight!"

"Let me see that!" he said, snatching the phone from my hands.

An evil grin spread across his face, "Ask him where and what time," he instructed.

My hands shook as I typed what he asked. I had mixed feelings about this whole situation. I know I was originally down with this plan, but after witnessing first hand how sick this nigga really was, I wasn't so gung-ho on pretty much placing my cousin in his hands. Then again...Venom wanted to meet me!

Venom was such a good catch. He already had money, but once he blew, he'd really be getting to a bag! Jules always seemed to land on her feet. She'd be ok. I needed to think about myself and Venom could be my ticket out of this Hell I created. Pressing the send button, I nervously waited for a response.

Rich snatched the phone back from me.

"I'mma cancel your appointments for tonight while I wait for this weirdo to respond. In the meantime," he said, unzipping his jeans and pulling out his flaccid penis.

Sighing heavily and finishing my water, I dropped to my knees and placed him inside of my mouth. My jaw was aching, but I did the best I could. Excited that tonight this would all be over.

Later that night, I sat on the passenger side as Rich's high ass drove like a fuckin' maniac. Nervously, I tapped my nails against the console as we merged onto I-95. I'd showered and felt a little more like myself, in some black, see-thru tights, heels, and a peacoat that flared out at the bottom. My wig was wrecked, but I'd brushed it back into a neat ponytail.

"Let's go over the plan again," he said.

I sucked my teeth, "We went over it like five times! Chill!" I said.

WHAP!

He backhanded me, leaving me seeing stars as I quickly covered my face.

"Why are you treating me like this?! What did I ever do to you?" I yelled, becoming more and more fed up.

"Nikki, are you serious?! You and your dirty ass pussy is the reason Jules left me! You the reason she even dealing with that lame nigga! Now tell me the fuckin' plan and stop asking dumb ass questions!" he barked.

I wanted to remind him that he was the one who

came on to me that night in the bathroom, but instead, I silently sighed.

"I seduce Venom and get him to fuck me. You'll be in the area taping it. You send it to me, and I send it to Jules, sending her running back into your open arms," I said, glad that he missed my sarcasm.

He grinned and nodded. I don't know why the hell he was so proud of this basic ass scheme that a third grader could have thought of, but whatever. I was just ready to be done with him.

"Aight, this is the street. Poplar street," he announced, slowing down the car.

I looked around, "Here?" I questioned, gawking at the abandoned buildings.

"Yeah. Right there." He pointed to a large warehouse.

I shook my head, "Uh uhn. This don't feel right. Why would he want to meet here?" I asked.

"'Cuz that's where you fuck hoes. In the bandos. Fuck you scared for? You think the nigga a real vampire?" he laughed, while I rolled my eyes.

"Of course not, Rich! But he don't have to be a vampire to be a serial killer or something!"

He shrugged, "If you die, you die."

I cut my eyes at him and thought about making a run for it, but I wasn't familiar with this part of Philly. The streets were deserted and abandoned buildings loomed everywhere. This shit looked like a scene from *Candyman.*

"I don't even see his car or anything," I stalled, not wanting to get out of the car.

"You know he get chauffered around and shit. Get your scary ass out and go head, man! I'mma pull down the block and walk up so I can catch y'all in the act. Shit, I might kill the nigga. Ain't like its witnesses around here," he said, glancing around and pulling his gun from his waistband and checking the chamber.

"What!? No! That wasn't part of the plan! You get Jules and I get Venom!"

He looked at me and shook his head, "Yo, you really are a grimy bitch."

I stared at him in shock. If this wasn't the pot calling the kettle black!

"Go!" he screamed, and I quickly opened the door, stepping out.

As soon as I closed the door, he pulled off. I looked around, nervously taking a deep breath. The ground was uneven, a mix of old crumbled cement and the grass that grew over it. Carefully, I made my way across the lot, glancing over my shoulder every other second. The cold wind whipped my ponytail, and I turned the collar on my jacket up to shield against it.

When I made it to the door, I noticed that the heavy steel was cracked open. As I reached for it, something jumped out at me.

"Ahhhh!" I screamed.

Observing a family of cats scampering across my feet, I clutched my chest, willing my racing heart to return to normal.

"Shit!" I mumbled to myself.

Once again, I opened the door and stepped inside. Pausing to allow my eyes to adjust to the darkness, I tried to look around. It seemed empty. I could hear the sound of water dripping making a small splashing noise somewhere nearby. Probably a leaky pipe.

"Venom," I called out lightly, my voice echoing in the empty space.

I got no response, so I cautiously walked in a little further. The smell of metal and decaying wood was thick in the air.

"Venom. It's me, baby," I called out a little louder.

A noise to the right of me caught my attention. It almost sounded like a footstep. Hesitantly, I headed in that direction, tripping over something on the ground, but quickly catching my balance.

"Venom?" I called again.

, Suddenly, a rickety, makeshift light flickered on.

"Surprise hoe!" my cousin spat.

I was shocked to see Jules! Shit! Why the fuck didn't I figure it would be her?! I watched her, open-mouthed, as she snatched off her coat and tossed it on the floor. When she pulled her hair back into a ponytail, I realized her ass was preparing for a fight.

"Wait! It's not what you think!" I said, backing up.

I wasn't scared of her, but I didn't have the energy to be wrestling around with her big ass!

"It's not? Let me tell you what I think it is! I think you been ignoring my mother's calls while you laid up sending Venom unsolicited pics of that has been you call a pussy. Am I on the right page?" she asked, cracking her neck and slowly walking towards me.

"No! I swear it wasn't me! Rich said–"

"Rich!? Bitch, I knew it!" she yelled, lounging for me, tackling me to the ground, my head just barely missing a cinder block.

She elbowed me in my throat, knocking the wind from me. She went to slam her fist into my face, but I hastily turned my head, causing her to smash her knuckles against the concrete.

"Ahh!" she yelped in pain.

I took that moment to kick her off me and scramble to my feet. I kicked off my heels as she stood. I was tired of everybody putting they hands on me!

"Oh, you want it for real, huh?" she said.

Confident that I could beat her, due to her injured hand, I threw my hands up. That confidence waivered when she ripped some fabric from her shirt and wrapped it around her hand like a motherfuckin MMA fighter! I rushed her, trying to get some hits off. She ducked it and hit me twice, landing one square in the middle of my nose. Blood gushed down my face, and the sting caused my eyes to water.

Dazed, I stumbled back, tripping over some debris. When my back hit the ground hard, I just knew her ass was gonna kill me in here. She hopped on me, throwing punch after punch. I clawed her face and pulled her hair trying to get her off of me, but she wasn't budging. Suddenly, I heard rapid, heavy footsteps nearing us.

"Yo! Chill!" Rich hollered, trying to pull us apart.

Thankfully, he managed to get her off me, but I used that second to sneak a hit.

"Didn't I say chill?!" he yelled, punching me in my head.

"Nigga, don't touch my sister!" Jules snapped, wriggling from his grasp and kneeing him in the groin.

I know I was dazed and confused but did she just say, *sister*? Rolling onto my stomach, I struggled to catch my breath.

Rich doubled over in pain, clutching his nuts,

"I was tryna help you! Wait, sister?!" he spoke, desperately trying to gain composure.

"Did I ask for your help? As long as you live, don't you ever touch her!" she yelled, picking up a pipe and swinging it.

It connected with his neck, and he fell over, just as I managed to get up. Using my bare feet, I stomped him while he was down, taking delight in his anguish. When I finally stopped, he moaned in pain, and I spit on him.

"You piece of shit!" I yelled, finally turning my attention to Jules, who stood watching me, cradling her hand.

"Why did you call me your sister?" I asked, spitting blood from my mouth.

Her face softened and she breathed out a small sigh.

"We're sisters, Nikki. My mom just told me, which is why she's been trying to get in contact with you so desperately."

My mouth dropped in total shock. I watched her face, waiting for her to say *sike* or something. When she didn't, I stepped closer to her.

"Are you serious?" I asked, my eyes beginning to water. "But...but my mom... Aunt Nia... I-"

"It's a lot to take in, but I think you'd receive it better if you heard it from my.... *Our* mom."

Tears ran from my eyes. I couldn't believe what I was hearing! A part of me was pissed that I'd been lied to all of these years, but another part, another part of me just wanted to hug my Aunt. Or mom. I was so confused. A loud sob exited my mouth and I was surprised when Jules hugged me tightly. In this moment, embracing her tightly, I felt bad for the things I'd done to her.

"Jules, I'm so sorry!" I cried.

She simply rubbed my back, as she cried with me.

"I hate to interrupt this moment," Rich's voice sounded behind us, causing us to break our embrace and spin around. "But Nikki, you not needed anymore. I got what I came for," he said, raising his gun.

He was still hurt from us tag teaming his ass, and his hand wasn't steady. As much as I had fucked up, it was time to redeem myself. I quickly pushed Jules out of the way, just as he fired.

POP!

POP!

POP!

"Nikki!" Jules yelled, as my body began to feel like it was on fire.

Glancing down, I saw the blood beginning to soak through my coat, and I fell to the ground.

14

VENOM

JULES THOUGHT her ass was slick. Like I wasn't gonna notice that she'd been through my phone. When I realized that she was going to meet her cousin or sister, and then tried to delete the messages, I instantly had a bad feeling, which is why I decided to pop up on her ass. I know she told me she needed space, and at first, I was gonna try to be a gentleman about it and give it to her.

But the more I thought about it, nah. If she wanted space, she could just take her ass to a different room or some shit. I wanted her, no, scratch that, I needed her around. I'd been feeling like shit since the night of our threesome, and I wished it would have never happened. I knew she wasn't used to the life that I live, but I didn't expect her to react the way she did.

It made me realize that her feelings ran deeper than she was letting on, so hell nah, I wasn't letting her go.

Which is why I was out looking for her in the middle of the night. I stood outside of a door to an abandoned factory, sensing she was inside. The metal door was bolted, so I snatched it off of the hinges just as I heard gunshots. The metal bent and snapped making a loud noise.

Tossing it out of my way, I rushed inside, quickly taking in the scene. Nikki laid on the ground, the smell of her blood overpowering the room. Jules was crouched over her. She jumped and her eyes widened when she spotted me.

"Venom!"

I looked past her, noticing a bum nigga holding a gun. When he snatched Jules by her hair and put the gun to her head, my rage reached a limit I didn't know possible. I started towards him but stopped when he cocked the gun. Jules looked at me, her eyes wide with fear.

"It's ok, baby. I got you," I told her in a calm voice.

"Nigga, you got her how?! This my bitch! Ain't that right, baby?" he said, narrowing his eyes at me, while planting a sloppy kiss on her cheek.

She tried to move her head, but he pressed the barrel tighter against it. I felt my fangs extending as my veins pulsed with anger. Finally, I remembered him from the club. The ex she smacked with the bottle. I laughed.

"Fuck is funny?" he asked, still grilling me.

"The fact that you 'bout to die and haven't even realized it yet," I chuckled, trying to get him to take the gun off Jules and point it at me.

Just like I thought, he aimed at me, still keeping an arm around her neck.

"You lettin' them whack ass bars you spit go to your head, nigga!" he spat, firing at me.

The bullet hit me in my chest, feeling like a slight pinch. Looking down at the entry wound, I dug my finger inside, pulling out the bullet and glancing at it before I plucked it away. His surprise was evident as he moved his arm from Jules, placing both hands on his gun. Silently, I urged her to get out of the way with my eyes. Slowly, she began to back away as he fired three more shots, one grazing me in the head.

Tired of playing with him, I appeared directly in front of him, snatching the gun and tossing it to the side. It clanked loudly and slid across the floor, out of his reach.

"What the fuck?!" he yelled, staring at me in shock.

Opening my mouth wide, I allowed my fangs to expand their entire length, "You about to find out why they call me Venom," I told him, gripping him by his throat.

He wriggled in my grasp, but it was a useless fight. He wasn't going anywhere until I loosened my grasp, throwing him into a wall. When he collided, I heard the unmistakable sounds of his bones shattering. He fell to the ground, struggling to crawl away. Giant cinder blocks were strewn at my feet and I kicked one. It hit his leg with the force of a car, crunching his knee.

"Take her! I don't want her!" he pleaded, as Jules ran past, dropping down to check on Nikki.

"You never had her playboy," I said, lifting him from the ground.

I snapped his head back and plunged my teeth into his throat as far as they would go until they emerged through the back of his neck. I gulped, swallowing blood, tissue, and bone until I got my fill. I then snapped his neck completely, damn near decapitating him, allowing him to fall, his lifeless body crumpling at my feet.

Wiping the blood from my face, I turned towards Jules, who was desperately trying to find a pulse on Nikki.

"Venom, I can't. I can't tell if..."

Drowning out everything, I listened intently. I could hear very faint breathing and the slow pumping of a heart.

"She's alive," I informed her. "Watch out."

Stooping down, I unbuttoned her bloody coat, ignoring the smell of the fresh blood permeating my senses and reigniting my hunger. As I did, Nikki's eyes fluttered open, and to the back of her head. Not seeing a wound in her chest area, I opened the coat further.

"It's just an arm shot," I said.

"An arm?! Nikki! Get your ass up!" Jules shouted.

Her eyes opened, and she focused on Jules before squeezing them shut.

"Lord, I haven't been the best servant, but I come to you humbly," she prayed.

Jules sucked her teeth, "Girl, you only got hit in the arm!"

Her eyes sprang open wide and she touched her wound lightly. "My, my arm?" she whimpered.

"Yes. You're going to be fine!" Jules told her, helping her to sit up.

"Damn that shit hurt! I thought..." she paused, finally noticing me.

"AHHHHHHH!" she screamed bloody murder.

"I'm in Hell! I did die!"

Jules laughed, "Venom, you wanna fix your face?" she asked me.

I forgot my body was still in battle mode. I probably looked like a crazed animal to Nikki. Forcing myself to morph back into my normal form, I felt my teeth retracting and my jaw closing. When I opened my eyes, they were both staring at me.

"My fault," I said.

"What the?!" Nikki said before passing out from shock.

Jules shook her head before standing to her feet.

"Thank you for everything, Venom, but I could've handled this," she said, glancing at the ground.

I made a *yeah right* face before approaching her. Gently cupping her face, I turned her head from left to right inspecting the cuts and bruises, before looking at her hand wrapped in a makeshift bandage.

"Why would you come here alone?" I inquired, biting my finger so that I could use my blood to heal her cuts and scrapes.

"Why would you follow me?" she asked, wincing as I rubbed the blood on her wounds.

"Because I care about you! You really thought I was gonna let you do some shit like this by yourself?" I paused, looking at her.

"I'm not one of your girls anymore! You don't owe me anything," she said, looking away and folding her arms across her chest.

I decided not to respond, 'cuz she was being childish as fuck! She had me wrapped around her finger and she didn't even know it. All she had to do was admit that she wanted me for herself and I'd drop everybody for her, but she wanted to play this dumb, fuckin' game. After healing her as best I could, I moved on to Nikki.

Her skin around the entry of the bullet was hot and I lifted her arm. Not seeing an exit wound, I knew that the bullet was still inside, probably wedged into one of her bones. Sure enough, I dug my fingers inside, and felt the bullet halfway through her shoulder, like I'd assumed. Gripping it, I yanked it out, and rolled it around in the palm of my hand, looking at the tiny bone fragments clinging to it.

"She's losing a lot of blood and I can't seal her because her bones are splintered. We need to get her to a hospital. And you too, for your hand," I said, scooping Nikki up.

She sighed, "Ok. I had to hide my car. It's–"

"I already had Corey take it back to your house. Let's go," I said, cutting her off, and using my free hand to pull her close.

Her mouth dropped open in surprise. "Stop stalking me," she smirked.

"You shoulda never gave up that pussy. Don't complain about a stalker now," I joked.

She sucked her teeth, but relaxed in my grasp, as I flashed out of the door and jumped on the roof of the building, still holding the two women tightly.

"Oh my God!" she said breathless, while trying to smooth her hair. "You could've warned me that you were about to do that special effects stuff!" she said.

Glancing around, I spotted my car from the advantage of the rooftop.

"I'm 'bout to do it again," I warned her, and she tightened her grip on my leather jacket.

Jumping from the building, I landed at the back of my car, in less than a second, barely making any noise at all. Releasing Jules, I hit the alarm on my old school black mustang, and she opened the door, so I could place Nikki in the back. Once she was secure, I closed the door and faced Jules.

"Aight. You had a couple of days. It's time for you to come back home," I told her, leaning against the car.

She looked at me before glancing away,

"Venom, I said I needed some time–"

"You had time. I gave you space. It's time for you to come back."

"I can't! Look, I know I signed the contract–"

"Fuck that contract!" I yelled. "You want me to rip that jawn up? It's done! I don't know what else you want me to do! What you want me to do?" I asked, stepping into her space.

All I needed her to say was that she wanted to be with me exclusively. If she couldn't admit that shit, then we had a fuckin' problem. She fidgeted nervously with her injured hand. Gently, I grabbed it and cupped it in mine, forcing her to look at me.

"Venom, it's just not for me," she said, her eyes watery.

I looked at her for a moment before letting her hand go. "Fine," I said, opening the door for her to get inside.

She paused for a second before sliding inside. I was a hundred and nine years old. Way too old to play these games. I'd been nothing but honest with her about everything, and if she wasn't grown enough to do the same, I wasn't gonna force her. Peeling off, I hopped on the highway, rushing them to Crozer hospital, since that one was closer to their house rather than taking them to one in Philly.

As I drove, I stayed quiet, feeling Jules watching me from time to time. The night passed in a blur as I sped down the road, pulling up to the emergency exit. After I helped get Nikki on the stretcher that the paramedics provided, they rushed her inside, leaving me and Jules alone outside.

"Venom, thank you so much for everything. Really."

"Anytime, baby," I told her, turning to get back in my car.

"Wait!" she shouted, and I turned to face her, waiting to hear what she had to say.

"I....um... I'll drop the car off at your house tomorrow," she said, referring to the new car I'd given her.

"Nah. That's you. Think of it as a parting gift."

"What?! No! I can't–"

"Damn, Jules! You gonna fight me on everything?! Even to the end?" I snapped, but quickly getting my anger in check.

When she took a step away from me, and a tear ran down her eye, I apologized, "Jules, I didn't mean to snap on you. I just want you to keep it."

She nodded, "Okay."

"Yo, you sure you want to end it like this?" I questioned.

She nodded again, "I-I'm sure," she spoke in a whisper.

Her lips were saying one thing, but everything else said the complete opposite. Why the fuck were women so confusing? I was a century and some change old, and I swear I hadn't met one that didn't baffle me at one point or another.

"Aight," I sighed. "Go head and get your hand checked out. It's not broke, but you probably sprained a finger or two. And Jules, don't go back to your job. I'm still gonna help you find something else," I told her before hopping inside of my car.

I was disappointed and ready to go before I did or said something I'd regret. She watched me as I reversed away from the hospital and into traffic. I needed a drink, so I decided to head to the club. Halfway there, my phone rang, and I hoped it was Jules. I couldn't hide my disappointment when I answered.

"Sup?" I said.

"Fuck wrong with you? You sound like somebody just killed your puppy," Sypher's voice blared through the car.

"I'm straight. What's good?"

"You cappin', but I got some info for you."

"Word?" I asked.

"That's my word. She dirty."

I raised my brow, not surprised that my assumption was right. I was pissed that I was right about Serina. I was hoping she couldn't be *that* grimy.

"What you got?"

"I pulled the phone records. She was giving up info on your whereabouts. Just so happened to be every night you got shot at."

Shaking my head, I sighed, "Where she at now?"

"At the house. I'm laying on it."

"Bet. Be there in a few." I told him, disconnecting the call.

"FUCK!" I shouted, stepping on the gas, doing damn near a hundred to get back to my house.

"This gotta be a fuckin' joke!" I spat, glancing in my rearview mirror at the red and blue lights quickly speeding up behind me.

I ain't have time for this shit and I damn sure wasn't in the mood to deal with no fuckin' cops! Calming myself, I decided to do a quick finesse on them 'cuz I didn't have time to do nothing else. Two officers slowly approached, one on each side, hands on their guns. Rolling down my tinted windows, I handed my license and registration out of the window. Snatching it from me, he studied it with his flashlight.

"Venom? The rapper, right?" he asked.

The hairs on my body stood on end and I sensed something was wrong. Just as he pulled his strap, I jumped into action, snapping his wrist and snatching the gun, but not before his partner fired at me. The hot silver setting my body on fire. I shot back, putting two in his chest. He yelled, smoke pouring from the wounds. His partner with the snapped wrist pulled out another gun. Firing and hitting me in the stomach, chest, and face.

I was so full of silver I could taste it, running rampant in my bloodstream like poison. He placed the gun to the side of my head and pulled the trigger, but it was empty.

"Fuck!" he growled, disappointed he couldn't give me the final blow.

I was getting dizzy, and I coughed up blood streaked with silver.

"Die a slow death, bitch," he said, before running to

the other side to grab his injured partner and help him to their squad car.

Blood pounded in my ears, sounding like the screams of a thousand waves. I was in and out of consciousness, but I managed to press the button on my phone to call Sypher.

"You close, bro?"

"S-sypher," I wheezed out.

"Venom? What's wrong?!" he yelled.

"Rogues. I'm hit. Bad," I managed to choke out over the blood filling my lungs.

"Where you at?!" he screamed.

I didn't have the energy to look around. All I could manage to sputter out was, "Highway."

Sypher continued to yell for me, but his voice was fading away, and my body felt as if it was engulfed in flames. Then everything went black.

"SHIT! I THINK HE'S DEAD!" I vaguely heard.

I felt my body being dragged from it's hunched over position inside of the car until I hit the cold concrete.

"Venom! Venom, you still here? Come on, man!"

I struggled to open my eyes, but I couldn't — too much pain.

"We've gotta get him to the Court!" another voice said.

"Let's get him in the truck! I know my nigga ain't dead! Venom, can you hear me?"

I tried once again to open my eyes, but it was useless. At this point, my body was filled with more silver than blood. I would be dead by sunrise.

"Give him the anti!"

I felt a sharp piercing in my neck, followed by a cooling liquid entering my body. It curved through my veins, feeling like it was putting out the fire inside of me. I tried again to open my eyes. This time they did, and I looked up at the sky, a faint purple, indicating the impending sunrise. I was weak. Even opening my eyes felt like a task.

"Venom!" Sypher called, his face coming into my view.

My throat was still to tight to speak, and I wondered why, until I felt a bullet lodged there. Now that the vac was taking effect, I could feel where each bullet was. My body was riddled with them. Two in my face, one in my throat, three in each arm, one in my back and five in the chest. Twelve fucking pieces of silver! I felt my anger rise and I tried to reach for my throat.

"Venom, chill! Hold up!" Sypher said, propping something under my head.

He dug his fingers in my throat, pulling out the silver. I could hear the sizzle of my skin as the bullet rubbed against my wound. Gritting my teeth through the pain, I squeezed my eyes shut, feeling a tear run out. A gust of air hit the wound and he immediately rubbed some more of the vac on it.

"We wasting time! Get him in the truck so we can get him to the Court!" Corey said, sitting me up and looping his arms under mine from behind, while Sypher grabbed my ankles.

My body was mostly muscle so they couldn't lift me, but they were able to drag me. They managed to slide me inside. Closing the door, I could hear them outside frantically cleaning up what was supposed to be the crime scene of my death. This shit was too close. If the silver managed to penetrate my organs, it was a good chance that I still wouldn't make it past today.

My mind drifted to my father and Talia. I was the only son and I wondered what would happen to the Court if I didn't make it? The Court was important to my Father, since it was originally started by his Father. It was selfish of me to disown it. Especially when he'd supported my dreams against the wishes of other members.

Trying my best to reach my hands to my pockets, I shakily pulled out the ring. Slowly, bringing it to my mouth, I bit it, using my teeth to hold it in place while sliding my finger through. Once it was back on, I caught my breath, because that simple act had taken a lot out of me. Next, my mind drifted to Jules. I hoped she knew that I loved her. In the short time I'd known her, she'd become an important part of my life, but somehow, I'd managed to fuck that up.

I thought about Kember. She'd just lost Val and her mental state was delicate right now. I hoped that she wouldn't hear about this, knowing it would push her over the edge. But if I died, of course, she'd hear about it. I thought about that snake ass Serina and wondered if she was somewhere taking pleasure in this. Thinking about her caused my fangs to slowly extend, but the bullets in my face made it painful, and I had to really concentrate to stop them.

I also wondered if Lexi knew about this shit. That hurt, considering I actually had some type of feelings for Lexi. But they were best friends. It's no way Lexi wouldn't have known. The more I thought about this fucking set up, the angrier I became. Reaching towards my face, I felt around for the bullets. My fingers burned as they grazed over the silver, but I didn't give a fuck about the pain anymore.

"AHHHHHH!" I screamed as I ripped the bullets from my face.

I heard footsteps rushing towards me.

"Come on, Corey!" Sypher yelled, climbing in the back with me, while Corey jumped in the driver's seat.

Just as we pulled off, I heard a loud explosion and bits and pieces of metal hit the truck.

"The fuck?!" I whispered, trying to sit up, but Sypher pushed me back down.

"It wasn't no cleaning that car, V. You lost too much blood in it. We had to blow it," Corey informed me.

Goddamnit! My fuckin Mustang! I loved that fuckin' car! I sighed as Sypher unzipped my jacket, examining my bloody chest.

"Here," he said, placing a towel in my mouth. "You know what to do."

Slowly, I nodded as he cut my shirt open. I bit down on the towel just as he ripped a bullet from inside of my chest. The pain was damn near unbearable.

"These are too deep. You gotta try to push them out."

Fuck! Closing my eyes, I took a breath and pushed. I could feel the bullets moving from their lodged hiding places deep in my flesh and bones, moving scorchingly to the surface.

"I got 'em!" he spat, furiously yanking them from my body.

I groaned in pain, darkness clouding my vision although the sun was rising.

"We almost there! Stay with me, Venom!" Corey shouted from up front.

I shook my head, and Sypher removed the towel from my mouth. My eyes shut again, and this time the pain was too much to bear. I drifted off, allowing his voice to drown out.

15

TASH

I STRETCHED MY BODY, still tired as hell. When Jules called me last night, I was chilling with Lucky, but she was so hysterical over the phone that I abruptly left and went to go meet her at the hospital. We ended up having an old school sleepover, where she filled me in on everything that had went down into the wee hours of the morning.

We both ended up falling asleep in her bed, but all night she had nightmares and continuously woke me up, which is why my ass is so tired now. A soft knocking at her bedroom door caused me to glance at her alarm clock. *9:15.* Turning to Jules, who was knocked out, snoring loudly, I ran my fingers through my hair and tossed the covers from my body.

Padding across the room, I opened the door.

"Good morning, Aunt Nia," I spoke to her mom, groggily wiping crust from my eyes.

"Hey, baby. I just wanted to check on you two before I go to the hospital to pick up Nikki. How'd you sleep?" she asked, poking her head inside to get a look at Jules.

"Barely. I still can't believe he did that to them!" I said angrily, referring to Rich.

"I know," she agreed, shaking her head. "Thank God he ran off when he heard those police sirens! I just hope he doesn't come back!"

I looked at her in confusion for a moment before realizing Jules probably told her that, instead of saying *oh, my vampire boyfriend killed him.*

I nodded quickly, "Yeah. I don't think he'll be trying anything else! Do you need me to drive you to the hospital?" I asked.

"No. I'm fine. Got a clean bill of health from the doctor. I'm back to the old me!" she grinned.

I smiled, "That's good, Aunt Nia. I'm glad you're feeling better."

"Me too! Now...you and Nikki..."

I waved her off, "I'm over it. I'm not excusing what she did, and I do expect an apology, but after hearing everything... I don't know; I guess I understand a little bit better."

Nikki was still not one of my favorite people, but I figured I could at least tolerate her. I loved Jules, and it would be selfish of me to make her choose or have her be uncomfortable. She couldn't help it that her older sister was a scandalous hoe. I would be open for a conversation but, Lord knows I pray she says the right things 'cuz I'd hate to have to put hands on her again.

Once Ms. Sonia left, I checked on Jules, pissed looking at her fingers in a splint, and grabbed my phone, heading to the bathroom. I had a missed call from Lucky, which made me smile. I was still in shock that we were kinda, sorta a thing. He wasn't my usual type, but he was a lot cooler than I expected. He even remained cool when I admitted that I didn't know the first thing about book-keeping.

Instead of snapping, or making me feel stupid, he hired someone to train me. Stason was my computer teacher, and she went above and beyond, even teaching me a few basic hacking techniques. I was still learning, but I was always the type of person that absorbed infor-mation quickly. My first test was effectively moving one of his accounts to the Caymans.

'I knew Lucky was involved in some shady shit, but as long as it couldn't be traced back to me, and I got paid, I gave no fucks. Speaking of paid, he gave me ten bands for that transaction! I was able to give half of that to my grand mom, since I was now living rent free in a town-house in Claymont, Delaware. Taking that trip to the Bahamas was one of the best moves I'd made.

Before I could call him back, I noticed I had a voice-mail from an unsaved number. Calling in, to listen, I frowned as Riq's voice came on.

Tash, I know I fucked up, but I miss you. I know you still love me. What we had just doesn't go away overnight. I just need you to hear me out. I was thinking maybe you could meet me at our spot. For lunch. And at least give me the chance to talk to you face to face. We owe each other that. I'll be there at two o'clock. Please don't stand me up.

I was annoyed at the tear threatening to fall from my eye. I wanted to delete the message and delete him from my life. But the pain and sincerity in his voice had me

considering it. Sucking my teeth, I listened to the
message again, deciding that I would go. I'd never take
him back, but what could it hurt to hear him out. Besides,
I wanted to know what made him cheat in the first place.
I wanted the truth.

Shooting a quick text to Lucky, I let him know that I'd
be spending the day with Jules, but I'd see him tonight.
Once he responded, letting me know that was fine, I
stood from the toilet and used Jules' Aveeno soap to wash
my face. Finding the extra toothbrushes under the sink, I
tore open the plastic and brushed my teeth. Grabbing a
brush from the counter, I styled my new, copper colored,
Brazilian hair into a high ponytail, giving me the appearance of a cute cheerleader.

Examining my face, I noticed the faint darkness
under my eyes from the sleepless night and remembered
my concealer inside of my purse. Exiting the bathroom, I
headed back to the bedroom. I was surprised to find Jules
sitting up, frantically texting away on her phone with her
good hand.

"Hey boo! How you feeling?" I asked, plopping down
on the bed next to her.

"Girl. A mess," she responded, still typing.

Finally, she finished and sat the phone next to her,
giving me her attention. Her face was slightly swollen,
and her eyes were bloodshot. My friend looked like she'd
been to hell and back and I was sorry that I didn't get the
chance to fuck Rich up before Venom did.

"Venom hasn't called, texted or anything, and that's
not like him. I think something is wrong," she said,
running her hand through her hair and wincing because
she forgot and used her injured hand.

"Jules! You told that man you didn't want anything to do with him!" I reminded her.

"I know! But I been telling him that for the past three or four days, and that never stopped him before! He would've at least checked on me when I was released from the hospital!"

I sucked my teeth, "I'm confused. Why would you tell him to leave you alone, when you really don't want him too?"

"I mean... you know how I felt about Rich and look at how that shit turned out!" she snapped, holding up her hand.

I sat up and made a face, "First of all, nobody liked Rich ass but you! If I remember correctly, me, your mom, and some of his own family told your ass that nigga wasn't shit! But you just had to find out for yourself! You hard-headed! My mom mom always say, 'a hard head makes a soft ass!' Now you being hard-headed with Venom. He saved your life, Jules! That nut ass nigga coulda killed you!" I yelled.

I was trying not to get frustrated with her, but I felt she was being dumb! Jules was like a sister to me, and I hated to see her making dumbass decisions based off of some clown ass, bum ass, dog! Like, damn! The nigga dead and still managing to fuck up her life!

"I know that, Tash! But you don't understand! You wasn't there," this bitch said, hitting me with a Cam'ron line, "It felt...it didn't feel good to watch him fuck somebody else in my damn face!" she snapped, tossing the covers from her body and hopping up.

I jumped up, blocking the door so she couldn't leave. Standing in front of her, a large grin broke out on my face, "You really like him! Wait, no! Your ass in love!" I squealed.

"What?! Girl no! Now move your simple ass, I gotta pee!" she whined.

"Kegels, bitch! Hold that piss! Jules, you really love him! I know you! Ok, you gotta get your man back. He really feeling you, I can tell, so it shouldn't be that hard to get him away from those other bitches," I said, trying to think of a plan.

While I was thinking, she tickled me, causing me to scramble away from her and she quickly opened the door and scurried out.

"You are so childish, you carpet muncher!" I called after her.

She paused, spinning around, "You just mad it wasn't your carpet! Get Lucky for that!" she shot back, sticking out her tongue and marching to the bathroom, while I laughed.

Hurrying over to her phone, I typed in her code and found the thread between her and Venom. Glancing over my shoulder, I hastily typed.

I made a mistake. I love you.

Quickly, I pressed send and tossed the phone back down and sat on the edge of the bed, crossing my legs just as she came back in.

"Ok, maybe I do like him...a lot. But don't you think it'd be selfish on my part to make him choose. I mean, I knew what it was when I signed that contract, right?" she asked.

"Things change! When you signed that contract, you was crushin' and thought it would be fun and exciting, right?"

She nodded.

"But, the more you got to know him the deeper your feelings grew, and I mean, who can blame you? The nigga fine!" I said, kicking my legs.

She laughed, "That he is!"

"I think you should at least tell him how you feel. Give him the option. Instead of, whatever this shit is that you doing," I told her honestly.

She leaned against the door for a moment, in thought. "You know what? You're right! I'mma tell him right now. The worst he can say is no, right?" she asked, walking towards the bed.

"Right," I replied nervously, knowing she was about to see the text I sent.

I stood, moving out of her reach as she grabbed her phone.

Her mouth dropped open, "I really can't stand you! Nosy ass always in somebody business!" she laughed, throwing a pillow at me.

I shrugged, "I figured you would smarten up and see things my way," I chuckled.

"Hmmph, since you all in my business, what's going on with you and Lucky? You was with him when I called you last night, right?" she asked.

"Yup. I told you. Nothing major. I enjoy spending time with him and I'm enjoying how plush my bank account is looking. I know how to keep my feelings in check, unlike some people," I teased.

"Whatever!" she said.

"I did get a call from Riq though," I told her, fidgeting with the bottom of the oversized t-shirt I wore.

Her eyes damn near popped out of her head, "Whatt?! When? What did he say?"

I sighed, "He wants to meet up at Cambridge. Two o'clock. I don't know; I guess he wants to talk face to face."

"Bet! I'm going too! Just let me get something to eat and get dressed and–"

"Sit your Rumble in the jungle ass down! You already hurt; you should be recuperating. I can handle him. Plus, I feel like I need to handle this by myself," I told her hype ass.

"Uh uhn! I'm not letting you go by yourself! What if it's a set-up? What if his sister shows up?"

I chuckled, "Girl, do I look shook? Besides, I told her to pull up as soon as I got back from the Bahamas and her scary ass didn't want no smoke!"

"Ok, what if Lucky finds out? I know you said he cool, but I still don't trust him, Tash! The nigga is dangerous. I just don't like this. You see what happened to me when I showed up to go meet somebody!" she said, holding up her splinted fingers.

"That was a completely different situation! Riq is nowhere near as crazy as Rich was. And I told Lucky that I was gonna be with you all day," I explained.

She shook her head, "I still don't like it."

"Trust me. I got this."

She gave me a look like she still wasn't sure, but she didn't say anything else about it. Later on that afternoon, I was ready to go face Tyriq. We'd all eaten and dressed, and Nikki and I had even had a little kumbaya moment. She apologized non stop and I was taken aback by how different she seemed. I hoped it was genuine, for Jules and Ms. Sonia's sake.

As I prepared to leave, I noticed Jules grabbing her purse as well. Now, I know I told this girl I was going by myself!

"Where you going?" I asked, stopping her at the door.

"I'm not thinking about you. I gotta go to Walmart. They never deposited my last check. They talking about I gotta come pick it up. They just mad because I didn't give them two weeks notice!" she huffed.

"Wayment, Venom padded your bank account! And didn't he tell you not to go back there?" I questioned, tossing a hand on my hip.

"He did, but I'm trying to save that for emergencies until I figure out what I'm going to do. And he said not to work there; I'm only picking up a check, then I'm out. Besides, he still hasn't responded to my texts, so he's not really in a position to tell me what to do!" she spat.

"It's one thirty in the afternoon! He probably sleep!" I argued.

"Um hmm, with who?"

"Oh my God! Y'all need to get it together, ASAP!" I chuckled, shaking my head. "You want me to run you over there real quick before I go meet Riq?" I asked.

"Girl, I'm fine! You go handle your business, and we'll meet up later so you can tell me how it went."

"Ok. Be careful," I told her.

"You too, boo," she said, hugging me before we got in our cars, pulling off in opposite directions.

I PULLED UP OVER TOWN, on Avenue of the States, and

luckily found a good parking spot, close to the little breakfast spot that Riq and I often frequented. I sighed, thinking about how he pretty much threw our whole relationship away. Pulling down the visor, I checked to make sure my concealer was still doing its job, hiding the fatigue around my eyes. It was, so I added a little light pink lip gloss and finger combed my long ponytail.

Even running off of three hours of sleep, I was still bad. I'd put on the jeans I'd worn last night, and borrowed one of Jules crop tops that she could no longer fit, since she was out here with a vixen body now. I threw my cute little college jacket over it and paired it with some fresh Timbs. My ears and wrists blinged with expensive gifts from Lucky.

I looked cute and casual, but also like I was with the shits. Taking a deep breath, I marched inside with my head held high. The little bell sounded as I entered, and I scanned the small diner, my eyes quickly landing on Riq. He looked good, with a fresh haircut. Immediately, I became irritated, because he should have looked like shit. Like he'd been suffering without me. How dare this nigga still be living!

He smiled and stood when he noticed me. I kept a blank face and sashayed towards him. I took my seat without acknowledging him and saw that he'd already ordered my favorite breakfast food and a glass of orange juice.

"You look good, Tash. I miss–"

I held up a hand to silence him, while signaling for the waitress.

Smiling, she approached. "Hey Tash! Long time no see! What you need?" she asked.

Crystal was our regular waitress, and we usually stopped in so much that she now knew us by name.

"Hi, Crystal. I would like the same meal again. I wasn't here, and I don't know if my food was tampered with at the table," I said, handing her the plate and glass.

She looked baffled as her eyes glanced between me and Riq.

"Uh, sure, ok. I'll have the cook make it again," she said, glancing between us once more before heading to the kitchen.

"Really?! Was that necessary?!" he asked, obviously embarrassed.

"Sure was. I can't trust you, so I can't put anything past you." I spat, narrowing my eyes at him.

"Wow."

"Yup, wow. Why am I here, Tyriq?"

He sighed, folding his hands in front of him on the table. "I asked you here because I wanted to apologize. On God, I wish I could take back what I did–"

"What you did repeatedly," I corrected him.

He nodded, "You right. I'm sorry. But I learned my lesson. How long are you gonna make me pay for a small mistake?" he questioned.

I stared at him, not believing the words that rolled off his lying ass tongue.

"*Small mistake??*" I repeated, "a small mistake is forgetting to take the trash out the night before trash day! Fucking my best friend's cousin is a huge mistake!" I shouted, causing people to glance in our direction.

"Look, I fucked up, aight!" he said.

"Here you go," Crystal interrupted, placing a fresh

glass of orange juice onto the table. "Your food should be out in a few minutes. Is everything ok?" she asked.

"Everything is ok except for these stray dogs out here, passing around fleas and biting on their little balls, chasing any bitch that's in heat! They need to be neutered!" I snapped, smacking my hand on the table, causing the silverware to shake.

Crystal glanced out of the window in confusion.

"Strays? Around here?" she asked, still looking for some damn dogs outside.

"It's cool, Crystal. We good right now," Riq told her, and she headed to the back to get my food.

"You really doing the most right now! Yeah, I was wrong, but you really gonna sit there and pretend to be innocent?" he asked through gritted teeth.

"Excuse me?" I asked, sitting my orange juice down.

"I seen you been running around with that fat moth-erfucker! You gon' act like that just started? You was prob-ably fuckin' that nigga all along!" he snapped.

"I know you fuckin' lyi'n! I just started dealing with him. I have never cheated on you, although God knows I should have!"

My phone chimed inside of my purse, and I pulled it out, just as Crystal came back with the steaming plate. After thanking her, I checked my texts. Speak of the devil.

Lucky: You still with your friend, ma?

Me: Yes. I'm going to stay for a few more hours. She's really shaken up.

Lucky: Alright then. Hope she feels better. I'll holla.

When I glanced up, Riq was staring at me with a murderous glare.

"So, you just gon' text in the middle of our conversation?"

I sighed, taking a bite of my omelet, "What conversation? All I hear is you trying to shift blame on me. You know, I was lowkey hoping for a different outcome, but I see that was foolish of me. Riq, it's over. After today, forget you know me," I said.

"I shoulda listened to my family. They warned me about messing with a little crack baby! You gonna end up a worthless whore just like your mother!" he spat.

My eyes widened, listening to the insults easily glide from his mouth. I couldn't believe that this man that I used to love, could hit me so far below the belt. Damn, I guess it really was a thin line between love and hate. In a fit of rage, I tossed the hot plate of food in his face, followed by my glass of orange juice.

"Ahh!" he yelled, as the hot bacon grease ran down his face.

Before he could react, I hopped across the table, throwing punch after punch until I felt someone pulling me off him. Our waitress and two of the cooks had rushed out to break it up.

"You fuckin' bitch!" he yelled, hopping up, like he was gonna do something, but one of the cooks held him back.

"He asked me if I wanted you dead. I said no. Don't make me regret it," I spat, snatching my purse from the seat.

"Here, Crystal," I said, handing her a crisp hundred-dollar bill. "Sorry for the disturbance. Keep the change," I said, walking out feeling bossed the fuck up.

I couldn't front like his words hadn't cut me deeply, but I thought I handled it well. Smoothing my hair and clothes, I got inside of my car and peeled off, never looking back. My hands shook as I reached for my phone to call Jules. When she didn't answer, I switched directions and headed towards Walmart, wondering if she was still there.

After speaking to some of her former co-workers, I learned that she'd been there, but left a little while ago. When I still couldn't reach her, I sent her a lengthy text, telling her the main highlights of my meeting with Riq. I figured Venom had probably responded and turned into a bat or something and flew to get her. They were probably busy having make-up sex, so I stopped bothering her and headed to my own house.

Parking in my assigned space, I got out, walking through the parking garage towards the elevator. Stepping on, I pressed the button for the top floor. Inside of my loft, I smiled, looking at the all white décor. Lucky had dropped some stacks to have it decorated nearly identical to the hotel suite in the Bahamas. The only thing missing was the tropical view, but I was fine with the view of the Delaware River and the city skyline that was right outside of my gigantic picture window.

Kicking off my boots, I stripped out of my food-stained clothes and carried them to the hamper inside of my room. Taking a quick shower, I decided to wear some purple, lacey lingerie. Inside the kitchen, I took out the ground beef so it could thaw for the spaghetti. While I waited, I chopped the peppers and onions, tossing everything into a sauté pan to lightly simmer. Once I had everything going, I was bored, so I turned on some TV and pulled out my MacBook.

"Now, why would they put her in that outfit? I

could've picked something better," I commented to myself, watching the Love and Hip Hop reality star talk shit in her confessional.

Powering on my computer, I went into the files I had for Lucky. I wanted to check and make sure the last deposit had cleared for him. Checking the statements, I noticed a large sum of money had been wired to him recently. Five million to be exact. Being nosy, I checked to see who had sent it. *Clay Bakerfield.*

Who the hell is that? I wondered.

It didn't say what it was for, but it looked sketchy, so I didn't expect it too. But why did that name sound so familiar? Guess it was time to put my FBI jacket on. Minimizing the screen, I went to Facebook, typing in the name. Of course, a million pages popped up, but the first one was Clay Bakerfield, Philadelphia City Councilman. Scrolling down his page, I paused, seeing him standing next to a man that was a dead ringer for Venom! Just older.

"Damnit!" I mumbled, realizing that he wasn't tagged. "Maybe I can find him on Venom's page. They gotta be related."

Going to Venom's page, my heart dropped when I saw all of the *RIP* posts. Frantically scrolling, thinking that it was a mistake, I came to a news clip that someone posted. A bunch of cop cars and a news reporter stood on the highway, with a wreckage as the background. Quickly I turned up the volume.

This is Monica Valesquez, reporting from what we are told is the deadly aftermath of a possible crime scene. This Mustang, belonging to Venom, a well-known Philadelphia rapper, was found engulfed in flames early this morning. Some of the rapper's belongings were found inside, but authorities have not released any further details yet. As more information emerges, we'll keep you updated. Anyone with information is asked to come forward...

I hopped up, desperately trying to call Jules. Her phone was now going straight to voicemail, and I wondered if she'd heard.

"FUCK!" I yelled.

I needed to think. Pacing my carpet, I tried to make sense of this. Ok, Venom was dead...maybe. They said they found some of his belongings but not a body. He could've made it out. Can explosions even kill vampires? My mind drifted back to the picture of the man who looked like Venom. The ring he wore was identical to the ring I'd seen on Venom's finger before.

"His father!" I said out loud, remembering Jules telling me about how much they resembled.

So, his father is friends with the city councilman who just happened to send Lucky millions of dollars hours after Venom is presumed dead. I thought back to last night when Jules had called me. She was hysterical, but she mentioned Venom had just left her. It would only be common sense to assume that he would have been headed towards the highway.

When she called, I had her on speaker. Lucky left out of the room to go make a call right after she mentioned Venom.

"Oh my fucking God! Lucky set him up!" I whispered to myself.

Hearing a key in my lock, I gasped and dove to the computer, shutting everything down, just as Lucky walked in.

"What's up?" he asked, looking around before turning to me.

"Huh? Oh, nothing. Chilling. Watching...this," I pointed at the TV, forgetting what the hell was on.

He glanced at the TV screen before looking at me. "You good?" he asked, raising a brow.

"Of course! I'm just...my mind is still on Jules. That's all."

Taking a seat on the armrest of the couch, he looked at me, "Is she good? What y'all do today?" he asked, his hazel eyes boring into mine.

"She's a little better. We just stayed at the house," I lied.

"Hmm. Has she heard about Venom?"

"W-what about him?" I asked, acting like I didn't know.

"He dead."

"Lucky, stop playing. That's not funny!"

"Am I laughing? The nigga gone."

"Weren't you cool? Aren't you upset?" I asked, my voice raising.

"Niggas die everyday, b. Bitches do too," he said, standing and heading towards the kitchen.

Quietly, I opened the side compartment of my coffee table and pulled out the small .22 my grandmother had given me as a house warming gift and stuck it under the pillow next to me. My heart was racing so fast it felt like I'd just run a marathon.

"Baby, you gonna make my plate?" he called from the kitchen.

I glanced at the pillow before answering. "Here I come."

I took a few deep breaths, readying myself for what was about to go down in history as the best performance of my life. Standing, I slowly walked towards the kitchen.

"That's nice. You put that on for me, or you had it on earlier?" he asked, referring to the new lingerie that I'd just popped the tags from.

I looked at him questioningly, "I wore it for you, silly! Why the hell would I wear this for Jules?"

"Hmm." He muttered with a slight smirk.

As I grabbed the plates from the cabinet, he watched my every move. Fixing a hefty plate for him, I sat it on the table and poured him a large glass of iced tea.

"Make one for you too. I want you to eat with me."

He was still hovering over me as I made my own plate.

"Really, Lucky. I don't know how you could think about food at a time like this!" I said, taking a seat.

He turned on the mounted TV and flicked through the channels until he found a football game.

"A time like what?" he asked, finally taking a seat.

He pulled his gun from his waist and placed it on the glass table top with the barrel facing me.

Trying my best to ignore my internal warning system, I replied, "Your friend just died! Do you want to talk about it?" I asked, placing my hand on his.

He looked at it for a moment before gently sliding it away towards his fork. He shook his head, "I'm straight."

I sighed as he twirled the noodles onto his fork.

"Is it anything you want to talk about?" he asked.

"No," I said, forcing myself to eat.

"This is good. You almost perfect, huh?" he said.

"Almost?" I smirked.

"Yeah, almost. Nobody's perfect and if they are it's

probably too good to be true," he said, turning his attention back to the television.

"Ok. So what makes me fall short of perfection?" I asked.

He looked at me but didn't respond. Instead, he finished his plate in silence, occasionally glancing up at the TV. When I ate all that I could, I gathered our dishes and rinsed them off before placing them inside of the dishwasher, while Lucky sparked up one of his Cuban cigars. I started back to the living room, but he grabbed my wrist.

"Sit down."

I sat with no objection, although I would have felt safer if I was closer to my gun.

"How was your day, Lucky? You seem stressed," I tried to make small talk.

"Same shit different day. You asked me a question earlier. Repeat it," he spoke calmly.

"Um, I asked what makes me not perfect to you?"

"Remember when we were in the Bahamas?"

I chuckled, "Yeah, it was only a week ago."

He nodded, "I told you I had a knack for knowing when I was being lied to."

"Okay," I nodded, trying to remain cool and calm, but he was unnerving me minute by minute.

"I asked you what you did today and what did you tell me?"

"I-I spent the day with my friend," I responded.

"Now see. I find that funny because some of my people saw her at the store. By herself. So my question is, if she was there, where were you?"

FUCK!

"I... she... I was with her mom. She–"

Before I could finish my lie, he backhanded me so hard I fell from the chair. When he stood, I darted between his legs, trying to crawl to the living room, but he caught my leg, pulling me back to him. Once he yanked me back, he gave me a hard punch to the stomach, causing me to throw up the spaghetti I'd just eaten.

"Lucky, stop! It's not what you think!" I wheezed, still trying to get away.

My hands slid over the vomited food as I struggled.

"Yeah. I think you went on a little date with your old nigga! Am I wrong?" he yelled, snatching me by my hair and slamming me through the glass table.

I felt the shards slice at my bare skin.

"You're wrong!" I cried, wrapping my hands around a piece of glass.

"Tell me how, doll baby," he said, lifting me again, this time by my throat.

"I wanted some closure. And to tell him that I officially moved on!" I said.

He looked at me for a moment, and I used that split second when his guard was down to plunge the glass into his chest.

"Bitch!" he roared, dropping me to the floor.

I scrambled away as he yanked the glass from his body. Standing, I tried to run as he managed to grab his gun that laid on the ground in a pile of glass.

"Bitch, I'mma kill you!" he said, aiming the gun at my head, barreling towards me.

Just as he pulled the trigger, he slipped on my throw up, causing him to miss my head by inches. Taking my moment, I hauled ass to the living room, grabbing my gun and hiding behind the sofa. I could hear his heavy footsteps, and I felt like a bitch in a scary movie. His big ass would probably skin me alive and hang it on his wall like abstract art.

I couldn't hide forever. Standing, with my gun pointed towards him, I slowly eased from behind the couch. We eyed each other, both pointing guns, both bloody.

"You know how to use that?" he asked, nodding at my gun.

"Sure do," I said, cocking it and aiming for the center of his head.

"You look sexy as fuck holding that. You as turned on as I am?" he asked.

"What?! Nigga, no! You just tried to kill me!" I screamed, looking at him like he'd lost his damn mind!

"But did you die though?"

My eyes widened and I burst into laughter. I couldn't believe this nigga!

He started laughing too.

"Something is really wrong with you!" I shouted.

"I finally found my match," he said.

"Not really," I laughed. "I don't even know how to use this."

"Yo, for real? You had me shook a little bit," he chuckled, putting his gun back on his waist.

"Just a little bit? Should have been a lot," I said, raising my gun and firing.

I'll never forget the shocked expression that spread on his face. He tried to reach for his gun, but I walked up, still firing. One in his hand that he wanted to reach with, one in his chest and finally, one in his head. He fell back, through the window and down the thirteen floors.

Running to the window, I looked down, watching his life-less body spread out over the pavement below.

I heard screams, followed by a rush of footsteps. Rushing back to my computer, I quickly made an account and transferred the wired money to my account before hastily deleting the files. Shit, I wasn't ending this rela-tionship empty-handed, and I damn sure wasn't going back to the struggle.

16

SERINA

FINALLY! I thought to myself, fighting the urge to twerk in my little black dress. Finally he was gone, and before sunrise, I'd be a vampire! My first order of business was to kill all of these hoes, except maybe Lexi. She had kept my secret after all. I guess I could spare her. I couldn't believe we'd finally pulled it off! I was so giddy that I accidentally laughed out loud, causing Lexi to glare at me.

I quickly disguised it as an outpour of emotion before anyone noticed. I was thankful for the big, dark Prada glasses I wore, even though it was ten o'clock at night. Feeling a chill, I pulled my gray, mink coat tighter around me, wondering when this shit would be over. I was ready to get down to business.

"Would anyone else like to say anything?" Xavier asked, looking drained, gaunt and thin, standing in front of the massive monument dedicated to Venom.

They'd had him cremated, and the solid gold urn that held his ashes sat in the center of all this gaudy shit. I was hoping no one else spoke. I rolled my eyes behind my glasses when Kember stood. Of course, I'd had to hear her whining all night.

Oh, first my girlfriend and now Venom! Wah wah wah.

Like, bitch, if you don't shut your woe is me ass up! But of course, she wouldn't. I hastily moved my feet before she stomped on them with those big ass horse clompers she was wearing. Who in the hell wore stripper shoes to a memorial? Come on now! Oh, I couldn't wait to kill her ass!

I glanced at Lexi to see if she'd noticed those horrible shoes, but she was too busy sobbing. Sypher consoled her by rubbing her back. Rolling my eyes again, I focused on the Amazonian Kember, who was now up front. She gently touched the urn and kissed the full-size photo of him, before turning to the podium. She cleared her throat.

"Before I met Venom, I was lost. Shunned by my family. No friends and surrounded by snakes. Venom was a bright spot. He *is* a bright spot. The many memories we have will always live on. He made me believe in magic and mystery, something the world beats out of us." She paused, crying again.

"I'm sorry. I feel like I just did this! I'm so tired of the people I care being taken away!" she sobbed.

Girl, get on with it!

Talia rushed to her aide, wrapping her in an embrace.

"It's going to be okay, honey. I promise," she told her.

Hmph! Cold bitch never hugged me!

"Do you think... I mean, well I used to sing for Val all

of the time. Do you think I could sing something now?" Kember asked.

Jesus Christ, now I had to sit through this bird tryna screech out a melody?! Lord, keep me near the cross!

"Of course! We'd love it! Right?" Talia asked, glancing around the large yard at everyone.

Most people (and I use the term loosely) nodded or clapped lightly. I sat stone-faced with my arms folded.

How original, I thought as she began croaking out a less than stellar rendition of *Amazing Grace.*

I tuned her out as I glanced around. The vampires all sat on one side of the yard while the humans sat on the other. Their first few rows were filled with his mom and dad and other prominent members of the Court. Behind them were other vampires from the area, some I recognized from the secret vamp club that I'd only gotten to go to once, and others, I didn't recognize as they must have traveled in from out of state.

On our side, it was just us. The woman of the house, (which would be me) and our tramps. I was glad that bitch, Jules was indisposed at the moment and couldn't make it. Corey and Sypher were here too. We used to be cool, but Venom had trained them to disrespect me, and now I couldn't stand their asses. I couldn't wait to tell them that their services would no longer be needed! When I heard everyone clapping, I was surprised that it was over. Some people were even crying harder than before.

If I'd have paid attention to that banshee, I'd probably be crying too. Talia wiped her face with a silk, crimson-colored handkerchief and helped Kember down from the podium.

"That was absolutely beautiful, dear," Talia lied, handing her handkerchief to Kember.

Kember sobbed, looking at the silk and stumbled. I sat up.

I know this bitch ain't about to fake pass out up here!

Talia whispered a few words to her, and she pulled herself together, making her way back to her seat.

"Don't you want to say a few words?" she asked me loudly, drawing attention to me.

Smiling through gritted teeth, I stood. I was gonna fuck her up for putting me on the spot! With my head held high, I strutted down the center of the yard, careful that my heels didn't sink into the soft, freshly manicured ground. I nodded at his parents as I passed, but they both ignored me. Whatever. I stopped at the urn and touched it.

I'm so happy you're gone, you bitch ass nigga. I'm just sad that it wasn't my own hands that took you out of here! I thought to myself.

Sighing deeply, I stood at the podium, surrounded by exotic flowers, incense, and pictures of Venom.

"Where to begin. I stand here a grieving widow, for Venom and our family. But I don't stand here in sadness or weakness. I stand here demanding justice! Justice for Venom. I demand a slow, painful death for the person responsible. The person responsible for dimming all of our light! Come on, everybody! Justice for Venom!" I stomped my foot, chanting.

When no one joined in, I pushed and managed to get some tears flowing. Pretending to be overcome with grief, I wobbled down from the podium, waiting for Talia to come and comfort me like she did for Kember. When no one moved, I hurried back to my seat. Next, Xavier stood again.

"My son, I release you into the night," he said, sprinkling the ashes over the green grass.

One of the vamps I recognized, opened his arms, releasing dozens of bats.

Ohh, magic tricks!

We all watched as the bats circled over us. One of them dived at my mink hat.

"Oh shit!" I yelled, frantically trying to wave it away.

My embarrassment elicited a few chuckles, especially from Corey and Sypher. I glared at them through my glasses. Finally, it was over, and we all filed inside of the huge old mansion. I wondered whose house it was or if it was just one of the houses that was owned by the Court. Looking at the old Hollywood décor inside, I figured this was one of Talia's homes.

Old bitch has good taste, I thought, running my fingers over the gold, satin curtains.

Everyone mingled about, vampires sipping flutes of blood, while we were served wine. I could get used to this. Everyday should be Venom's funeral. I sipped my wine and grabbed an escargot hors d'oeuvre, noticing Clay walk off upstairs. Glancing around, I saw that no one was paying any attention and I followed him. He went up another flight of stairs, and I quietly tiptoed behind him.

"What in the fuck are you doing?" he whispered, grabbing me roughly and pulling me into a room.

Once he shut the door, I spoke, "Is he really dead?" I whispered, bouncing on my toes.

"Yes! And you could pretend to be a little more hurt!

Xavier and Talia are powerful, and if I can feel it, I know they can!" he scolded me.

"I don't care what they feel! Once I'm a vampire, it won't matter!" I spat lowly.

He sighed, walking across the hardwood floor and taking a seat on the brown leather recliner.

"Why should I turn you when it was Lucky who actually helped get the job done?"

My eyes widened and I couldn't believe my ears!

"Lucky?! He may have delivered you the final blow, but it was me who has been helping you since the beginning! I blame your shooters! How many tries do they need before they hit a mark?!"

He jumped up, and in a flash, he was in my face.

"Keep your fucking voice down! I'll turn you, but once I do, I want you gone! No one can know that you're a vampire, or so help me, I'll stake you myself!" he threatened.

Once I was turned, I had no plans on leaving! I wanted to take over the Court and make all of these motherfuckers pay! But I played it cool.

"Of course I will, daddy," I said softly, dropping to my knees.

Unzipping his pants, I pulled out his stiffening member and slowly ran my tongue over it. Clay was two thousand years old, but still wasn't the oldest vampire. He was Xavier's right-hand man in the Court, but his fake human job was as a city councilman. The Court was divided on Venom. Some agreeing with Xavier that he should be allowed to pursue whatever he wanted, and others, like Clay, who lowkey agreed with the Rogues that Venom was a threat to their way of life.

Clay and I started our affair about a year ago, when I showed up to a council meeting, and we had a little private *chit chat*. In all his years, he'd never been with a human. I was his first, and he was strung out on this pussy. But who could blame him? Slurping him down my throat, I allowed him to grab my hair and fuck my face. He wasn't as good or as big as Venom, but he served his purpose.

Finally, he came down my throat, and I stood tilting my head back, ready for a bite.

"I can't bite you here. They'd all smell it!" he said, tucking himself back inside of his pants.

"Fine!" I sighed. "Where are your people keeping that skank?"

"She's at Stefan's house. I'm going to let her go. We only snatched her to try and pull Venom out of hiding if he was still alive. Since he's really gone, there's no point–"

"No! Clay, please let me have her!" I whispered.

"For what?" he asked, staring at me.

"It's personal. I'd be forever grateful," I said, running a nail down his chest.

"Fine. Whatever. I'm just ready to be done with this!" he said, leaving out of the room.

Grinning, I reapplied my lipstick, forced out more tears and headed back downstairs. I noticed Sypher watching me as I strolled around, gracing the room with my presence. When I finally got tired of the gloominess, I went back outside. Me, Lexi and Kember had all rode over together with Sypher and Corey, but I was ready to leave now. I desperately wanted to pay that bitch Jules a visit.

"I bet he would have turned her," I mumbled, sparking a cigarette.

I paced around, heels clacking on the cold pavement, until I finally figured I would go. Using my phone, I ordered an Uber and put in Stefan's address as my destination. I was supposed to wait for Clay, but he'd get over it. Eventually, the silver Kia pulled up, just as I noticed Kember stick her head out of the doorway. I rushed to the car, not feeling like talking or explaining myself to her.

Once we hit Lansdowne, my excitement hit it's pinnacle. I'd really pulled this off! And I managed to do it without getting myself killed! I was a smart cookie! Venom should have realized what he had. If he'd have turned me the first time I'd asked, not only would he still be alive, but he would have been lucky enough to be connected to me permanently.

When we turned onto Union Avenue, I spotted Stefan's house. He was obsessed with cars and had two out front, and I knew there were two in the garage. I knew Stefan because I'd attended a couple of their little Rogue meetings that were held at his house.

"Have a good night and please rate me five stars–"

I slammed the door while the driver was still talking, not concerned with whatever bullshit he was babbling about. Pulling the collar up on my fur to fight against the chill, I hurried across the street and up his walkway. Laying my finger on the bell, I held it there until the door was snatched open. Stefan stood there, looking like he was ready to attack until he saw it was me.

He peeked out, glancing around. "Where's Clay?" he asked.

"Still at the memorial. You know he has to keep up appearances. Are you going to let me in?"

He looked at me cautiously before stepping to the side so that I could enter. Stefan was a cutie, but he wasn't powerful enough for me. He was one of the weaker vampires, and he was debilitating himself even more by separating himself from the Court. That's where the power source was and the further away from it you were, the less you could connect with it.

"Why are you here without Clay?" he inquired, still looking at me, suspiciously.

He didn't trust me, and I didn't understand how you wouldn't trust someone that's been looking out for your team.

"Where is she?" I asked, exasperated with his questions.

"Why?" he demanded.

Just then, I heard a scream coming from his basement. Turning, I headed in that direction, but Stefan appeared in front of me, lifting me off of my feet by my coat collar.

"You are not a vampire despite what you think! You aren't welcomed here without Clay! This is why I'm glad Venom is dead! He got you human bitches thinking you have input about vamp shit! Nothing we do concerns you!" he growled, his eyes burning a bright red.

"I helped kill Venom, in case you forgot!"

"Oh, I know! Lived in his house and ate his food and still wasn't satisfied. Dogs have more loyalty. That's exactly why I don't trust you!" he spat, letting me go.

"Hah! Loyalty? You conspired to kill another vampire!

Who are you to talk about loyalty?" I questioned, straightening my coat.

"I'm loyal to my Rogues. The only motherfuckers I owe anything to! Now, what the fuck do you want with Jules?"

I rolled my eyes, sick of everyone trying to protect her, like she was something special!

"Does she know about Venom?"

"No."

"I want to tell her," I said, once again making my way towards the basement.

He yanked me back, "YOU DON'T RUN SHIT AROUND HERE!" he roared.

Just then, Clay entered the house. Breathing a sigh of relief, I ran to him, squeezing out some tears.

"Oh my God! Clay! All I've done is try to help your cause! Why am I being treated like this?" I whined on his alpaca coat.

"She's right. Stefan, stop it. There's nothing wrong with having human allies," he said, coddling me.

I turned around, smirking at Stefan while he narrowed his eyes at me.

"You so blinded by some pussy that you can't see a snake in your mist?" Stefan questioned.

In a flash, Clay was in his face, "Question me again!" he demanded.

Like the punk he was, he lowered his head, not daring to repeat himself, while I folded my arms, watching him smugly. Before I could rub it in, I heard crying from the basement, and I marched towards it, snatching open the door. Walking down the flight of stairs, I cringed at the unfurnished basement. It looked like something out of *Hostile*. It was a perfect place to keep the bitch.

As I looked around, I spotted two other vampires, both watching me like a hawk. Ignoring them, I glanced behind them to see Jules. My heart jumped for joy, spotting her ripped clothing, and the bite marks up and down her arms and chest. Slipping off my long, heavy fur, I carefully placed it on the cleanest chair I could spot. I'd just have to get it dry cleaned later. Taking off my hat, I shook out my bundles.

"Hello, Jules," I spoke, cheerfully.

She slowly looked up, disoriented. When her gaze finally landed on me, she narrowed her eyes, gaining a burst of energy as she struggled with the ties that bound her wrists. I chuckled at the dirty look she gave me.

"Hey, boo! How you been doing?" I asked, stopping to wipe a smudge from my shoe.

She grunted, "I should've known you had something to do with this bullshit! When Venom finds out–"

"Oh! You haven't heard?" I asked.

"Heard what?"

"It's so sad really. Our poor Venom is dead," I said, faking sadness.

Her eyes grew wide, and then she... she laughed! "Yeah right, bitch!" she laughed.

She glanced around the room, "You've been working with the Rogues. I'm not surprised, but I don't understand why? Venom–"

"First of all, stop talking about him like he's still alive! He's gone! And yes, I've been helping them," I admitted, waving my hand around the room. "They know how to repay loyalty!" I said, ignoring Stefan scoffing at me.

"Loyallttyyy!? Hoe, you wouldn't know the first thing about it!" she responded.

Stepping closer, I roughly smacked my hand down over hers. I made sure it was the one with the fingers in the splint, and she winced, but remained quiet.

"And how about you? Where has your loyalty gotten you? Where's your Lord and savior Venom now? No one's coming to save you." I told her, leaning closer.

She shook her head, "You really believe that, don't you? If you really believe he's gone, it's obvious you don't know him at all. Never did!" she spat indignantly.

I hauled off and slapped her, the loud sound echoing through the room.

"He couldn't save Val, and he can't save you!"

Her eyes burned with hatred, "I knew it! I knew you had something to do with her death. Bitch, untie me and let's see who needs to be saved!"

Laughing, I hit her again for the hell of it. "Girl, please! Even if I untied you, you wouldn't be ready for these hands! Obviously, I'm a pro when it comes to murdering weak hoes!"

She hawk spit in my face, surprising me.

"Disgusting bitch!" I yelled, punching her in the face.

When she didn't seem fazed, I grabbed her fingers, twisting them. She screamed, and I wiped her spit from my face and rubbed it in her hair, surprised I didn't feel any tracks.

"Bitch, on my mama, I promise, before this is over, you're gonna pay for this shit!" she yelled.

I raised my hand to hit her again, but a cold hand grabbed my wrist.

I turned. "Clay! What–"

"Serina! You told me you had nothing to do with that girl's death! She was an innocent!"

"Oh God!" I yelled, snatching my arm back "She was not! She laid her thot ass up in *my* house, fucking *my* man! She got what she deserved, just like this bitch is about too!"

"It was your idea! Tryna keep a man that didn't want to be kept! Introducing other females into your relationship. You dumber than you look, sweetie," Jules said.

I was beyond pissed that nigga had been pillow talking with this bitch! Telling my business! Angrily, I snatched my phone from my purse, and clicked on the news report about Venom. Shoving it in her face, I forced her to look at the barely recognizable Mustang. As she watched, it seemed as if all the air left her body.

She shook her head, "No! I don't believe it!" she proclaimed.

"Believe it, hun. But no worries, you'll see him soon," I promised.

"Kill her," I said to Stefan and his two musketeers.

When he didn't move, I turned to Clay. He looked at Stefan and nodded. Begrudgingly, he walked over, snatching the ties from her wrists and ankles, roughly pulling her from the chair.

"I told you to stay away from him," he growled, his face morphing and teeth extending.

Her eyes watered but she didn't say anything, which annoyed me. I wanted to hear her begging and pleading for her life. He tilted his head back and forcefully plunged his teeth into her throat. The sound of skin breaking, and blood dripping filled the room. I watched, elated, as her eyes closed, and she stopped struggling.

When he was done, he tossed her body into the corner and turned to me and Clay. His eyes pitch black and his face covered in blood.

"SATISFIED?!" he roared.

"Very," I replied, sparking a cigarette and sighing in satisfaction. "Just one more thing," I said, turning to Clay.

"Clay, you can't be serious?" one of the no-name Rogues spoke up.

He cut his eyes at him before focusing back on me. I jumped a bit as his cold hands grasped my bare arms. Gently, he moved my hair aside, his eyes burning red as his teeth extended.

"Don't make me regret this, Serina."

I shook my head, urging him to continue. I gasped as I felt his sharp teeth intruding into my skin. As he hungrily gulped my blood, snippets of my life flashed before my eyes, from childhood to when I graduated college. Meeting Venom all the way up until now. I could feel my limbs going numb and it scared me. I'd never had this much blood taken before. My heartbeat slowed and I could feel the cold, shallow waves of death washing over me.

My vision blurred and just as I felt like I was going to take my last breath, he pulled back, using his nail to make a small gash in his neck.

"Drink!" he growled.

Weakly, I tried my best to suck his blood, but I didn't have the energy. He lifted me, cupping my head and pressing it to his throat, until his blood practically rushed into my mouth and down my throat. The first few sips nauseated me, and I wasn't sure if I'd be able to do it. But after a few gulps, his blood began to taste like the sweetest honey I'd ever tasted, and I drank him down, greedily.

"That's enough," he said, but I latched on tighter, suckling like a hungry child, not caring about the drops that ran down my face, staining my dress and the floor.

"Enough!" he roared, dropping me to the ground.

My body was on overload as I writhed in a mixture of ecstasy and pain on the floor. I could feel every sensation to the hundredth degree, so much that it hurt. Suddenly, everything stopped, but the relief was brief.

"AHHHHHHH!" I screamed as my body began to spasm, locking in painful cramps.

"WHAT'S HAPPENING?!" I yelled, tears running from my eyes.

"Your body is dying. You have to die before you can become immortal."

"NO! I DON'T WANT IT ANYMORE!" I pleaded, losing control of my bowels, trying to crawl away.

I stopped when my limbs shut down leaving me paralyzed. My body involuntarily twisted, almost as if rigor mortis had set in before I'd died completely. My throat began to close, cutting off my oxygen supply. Closing my eyes, I prayed for death, and it came. Engulfed in darkness, I kept hearing a rhythmic beating, and it was driving me crazy!

Searching the darkness, I anxiously tried to find what the noise was that was disturbing the quiet. It seemed to be coming from behind a door. Hastily I clawed at it until I found the handle. Snatching it open, I was blinded by the light. Taking a deep breath, my eyes sprung open.

"Ahhh!" I screamed, sitting up, gasping for air, clutching my chest, hearing the loud thump of my heart.

Looking around, I saw I was still in the basement. I could hear something crawling. Glancing over my shoulder, I saw a tiny spider in the corner way across the room. I could hear its footsteps! Focusing on it in the dim light, I could see each of its microscopic hairs. My mouth fell open, and I looked at my hands. My skin practically glowed, except I could see the tiny particles of dust sitting atop of my skin cells.

I hurriedly tried to wipe my hands, like a mad woman.

"How do you feel?" Clay asked.

I looked up at him and grinned, running a tongue over my newly sharpened teeth, "Powerful."

17

TASH

I COULDN'T WAIT to go get my bitch! These damn vampires got me fucked up! This was the second day she'd been missing, and I didn't know how much longer I could lie to her mom about her whereabouts. Once I'd gotten everything straight with the police concerning Lucky's murder, (which they found was self-defense), I went on a hunt trying to contact anyone that had any connection to Venom.

After scrolling his page, I found a picture of him and Sypher, who thankfully was tagged. He finally responded to my fifteenth inbox, and once I told him I had some information he could use, he agreed to meet me. I suggested a public place because, at this point, I didn't know who in the hell I could trust, and I wasn't sure how many more crimes I could get away with! Sitting on a bench, outside of Ruby Tuesday's, at the Springfield Mall, I nervously checked my watch every five seconds.

When I saw him enter the glass doors, I jumped up. He was usually a jokester but today he looked stressed, tired and frustrated. Spotting me, he walked towards me, offering a light hug.

"You hungry?" he gestured towards the restaurant.

I shook my head, "I haven't had much of an appetite lately," I said, smoothing a strand of hair from my face.

"Well shit, I at least need a drink. Come on," he said, waiting for me to enter before him.

Once we were seated, and placed our drink orders, he turned his attention to me.

"What's the important information you have?" he asked, checking his phone and folding his hands in front of him.

I cleared my throat and glanced around, "I know who set Venom up," I spoke quietly.

He stared at me as if he was trying to figure out if I was telling the truth. "What'd you say?" he asked.

I started to repeat myself, but shut up as the waitress brought our drinks over. Once she placed the glasses on the small square napkins and left, I pulled my phone out of my purse. Unlocking it, it opened right up to the councilman's Facebook page since I'd been on there earlier looking for more clues. Sliding it across the table, I tapped the picture.

"Do you know these men?" I asked, looking up at him.

He nodded, "Yeah."

"I think they may be responsible for Venom's... accident."

He looked at me before shaking his head and downing his drink, "This is crazy. I thought you had some real shit. Look ma, I got shit to handle," he said, preparing to stand.

"Wait! Why would he," I paused, pointing to Clay, "wire five million dollars to Lucky Farigamo, hours after the hit on Venom?"

He stopped, sitting back down. "He did what?! How do you know?!" he demanded, his voice rising.

"Shhh!" I snapped, glancing around.

Lucky was well connected, and there was no telling if one of his goons were after me or not.

"I was working for Lucky. A little bookkeeping, funds management, and..."

"A cleaner of bullshit, huh?" He finished.

"You could say that. Anyway, I ran across the wire transfer and put two and two together. Not only that. He mentioned something about my friend, Jules. He said someone he knew saw her in the store and now she's missing! Venom told her not to go back to Walmart, but she had to pick up her check, now–"

"Hold up! She went back to that store?" he asked.

"Yeah. But only to–"

"One of the fucking Rogues works there! That's why Venom didn't want her going back there! To get to him, they would get her. They probably snatched her up to see if he was really dead! Fuck!" he shouted.

"What?! Well, where would they take her?!" I demanded, jumping up.

"I don't know, but I know who may. Let's go," he said, tossing some money on the table and walking out as I hurriedly followed behind him.

"I'll follow you!" I said, out in the parking lot, speed walking to my car.

"No, you won't! You riding with me. No offense, sis, but I don't know you like that yet. I need to keep an eye on you," he said, reaching for my arm.

Snatching out of his reach, I threw a hand on my hip, "I don't know you like that either, *bro!* You have no idea what I've been through the last few weeks, so excuse me if I don't exactly trust you either!" I spat.

"You don't know what I've been through the last few days! I watched my nigga bleed out!" he shouted, causing some lady to put some pep in her step and head in the opposite direction of us.

I thought about it for a second before huffing, "Fine. But if you try anything I'm fucking you up!"

He rolled his eyes, waving me off, "Come on."

I followed him to his truck and walked around to the passenger side. Once I got in, he screeched off like a bat out of hell. Cutting my eyes at him, I put on my seat belt. We rode in silence for a few minutes, before I spoke.

"Do you think... I mean, you don't think...you don't think they...killed her, do you?" I asked, hating that those words even had to leave my mouth.

He looked at me and uncomfortably shifted in his seat, "The sooner we get where we're going, the more her odds increase."

I nodded, deciding to shut up. Glancing in the mirror, I noticed a car taking every turn we took. Turning in my seat, I watched as we switched lanes, they did the same.

"You see that?" he asked, taking a hard turn.

"Um hmm. The Audi," I responded.

"Who the fuck are they?!" he said, more to himself, but I answered anyway.

"Lucky's people."

He glanced at me, driving down a one-way street,

"Why the fuck would they be following us?"

I sighed, "I don't know."

He looked at me as if he didn't believe me.

"Open the glove compartment," he instructed.

I did as he said and pulled out the gun that was inside.

"You know how to use that?" he asked.

I chuckled but didn't respond. Flipping it open, I saw that it was fully loaded. Rolling down my window, I waited until they sped up on us. Quickly, I poked my head out, the wind whipping my hair. Closing one eye I fired two shots, hitting the passenger. Their car swerved, but stayed on our ass.

The driver switched tactics and tried to pull up to Sypher's side.

"Hand it to me!" he yelled.

"Just drive!" I shouted, climbing on his lap.

He swerved a bit, barely missing a mailbox as he tried to see around me. Rolling down his window, I took a breath and fired, missing because we hit a bump. The car was now up on the sidewalk, side by side with us. The driver of the Audi raised his gun. Before he could fire, I did, getting off a clean shot to his neck. Losing control of his car, he crashed as we sped off towards the highway exit.

Carefully, I climbed off Sypher's lap and plopped back in my seat. Using my shirt, I wiped my fingerprints from the gun and tossed it back inside of the glove compartment. Pulling down the visor, I looked in the mirror, trying to fix my hair. On the highway, he slowed to the normal speed and looked at me.

"Damn! You Jamaican?" he questioned.

"I don't know. Why?" I asked, flipping up the mirror and turning to him.

"'Cuz them niggas crazy as fuck! Shottas!" he yelled, and I giggled.

"If I didn't trust you before, I trust you now!" he said, still amped from the chase.

"Well, I still don't trust you," I said, folding my arms across my chest.

He chuckled, "Don't act like you didn't enjoy climbing up in my lap."

I frowned, "I was trying to save our lives, not ride your little dick!" I told him.

"Yeah, whatever," he said, waving me off. "You gon' tell me the real reason why Lucky's hittas was gunning for us?"

"Nope," I replied.

"What? You a scammer? You robbed the nigga?"

Whipping my head towards him, I screeched, "Excuse me?! Nigga, I know you just ain't call me a scammer!"

"It is what it is," he shrugged.

"I told you I worked for him! His big ass would have killed me if I didn't kill him first–" I shut up, realizing that I just told on myself.

He grinned, "I knew it. I heard on the news last night he was killed in a *domestic disturbance*," he said, making air quotes with his fingers.

"Yeah, well...shit happens."

He glanced at me again, before turning his eyes back to the road.

When we pulled up to a large home in German town, I looked around. "Who lives here?" I asked.

"The Court," he responded, parallel parking the truck.

"The Court?! Like a judge?! You snitchin' ass mother-fucker!" I spazzed, reaching for the glove compartment.

He quickly grabbed my wrist, "Bonnie, if you don't chill the fuck out! Not that kind of court, a vampire Court!"

"Oh," I said, relaxing.

He sucked his teeth, "Man, bring your crazy ass on!" he said, stepping out.

Following closely behind him, we walked up the driveway to the door. He knocked and waited. I watched someone peek out of the heavy curtain, before hearing the many locks unclicking. The door opened and I spotted an older man.

"Mr. Butch," Sypher spoke to him.

The man nodded, before stepping to the side. We entered, and I looked around. It was a lot bigger on the inside than it appeared from outside. It was very taste-fully decorated with antique furniture. Even though it was bright and sunny outside, the heavy drapery gave the appearance of dusk on the inside.

"Wait here," he said.

Grabbing his arm, I shook my head, "You not leaving me here with Lurch!" I whispered, glancing at the man as he dusted a lamp.

Sypher chuckled, "He should be the one scared. You can't go a day without poppin' somebody."

When I frowned, he said, "I promise, you good. Have a seat."

Sighing, I sat on the dark, soft chair as he headed upstairs. Not knowing what to do, I pulled out my phone, pulling up my new account. I smiled when I saw all of the zeros. A part of me felt bad, knowing that the stolen cash was blood money for Venom. But I couldn't send it back, and Lucky damn sure wouldn't be using it. Sighing, I wished Sypher would hurry up! I wanted my friend back.

When I heard footsteps, sounding like a damn marching band upstairs, I froze. A woman who resembled Phylicia Rashad, gracefully walked down. Her heels clicking against the shiny hardwood floor. Her eyes glowed purple as she appeared to stare right through me. She was followed by the man I assumed was Venom's father. Standing, I backed up, scared to death that Sypher had set me up.

Two more people, or vampires, or whatever, followed. One was tall, dark and handsome. He peered at me, raising his brow in interest. The other, a woman, had flawless chocolate skin and a sleek faux hawk. She reminded me of a video game character. She looked me up and down before making a move towards me. Phylicia grabbed her arm to stop her.

Finally, Sypher came down.

"Tash, this is Talia and Xavier, Venom's parents. These are some friends, Potion and Milli."

None of them spoke, so neither did I. Instead, I stood in a dark room with four fuckin 'vampires, not knowing what to say or do. I was already making a mental list of shit Jules was going to have to do to get back on my good side. If I made it out alive.

"Tell them what you told me," Sypher said, stepping closer to me.

I glanced at Xavier before looking back to Sypher. I still wasn't a hundred percent sure that he didn't have anything to do with the set-up. Almost as if reading my mind, Sypher nodded,

"It's cool."

Reiterating the whole story, I closely watched their reactions. They all seemed genuinely stunned, but I still couldn't tell if it was real, so I made sure to stay close to Sypher.

"How could we have missed this?!" Xavier shouted, and stumbled back against the railing.

"Calm down, dear. You've lost a lot of blood." Talia spoke in a calm tone, ushering him to a seat.

"How did you lose blood?" I asked, still behind Sypher.

They all shared a glance before Talia nodded, still tending to her husband.

The sexy one, Count Chocula, as I was calling him in my head, approached, "He lost blood giving it to Venom. We all did, but Xavier gave the most. I'm Millennium, by the way," he said, holding out his large hand.

"I already introduced you, Milli," Sypher spoke.

Count Chocula shrugged, "I'm doing it officially," he retorted, still holding out his hand.

Nervously, I reached out my hand, allowing him to grasp it. I gasped as he slightly pulled me towards him, but Sypher snatched me back and shook his head.

"Not this one, Milli," he spoke.

Potion sighed, "Can both of you stop thinking with

your dicks so we can figure out what the fuck is going on!" she growled.

Milli eyed me again, before cutting his eyes at Sypher. Shaking off the feeling of his touch that was having a mild sexual effect on me, I focused on what he said.

"So... Venom is alive!" I said.

"He is. But we thought it best to let our enemies think otherwise for the time being," Talia spoke, finally giving me her attention.

"No! I need him! The Rogues kidnapped my friend!"

"What? Who?" Xavier asked.

"Jules! I need Venom's help to find her!"

Milli threw his hands in the air, shaking his head.

"Please, can I just speak to him? He loves her and I know–"

"I'm afraid that's impossible, dear. He's alive but in a coma from all of the silver," Talia informed me.

My shoulders slumped in defeat as I began to cry. I blamed myself for forcing Jules to go to Venom's show in the first fucking place. I should've just let her ass stay home in bed! Sypher tried to comfort me, but it was awkward. As if he wasn't use to being nice.

"Listen, nobody spends more time with V than me, and I know for a fact that when he wakes up, he's gonna be tight if we let something happen to his girl. I came here because I thought you'd be able to help, but if not," Sypher paused, grabbing my hand and heading towards the door.

"Wait!" Xavier said, standing. "Potion, take them to Venom."

"Are you sure that's safe?"

He nodded and Potion waved for us to follow her. She

led us down a maze of stairs, so far down, I knew we'd passed the basement and were now in some type of underground bunker. I tried not to gasp as we passed rows and rows of giant coffins. When we finally stopped at one, I watched as Potion typed in a code on the keypad built into the wood. Slowly, the lid slid to the side, and I covered my mouth to stifle my scream.

Venom lay inside almost motionless except for the tiny breaths he took. His honey brown skin was so bruised and ashen, it appeared gray. His normally shiny, maintained dreads looked dry and damaged. His body was sunken in, and I could clearly see the outline of his skeleton. He reminded me of a couple of crack heads that used to hang with my mother. Even his lips were ashy.

"Talk," Potion instructed me, and I knew I needed to get myself together.

"Uh, hi Venom. I know you don't know me very well, but we did meet. I'm Tash, Jules' friend."

At the mention of her name, I could've sworn I saw a movement in his body.

"Listen, I'm so sorry for what happened to you. Jules is too, but she couldn't be here because... um," I glanced at Sypher and he nodded for me to continue.

"She was kidnapped, by the Rogues."

A small sound rumbled in his chest and Potion, and Sypher both looked surprised. They motioned for me to continue.

"Venom! Please wake up! I don't know where to look, and I need your help! Jules is strong, so I know she's still alive but–" I paused, tears falling from my face.

"Aye, nigga! Wake your ass up! Those motherfuckers got your girl and–"

Suddenly his hand shot up, gripping Sypher.

"Ahhh!" I screamed.

"Oh shit!" Potion yelled at the same time.

"Blood," he whispered in a hoarse voice.

"Here!" Sypher yelled, putting his arm up to Venom's mouth.

At first, nothing happened, but soon, I heard the crunch of skin ripping. I could see the pain on Sypher's face, but he masked it as he clenched his jaw, allowing Venom to drink. Slowly, the color began to come back to his skin, and his lips looked like they got some much needed chapstick.

"Venom, stop!" Potion said, prying Sypher's arm away.

Using her stiletto nail, she sliced her wrist, holding it to his mouth as he hungrily drank. His eyes popped open and he sat up, gulping.

"Go get the others! He's going to need more blood!" Potion ordered.

Turning, we hurried back the way we came, hustling into the main room.

"He's up!" Sypher announced, waving his bloody arm, "He's feeding on Potion, but he's going to need more!"

In a flash, the vamps disappeared. I looked to Sypher in confusion.

"They ran out of the room. They're probably down there now," he explained.

The butler entered, carrying gauze and began wrapping it around Sypher's bite.

"Oh my God! We're really about to get Jules!" I exclaimed.

Sypher nodded, "Now that we know it's more than

one snake, we gonna let them bastards slither right to her. We can get everybody in one spot."

"Bet! I'm down! What do we do now?" I asked.

"You can help me shop."

"Shoppp?! Huh?" I questioned.

"I need a suit. Venom's funeral is tonight."

18

VENOM

"*SHE COULDN'T BE HERE...SHE was kidnapped by the Rogues.*"

"*Aye nigga...they got your girl.*"

I was listening to the voices cutting through my deep, dark slumber. I had no idea how long I'd been out, but I'd been struggling to wake up for what felt like forever. At one point, my body was racked with so much agony that I was ready to say fuck it; death gotta be easy 'cuz life is hard. But listening to my father's cries of anguish, a man I'd known my entire life and never seen him shed a tear, made me want to hold on.

Every few hours or so, I could feel his blood seeping into my body, and I wanted to tell him to stop before he gave too much. His blood was strong, and probably the only reason I wasn't dead. Each time he gave me blood, I could feel my body slowly strengthening, but still, I didn't have the energy to wake... until I heard the new voices. I woke due to sheer willpower and pure rage.

Reaching out, I snatched someone. Hearing the voice again, I realized it was Sypher. I was thirsty as fuck, and when he offered his arm, I paused, knowing that I might not be able to control myself once the blood started to flow. When I couldn't resist it any longer, I opened my mouth and chomped into him. My skin was so dry that I could feel it cracking when I opened my mouth.

His blood rushed inside of my mouth and down my throat like a cooling river. I could feel his heartbeat thumping through his veins, and I knew I needed to stop, but I couldn't. Thank God Potion was able to pry him away and replace her blood with his. Where his was cooling, hers was the opposite. A fiery flow of lava that caused my eyes to pop open. I was still feasting when the others appeared.

They each happily offered their blood, but when my dad tried to give me his, I turned my head.

"Venom, drink!" he demanded, his voice echoing throughout the lower chambers.

"You've given me enough," I spoke, so raspy that I didn't even recognize my own voice.

"I know when I reach my limit. Drink," he said again, slicing the side of his neck.

I glanced around, although my vision was still slightly fuzzy, I could sense the urgency from them. Moving his gold chain out of my way, I locked down onto his neck. Each sip gave me renewed strength, and I could feel my muscles pulsating with energy. When I felt his blood-stream begin to slow, I forced myself away and looked at him.

Now I could see them all clearly. Actually, my vision was probably better than before! I felt stronger. Looking at my dad, I watched as his wound healed slower than usual. When he embraced me tightly, I felt how thin he'd become.

"Thank you," I said into his shoulder.

"I'm not ready to lose you yet. You're still a baby."

I chuckled, "Dad, it's a whole different century from when I was born."

"I don't care! Now, you should continue to rest and let us–"

I stopped him,

"I can't do that. Jules is in trouble, and I'm responsible," I said, swinging my legs out of the casket.

I wore a pair of jeans and socks, but no shirt or shoes. I looked to Millennium, who flashed away, returning in a split second with a t-shirt and some Timbs. After pulling on the shirt, I slipped into my boots and began lacing them.

"Venom, it's worse than you think," my dad spoke, placing a hand on my shoulder to get my attention.

My heart dropped, and I glanced up, preparing myself to hear some bullshit.

"This Rogue thing. It's deeper than we thought. Clay is in on it as well," Talia explained.

"Clay?!" I yelled, jumping up, "Where that nigga at?!" I spat, my fangs extending.

"He's at a council meeting. But we have a plan in place, and he will fall right into it," my father spoke.

When I noticed how fatigued he looked, I moved out of the way and gestured for him to sit down. Which he did, taking a seat on the edge of the coffin.

"What's the plan?" I asked, remaining calm on the outside, but fuming on the inside.

"We're faking your death. Your funeral is tonight," Potion spoke, while offering some of her blood to my dad.

"It's gonna be a lot of funerals tonight," I mumbled.

"Damn straight!" Millennium agreed, giving me a handshake before pulling me into a quick hug, "Glad to have you back."

"You can't be here when Clay returns. If this is to work, he has to believe you're really dead. Him and that little sneaky hussie, Serina. I'm positive they'll lead us to the rest of the Rogues and Jules. You go to my old house. That's where the funeral is taking place. There's a secret room upstairs. I want you to stay there until we tell you otherwise," Talia informed me.

I wanted to go get Jules now, but I knew that would only alert the others, who may still be in hiding. My family was right. We needed to exterminate all of them at once or we'd always be at war. Begrudgingly, I nodded.

"What about a body?" I inquired.

"I got that handled," Potion spoke, "I got a little too..." she paused, glancing at my parents. "A little too frisky with one of my humans and he had a heart attack," she pointed to a nearby coffin.

Opening it up, I looked at the poor man that met his end because of Potion's pussy. She grabbed my finger and punctured my skin, squeezing out a few drops of blood over the body.

"We'll cremate him. Ashes to ashes. With your blood mixed in, he'll believe it's you."

"Now go! He could be back any minute!" Talia said, shooing me.

Planting a kiss on her cheek, I said, "Missed you too," before running off.

I WAS IMPATIENTLY WEARING a path in the soft carpet from pacing back and forth. Finally, everyone began to arrive for my *funeral*. I was fuming! I could sense that Jules was still alive, but that didn't mean she wasn't in danger. Everything in me wanted to go on a warpath, but I had to wait for the right moment. On God, everyone involved was gonna feel my wrath! The small secret room I was in, faced the huge garden below, which was decorated with pictures of me and a huge gold urn that was supposed to contain my remains.

Peering from the disguised window, I let out a low growl as I watched Serina take her seat. Fighting the urge to rip her throat out, I focused on the others, only feeling bad for Kember. I hated having to put her through another death, but this one was necessary. It was torture, watching the entire thing play out, waiting for the moment that I could run up on the Rogues. When Millennium stood, releasing the bats, I focused my energy to get them to attack Serina.

It was petty, but I didn't give a fuck. Her slimy ass deserved a lot more. When everyone filed inside of the house, my anticipation grew. What I didn't expect, was to hear a conversation between Clay and Serina. They were in the room directly below me, and I could hear every word they spoke, even down to her dry ass dick sucking lips.

I shook my head, expecting as much from Serina, but surprised at Clay. He'd been my father's right-hand man for as long as I could remember. The nigga was even my godfather! Damn! This shit was crazy! Finally, there was a knock at the door, and I flew down the stairs, snatching it open so hard I took it off of the hinges.

"It's time," Milli said, grinning, "Clay's car is tracked, so we can follow him."

"Bet," I said.

Zooming down the stairs ahead of him, I looked around as everyone watched me. I made brief eye contact with Lexi.

"Venom, I'm so sorry I didn't tell you," she cried, attempting to touch my arm, but I moved around, giving her a death glare.

Kember rushed me, "I'm coming with you!"

I shook my head, "It's not safe, Kember."

"I want that bitch! Venom, I know she had something to do with Val's death! Especially now, knowing what that bitch is capable of!"

Lexi and Kember had just found out tonight that I was actually alive. I'd overheard when Talia had whispered the secret to Kember during the funeral. We couldn't chance them knowing earlier, because we didn't know who to trust, especially Lexi. Shit, even Lucky had been in on it! Once this fuck shit was over, I vowed to cut my grass so I could see the snakes.

"Kember, no. I'll make her pay," I promised, and I meant that shit from the depths of my soul.

I assumed the same thing as her. The bitch was foul, and it would be no surprise that she'd been involved in what went down with Savalia.

"We gotta move," Potion said, glancing at her phone.

Me, Potion and Milli hopped in the truck with Corey

and Sypher, while Talia and my father followed closely behind. Leaving Lexi and Kember at the house with the other vamps. Murder was the only thing on my mind as we jumped on the highway. I could still sense that Jules was alive.

Hold on, baby. Just hold on. I thought to myself.

If anything happened to her behind my bullshit, I'd never forgive myself. Exiting the highway, we flew down the dark, quiet streets and I figured we must be close, noticing Sypher loading silver bullets. After what I'd been through, just seeing that shit caused my chest to itch. Glancing behind us, I checked to make sure my dad and Talia were still there. Talia was driving and keeping up with our every move.

I noticed a sign that read Union street, as we began to slow down. When I spotted Clay's car, I spoke.

"Stop."

Corey eased on the brakes, and I jumped out before we came to a complete stop, walking in front of Talia's Jaguar, heading to the passenger side. Opening the door, I crouched down to speak with my father.

"I want you to wait here."

He looked at me like I'd lost my mind, "What? Son, move out of my way."

"Dad! You lost a lot of blood! You don't have the energy for this! Let me handle it."

Talia watched our exchange silently.

"Hey Venom, listen! I'm the leader of the Court. The most powerful–"

I cut him off, "I know this! But right now, you're weak! I'm not taking any more losses behind my shit! You feel me?" I said, placing a strong hand on his shoulder to let him know I'd keep him here by force if I had to.

He glared at me angrily and Talia placed a hand on his leg.

"Venom is right, dear. Not tonight," she said.

He sighed, "Fine. But if I feel anything isn't right, I'm coming in!"

I nodded, "Deal, old man."

He waved me off and turned to WDAS on the radio. Talia winked at me before giving him a quick peck on the cheek and stepping out. We all headed towards the house except Corey, who stayed behind the wheel, and my father. As we moved closer, I could sense a gathering. Getting the attention of the others, I silently told them where to go.

Talia, Potion and Sypher went to the front, while me and Millennium crept towards the back. I could sense Jules was close. Something was wrong. I couldn't feel her as much as I had earlier. Not only that, I sensed a new energy!

"You feel that?!" Milli whispered in surprise.

"New blood. I think these dumb motherfuckers might have turned Serina!" I spat.

Feeling my connection to Jules beginning to fizzle out, I snapped, "Now! We can't wait any longer!"

Snatching apart the bolted, metal cellar door, I threw the pieces and flew down the stairs. The smell of blood was heavy in the air as I quickly morphed.

"Venom!" Clay shouted, looking like he'd seen a ghost.

Serina, who was on the floor, scrambled to her feet, moving closer to Clay. I could see the immortal blood flowing through her veins. Stefan, the one I encountered at Walmart, eyed me and Millennium, his fangs extending. Two other Rogues glanced nervously between all of us. Scanning the room, I spotted Jules, barely alive, crumpled on the floor.

Fury erupted from my chest as I dove for Clay. Out of Serina and the Rogues, he was the strongest and I wanted to take him down first. He quickly shook off his surprise and dodged out of my way. One of the weaker Rogues took the opportunity to try me. I hastily snapped his neck and punched my hand through his chest, snatching out his still beating heart and sinking my fangs into it. He fell to the ground, writhing in agony as his body immediately started to dry up.

Behind me, I heard Millennium spring into action as I focused back on Clay, who started towards the stairs, but paused when the sound of the front door caving in, sounded throughout the house. In the back of my head, I could faintly hear Jules' heartbeat. I knew I had to act quick or she'd die.

"Fuck!" I roared, as I realized I wasn't gonna be able to save her and fuck shit up at the same time.

Leaving Talia, Potion, and Sypher to handle Clay, I darted to Jules and cradled her in my arms. She was soaked in her own blood, and I spotted multiple bite marks.

"Baby, I'm here! I got you!" I told her, watching her eyes slowly flutter open, creating small narrow slits.

"I knew you weren't dead," she whispered so low that if I wasn't a vampire, I doubt I would have heard her.

I smiled, moving the hair that was coated in blood

and stuck to her face. "You know I'mma stalker. I ain't leaving you."

She let out a tiny noise that sounded like a chuckle before speaking.

"I love you, Venom. I should have told you sooner-" she stopped, interrupted by a coughing fit, that caused blood to gurgle in her chest.

"I love you too, Jules," I said, my eyes filling with tears.

They spilled down my face, blurring my vision, as I came to the realization that she wasn't gonna make it. Time seemed to slow down as I glanced around the room. Talia and Potion were going at it with Clay. Millennium and Stefan were each landing blows, while Sypher fired a bullet at a Rogue. I turned back to Jules, who was beginning to go cold in my arms.

"I gotta do this, baby," I told her, gently biting into her already ravished neck.

She was damn near on the brink of death, so I pulled a few sips to bring her closer. She didn't fight me as I punctured my own throat, pouring my blood into her mouth. Rubbing my hand down her throat, I forced her to swallow. I did this until I could feel her pulling the blood from my wound on her own. My tears were now tears of relief as I felt her lightly grip my arms as her suction became tighter.

I glimpsed the room as she drank, becoming stronger and more alive with each sip of the immortal elixir my body produced. I was glad to see my family appeared to be coming out on top of the war, but one person caught my eye. Serina, who'd been hiding in the corner the entire time, was watching me with a pained look on her face. Tears streamed down her face as she watched me give life to Jules.

Gradually, her face began to change. Her jaw widened, and her newly gotten fangs emerged. Her eyes burned a raging deep red. Fuck. Now, this bitch was a vampire scorned. I had to pry Jules away from me. I'd tried to give her enough blood so that her transition wouldn't be so painful, but still keep enough so that I wouldn't get weak.

I hopped up, the same time that Serina emerged from her hiding place. I was gonna make this shit quick. I was tired of playing with her ass. She growled, punching her hand through the brick wall and snatching out a copper pipe, which she hummed at my head with beastly strength. I quickly ducked it as it whizzed past my head. I glanced down, as Jules whimpered in pain. I wanted to coach her through it, but I had to keep this bitch away from her until she fully changed. When Serina noticed that Jules was changing over, she charged.

19

CHAOS WAS EVERYWHERE, including inside of me. As a battle ensued all around the room, a battle was being fought inside of my body. I was dying. I could feel it. Venom had tried to save me, but I could still feel my body going cold. Crawling into the corner, I balled up in a fetal position, just as I felt my legs and stomach cramp up.

There was so much that I wanted to do. Places I wanted to visit. A life I wanted to live, but it wasn't meant. There were many things I'd do differently, but meeting Venom wasn't one of them. My only regret was that our time together was so short lived. As I took my final breaths, I glanced around.

The vampires were going hard, fighting as if their lives depended on it, and I guess they did. That simple bitch, Serina, was even a vampire now, and when she noticed me, she charged at me. Gasping in pain, I was paralyzed and all I could do was watch, and pray that I died before she got to me. Something flashed in front of my eyes and I saw that it was Venom. He clothes-lined her, and she flipped over his arm, hitting the floor with a thud.

I gave a weak smile, glad that would be the last image I saw. Closing my eyes, I took my last breath and waited for death... and waited. Peeking open an eye, I was shocked that I was still alive. The pain left my body and I began to feel rejuvenated from my toes up to my head.

What in hells bells?! I thought, slowly sitting up.

Looking around, I could see everything clearer. I could even see that the vamps weren't just flashing around; they were running in super speed! I ducked with cat-like reflexes as something flew past my head and crashed behind me.

THE FUCK?! I thought, jumping up.

I looked down at my arms and hands, noticing all of the bite marks and bruises rapidly disappearing. When my damn gums started to hurt, I felt my fangs and finally realized that I was a vampire!

This nigga done turned me into a damn vampire! I thought.

I had to! You would've died! Venom's voice rang inside of my head, causing me to jump.

Now he could read my mind?! Oh hell no!

Nigga, I might coulda made it! I probably just needed to go to the ER!

Aye yo, Jules! We can discuss this later! I'm a little busy right now!

Sucking my teeth and wincing a little because I accidentally bit my tongue, I looked around. He was fucking

Serina up, but the bitch was dodging some of his hits. Seeing her sent me into a fit of rage, and I felt hot. Like literally. My blood boiled in my veins, and my jaw painfully extended, making room for my long fangs. I flashed over to him.

"I got this bitch, go help your family," I grinned, cracking my neck and narrowing my eyes at her.

Venom glanced at me, unsure. When I snatched her by her arm and snapped it off, he smiled and ran off to help Talia with Clay.

"AHHHH! You stupid bitch!" she growled, trying to swing at me with one arm.

"Let's see your hands now, sis!" I yelled, waving her arm in the air like I didn't care.

When the bitch popped me in my jaw, causing me to stumble back, I was pissed and embarrassed that I just got rocked by someone with one arm, so I backslapped her with her own dismembered arm, and kicked her as hard as I could. She flew back, crashing into the wall, leaving an indentation of her body as she fell to the floor, gasping for air. Darting over before she could regain her wits, I stomped her head, praying it would smash open.

As I lifted my leg for what would hopefully be the last blow, she quickly rolled out of the way and used her arm to clip me. I hit the ground roughly, and she hopped on top of me, trying desperately to sink her fangs into my throat. I was holding her off and still holding her ripped arm. I used it to block my neck just as she bit down. Instead of biting me, she was ripping apart her own flesh.

I watched her for a second, because she really thought she was doing something, before kicking her ass off of me. She looked in shock as she realized she was biting and gripping her own arm and not my neck. I chuckled at this goofy hoe before hopping up, running up a wall and jumping down, landing in back of her. Wrapping my arm around her neck, I put her in a death choke hold, before snapping her neck.

She fell to the floor, and I gently kicked her to see if she was dead. I didn't know if I needed to put a stake through her heart, chop her head off or what? Since I wasn't sure of the protocol, I kicked her head, and it flew off her neck. Placing my hands on my hips, I did a little dance. I was good at this vampire thing!

Glancing around, I tried to decide who to help. Millennium and Stefan were still fighting each other, but Millennium seemed to have the upper hand. Venom had finally gotten Clay. It seemed as he snatched him off of his feet by his collar, sinking his teeth brutally into his throat. His body shook as Venom drained him. Talia was hurt, not bad, but enough that Potion was giving her blood. Finally, my eyes landed on Sypher.

He was firing, but the Rogue was quickly dodging the silver. One managed to pierce his shoulder, and he screamed in agony before rushing Sypher, knocking him to the ground and the gun out of his reach. I darted over, snatching the Rogue off of him and burying my new teeth into his skin. Blood gushed into my mouth, setting my taste buds on fire!

Wanting more, I ripped open his chest cavity, slurping hungrily. I saw brief flashes of his life as I feasted. It was like Netflix with food. I devoured him, until I could drink no more. Letting him go, he fell, his skin drying up. Sypher stared at me with large eyes,

"Good lookin'!" he nodded, wiping the blood and bits of flesh that had splashed on him.

"GODDAMN!" Millennium yelled, causing us to all turn towards him.

He was grinning, holding Stefan's severed head.

"I ain't had a good workout like that in years! Nothing like a good vamp fight to get the blood pumping," he said, swinging the head back and forth.

Venom laughed, as he caught Stefan's head that Millennium tossed to him.

"Speak for yourself! This the second pair of boots I fucked up in a week!"

Shaking my head at both of them, I moved towards Talia and Potion. Talia was waving Potion off.

"I'm fine! It was only a surface bite. I'm more upset about my necklace," she said, holding the bitten gold in her hand.

Noticing me, she looked at me in surprise before smiling.

"Well, look at my new daughter in-law! You look stunning. Death, or should I say eternal life, becomes you," she said, circling me.

"Wait! Huh?!" I questioned in surprise.

Potion laughed, "Venom turned you. Y'all have a blood connection now. Wow. I didn't think he'd ever settle down!"

So that explained why his ass was all in my head!

"Yes. Welcome to the family, dear," Talia spoke.

Still in shock, I couldn't speak. Instead, I peered at Venom, who was engrossed in a conversation with Millennium and Sypher. He looked up, giving me a sly smirk, which I returned.

He strolled over. "You got a little," he said, pointing to my face.

Sucking my teeth, I wiped the blood from my mouth and threw a hand on my hip, "So what you think you my husband now?"

"Something like that," he said, wiping the splatters I'd missed from my face.

"You could've asked," I said, folding my arms across my chest.

"I can release you if you're not happy," he said, stepping closer.

"I didn't say all that! But you could still act like you have the home training I know you were raised with!"

"She has a point, Venom. I know you only wanted to save her, but you didn't give her a choice," Talia agreed with me, and I stuck my tongue out at him.

He chuckled, shaking his head, "If y'all think this double team shit is gonna be a permanent thing, think again!"

Talia and I looked at each other before sharing a *yeah right* look.

"I do appreciate what you did, though," I told him.

He raised a brow, "How grateful are you?" he whispered in my ear, his hand sliding down to my ass.

I giggled, moving his hand, "I'll show you later."

"Alright, enough! I'm going to finish this once and–"

We all turned as his father came storming into the room. He paused, glancing around at all of the carnage that littered the cement floor. Venom laughed at his shocked expression.

"You just like the cops. You come when everything is over!" he said, causing us all to laugh.

"Hmmph. Well, good job, I guess. Rather sloppy though. I like clean kills," his father responded as he flicked a piece of flesh from his shiny, black shoes, determined to have the last say.

"Oh, Xavier, please! Remember that bar you destroyed back in eighty-two? He went on a rampage because one of the vamps offered me a drink!" she explained.

"Anyway!" he said, cutting his eyes at her. "Let's clean this up so I can finally relax."

"I got one better, X," Potion spoke. "Let's burn it!"

I was starting to think this damn girl was crazy. She'd probably get along well with Tash. We left out, leaving Potion to pour gasoline.

"Your crazy ass friend is waiting for you at the Court. Textin' me talking about hurry up before somebody try to eat her," Sypher told me as I laughed.

"Why in the hell is she at the Court?" I asked, looking around for an explanation as we headed across the street towards the vehicles.

"I'll tell you on the way, but she's the one that figured out Clay and Lucky were associated with the Rogues," Venom informed me.

"LUCKY?!" I hollered, pausing in the street. "Oh my God! Is she ok?!"

"Is *she* ok?" Sypher repeated. "Shid, she straight! Lucky the one restin' in pieces out this jawn!"

They all chuckled while I was still lost.

"You know what? Y'all go head and drive. I'mma head to the Court now, to check on things," Millennium said, smirking at Sypher before hopping up onto one of the rooftops and disappearing into the night.

Sypher's mood seemed to instantly change and he clenched his jaw, eyeing the path Millennium had taken. I looked to Venom in confusion, desperately trying to piece together what I had apparently missed in the few days I'd been held hostage. Venom shrugged.

I think both of my homies got a thing for your girl.

I'd almost forgotten about our telepathic connection. I looked at him with wide eyes before glancing back at Sypher, who was still visibly steaming. Shaking my head, I turned my face to hide my smirk, wondering what the hell Tash did to have both of these men on her top. I couldn't wait to holla at my girl and catch up.

WHEN WE ARRIVED at the Court, it was full of life even though it was about two in the morning, but I quickly remembered they were vampires, and now, so was I. Cars were everywhere and I marveled at how much it seemed like a regular home from the outside, but inside, I knew was packed with supernatural killers. Bats circled the house, which I guess would have been a clue if anyone was looking for it. I was lowkey nervous about meeting all of these vampires, wondering if they would accept me or frown upon me. I finger combed my hair, hoping I looked presentable despite my ripped clothing.

Sensing my apprehension, Venom grabbed my hand tightly, interlocking his fingers through mine. I smiled, feeling a little calmer. An older man opened the door as we approached, allowing Talia and Xavier to enter before the rest of us. As Venom and I stepped inside, we were met with loud, excited cheers. Everyone was excited to see Venom and his family safe and sound. They clamored to congratulate them, and the entire time he never let go of my hand, introducing me to everyone until their names and faces became a blur.

To say I was overwhelmed would be an understatement! This was pretty much all of the vamps from Philly, Jersey, Delaware, and Maryland. Who the fuck would have thought that the tri-state area was flooded with vampires? Sheesh! Once I'd damn near met everyone in the large, crowded room, I finally spotted Tash, chatting with Millennium.

"V, I'mma go and talk to Tash! I see her over there," I said, pointing across the room.

"Okay, I'll be over in a second," he said, loosening his death grip on my hand.

Making my way through the crowd, I remembered I was a vampire, and flashed behind her, catching Millennium's eye. When she turned to see who he was looking at, her eyes widened to see me.

"BITCHHHH!! Oh my God, I was tryna get to you earlier, but y'all was surrounded by all these damn secret service vampires!" she exclaimed, waving her hand around animatedly, causing Millennium to chuckle.

"I'm so glad you're okay! I was so worried!" she said, throwing her arms around me.

"I missed you too, boo! Girl, thank you for the look out!" I squealed, squeezing her back.

Venom had explained everything and I should have known her nosy, scheming, Inspector Gadget ass would have figured everything out!

"I heard about Lucky. Are you ok?" I inquired.

"Girl, I'm more than ok, but that's a story for a girls day lunch!" she winked, and I laughed, knowing her ass was gonna give me all the tea later.

"But, um, what's going on with you? What the hell? They had you kidnapped in a gym or some shit?! You look toned as fuck! And why your skin look so damn bright and smooth? You the sexiest hostage I ever seen!" she said, staring me up and down.

"Awww shit! Bitch! Did he turn you into a vampire?!" she asked, touching my face and quickly removing her hand from my cool skin.

"He did! Oh my God, what does this mean? We can still be friends, right? Like, are you allowed to hang with humans? What am I gonna tell your mom?" she talked non-stop.

"Tash! Calm down! I'm still me... just..."

"Just forever! Your immortal ass is you forever!" she said, causing Millennium to laugh again.

"I'mma let y'all catch up," he said, glancing between us. "You got my number. Use it when you need it," he said to Tash before strolling off into the crowd.

I noticed she blushed a bit before turning her attention back to me. Before she could start grilling me again, I started on her.

"And what the fuck is going on with you and Millennium?" I grinned, placing my hands on my hips.

"I, uh, nothing, girl. Listen when I tell you! I'm over men! Me and Milli are just cool. I–"

"*Milli*," I repeated, "You calling him by his nickname? Hmmm," I questioned, staring her down.

"It's just a nickname, Jules! Besides, we've both made

it clear that *IF* anything was to go down, it would only be sexual! Nothing serious!"

My mind flashed to the club and the sexy show that he and a human woman had put on for the audience. My cheeks burned remembering the way I'd felt watching it and then my eyes widened.

"Did he tell you what he likes to do?" I whispered.

Grinning, she nodded and glanced around before speaking,

"Girl, he a freak! Now I don't know if I would be down with all the shit he was talking about, but a little excitement here and there never hurt nobody!" she said, raising her brows.

I laughed, "You such a hoe! Bust down thotiana!"

She laughed too, "Takes one to know one! Y'all still gonna be having threesomes and shit?"

"Doubt it!" I said, folding my arms.

"Hmm. Well, who the fuck is that all in your mans face?!" she asked, pointing behind me.

Turning, I spotted Lexi trying to talk to Venom. When I really concentrated, I could feel his annoyance and anger.

"Let me go handle this!" I spat.

"Wait! I'm coming too, so don't do that flashy thing!"

Snatching her hand, I flashed over to Venom with my bestie in tow. Lexi appeared shocked and nervous as I narrowed my eyes at her.

"So, you're..."

"That's right, bitch! She's the queen of the damned! And who do you think you are–"

I slapped a hand over Tash's mouth and sighed shaking my head. I couldn't with her!

"Tash, I got this, boo," I told her, uncovering her mouth.

She glanced at me, and I nodded as she folded her arms, giving Lexi a silent death glare.

"Lexi, did you know that Serina murdered Val?" I asked, causing Tash to gasp, placing her hand over her mouth.

Venom stared at Lexi, and Kember slowly approached. It seemed like a hush fell over the party with only slight murmurs echoing around. Lexi's eyes grew round, and she shook her head.

"I knew it! Jules, she admitted it?" Kember asked, stepping closer.

I could see the tears building in her eyes and I hated having to tell her the ugly truth, but she needed to know for sure if she was ever going to get some closure from all of this. Grabbing her hand, I slowly nodded my head, and more tears streamed down her face.

"She was pure evil. I got her, Kember. I got her for you, for Val, for Venom and for me! Val is probably resting somewhere beautiful and peaceful, while that bitch burned and turned to dust!" I said, trying my best to make her feel a small amount of vindication.

She broke down, and I hugged her tightly, allowing her to let her grief out.

"Are you sure she's dead?" she asked.

I nodded.

She sighed, "I'm grateful, but I wish I could've been the one to kill her!"

"Kem, the Rogues had turned her into a vampire. It would have been too dangerous for you," I said, rubbing her back.

She got herself together and nodded, taking a deep breath before turning to Lexi,

"You knew, didn't you?! All this time!"

Lexi shook her head, wiping her own tears, "I swear I didn't! Not about Val! I knew that she was speaking with the Rogues and that she had some type of deal with them, but I didn't know the details! I promise! I should've said something! I-I just didn't know what to do! I'm not a bad person! I'm not!" she cried.

"Venom, I still love you–"

"Hold up! That's where I stop this shit!" I said, interrupting, "Lexi, I know you were here before me and you and Venom had some feelings–"

"That shit dead," Venom interjected coldly.

"I said *had*. But shit, bitch, you could've gotten him killed! Hell, all of us," I said, waving my hand around wildly.

"I know that's right!" Tash backed me up.

"Whatever y'all had, it's finished. You gotta go! One of us will go to the house with you so you can get your shit."

"Now, wait a minute! I know I made some mistakes, but since when do you speak for Venom?!" she demanded.

Chile! See? Try to be an adult and handle things in a mature matter and bitches wanna try you. Tash was already taking off her earrings, ready to go. I had to take a deep breath to calm myself, but the shit wasn't working. I felt my face transforming and I couldn't stop it. Lexi watched in horror as I morphed in front of her eyes.

In an instant, I'd gripped her ass up, "I'm trying to be civil about this, Lexi. In case you haven't noticed, Venom and I share a connection. Something you'll never have!

So, if I wanna speak for him, I fucking will! There's a new vampire in town, and I'm hungry and agitated! You wanna test me, or you wanna do what I said and go get your shit?" I asked, holding her so close I could smell what kind of deodorant she had on.

Her mouth gaped open in fear and surprise. She glanced at Venom, but he simply shrugged. When she finally realized that I had the last say, she nodded, and I let her go, causing her to stumble back.

"Fine. I understand. I'll go now," she whispered.

"Corey–" Venom started.

"I got it," he said, escorting her out.

"Whew, girl, she tried it!" Tash said, putting her earrings back on.

"Didn't she though!" I chuckled, shaking my head.

"Do you want me to go too?" Kember asked, glancing between me and Venom.

"Kember, I know your situation and what you've been through. Of course, you can stay as long as you need to. But, um–" I paused, trying to figure out how to tell her that the whole sister wife thing was over until further notice.

"I get it! You don't even have to say it! I knew Venom was in love with you the first night he brought you home. You don't have to worry about me and Venom. We were always more friends than lovers," she admitted.

Nodding my head, I breathed a sigh of relief that she understood how I felt. Who knows what the future held? Maybe I'd be down for it later on in life, but right now, I felt selfish, and I wanted my man to myself. We didn't start off in a normal relationship and hell, we still weren't, but I wanted our strange love kept just between us two.

"She probably more interested in what's between your legs than Venom!" Tash chuckled in my ear, causing me to elbow her.

"Dear, you handled that like a class act!" Talia said, approaching, her hands clasped together. "Let's get you out of these rags and find you something more fitting," she insisted, grabbing my hand and leading me away.

"Aнhh! Uhh! Oh God! I'm grateful! I'm so grateful!" I screamed out as I rode Venom.

He gripped my hips forcing me to bounce harder, bringing me to my... I lost count of how many times I'd cum, but I was cumming again. I thought I'd never have better sex than our threesome, but I was wrong. Dead ass wrong! Having sex as a vampire was a religious experience! Everything was heightened, and my orgasms hit harder than ever before.

"Yeah? You grateful I saved your life or you grateful for this dick?" he grunted, flipping me off of him and entering me from behind.

My razor-sharp nails shredded his sheets as pleasure overtook my body.

"Both!" I screamed.

When he began pounding into me with supernatural strength and speed, I squirted, feeling my juices soaking the sheets under me. Wrapping my hair around his hand, he yanked, snatching my head back before sinking his fangs into my shoulder. The bite pushed me over the edge as I came again.

"FUCK!" I screeched.

"This dick hit different when a nigga come back from

the dead for you," he said, digging his fingers painfully deep into the flesh of my ass as he bounced me on his dick.

I couldn't even respond as my eyes rolled back into my head. My mouth hung open, but no words escaped. Only guttural grunts and groans of pure ecstasy. Shit, if I didn't love his ass before, I did now!

"I know you do!" he spoke, reading my mind.

Using my pussy muscles, I gripped him and threw it back, the wet, slapping sounding obscene.

"Oh shit! Jules, hold up," he grunted.

Hearing his grunts and moans of pleasure turned me on, so I sped up.

"Fuucckkk!" he moaned, releasing his thick, warm cum deep inside of me, the feeling causing me to explode once more.

"Damn!" he huffed before collapsing on top of my back, his weight causing me to sink deep into the soft bed.

Blowing a piece of hair from my face, I exhaled. The night's events had finally caught up to me, and I was exhausted. We laid like that for a few minutes, catching our breath before he lifted himself off of me. Flipping over onto my back, I propped myself up on my elbows, examining my new body. I was still thick, but Tash was right, I did look toned as hell! Shit, I could probably compete with Kember for best vixen body!

"Your body was always sexy," Venom mumbled next to me, his arm resting on his forehead.

I laughed, "You're newsy as fuck! How do I keep you out of my head?"

He chuckled, "You have to guard your thoughts. I'll teach you everything later."

Pulling me across the bed, he cuddled me, draping his arm across my stomach.

"I'mma get you knocked and fuck up your whole summer," he said.

I giggled, slapping his hand, "Boy bye! I'm a vampire; I wanna be all magical and stuff before I have kids!"

He laughed, "Magical?"

"Yes! I know I'm technically dead, or undead or whatever, but for the first time, I feel alive," I tried to explain.

He sat up, watching me before he spoke.

"This is just the beginning. On everything, I'm gonna make you feel alive forever," he said, kissing me.

We laid there talking and tonguing for the rest of the night until the sun began to rise, and my body started to feel heavy. I couldn't keep my eyes open as the sun rose higher in the sky. I dozed off into a dark, peaceful slumber, next to my man for life.

"Venom, I don't know. I think I should talk to my mom and Nikki by myself first," I told him as we sat in front of my house as the sun set.

"If you want to, you can. But I'm here to support you," he said, looking exasperated because we'd been having this same conversation the entire drive here.

Sighing, I spoke, "You're right. Okay. Let's get this shit show started," I told him, exiting the car.

He grinned, hopping out. I didn't know how he was so calm when I was about to tell my mom and my new sister that I was a damn vampire! Using my keys, I entered, spotting my mom and Nikki watching some old episodes of *Power*. They both jumped up when they noticed us. I smiled at how healthy they both looked. Nikki had enrolled in the Art Institute for Fashion, and I was proud of her even though her classes hadn't even started yet.

"Hell must be frozen over! Jules, don't you ever pull something like this again! You must have bumped your head!" my mom scolded while pulling me into a tight hug at the same time.

"What happened to your phone?!" Nikki questioned before squeezing herself into the hug.

"I.... I..." I paused, looking to Venom.

"Nikki, Ms. Nia, it's my fault. I pulled her on a last-minute trip with me, and I didn't even give her enough time to grab her things or her phone," he spouted the same lie that Tash had been telling them for days.

I looked at him confused because I thought we were going to tell them the truth.

"Listen here, Venom! I like you, and I gave you a chance, but don't you ever whisk my baby away without letting her call her mother! I know you were raised better than that!"

"You're right. I apologize. But the reason it was so urgent was because I needed to talk to her about something important."

Now I was really confused. What the hell was he talking about.

"It was so important you couldn't talk to her here?" Nikki asked, sounding just as confused as I felt.

"Kind of. But then I realized that I should do it here," he said, digging in his pocket and producing a small blue box.

"Oh shit!" Nikki and I both yelled at the same time.

When he dropped to his knee, I would have fell except for the grip my mom still had on my arm.

"Ms. Nia, I know I've only known your daughter for a short period of time, but in my life, I realized that time moves so fast. People we love disappear before our eyes, and before you know it, it's just you. Wishing you would have done certain things, but the opportunity is gone. I don't want to waste one second. I wanna live in the moment. I want to experience each moment with Jules. I know y'all got a tight relationship, so I couldn't ask her without asking you first," he said, flipping open the box, blinding us with the giant, clear diamond.

"Did I miss it?!" Tash asked, running in the house, out of breath.

"You knew?!" I asked.

She grinned, "I sure did! And it damn near killed me to keep it to myself!"

"Well?" he asked.

"Oh my God," my mom whispered like he just proposed to her and not me!

"Mom!" I yelled, snapping her out of her trance.

"What? Oh of course! You have my blessing!" she said.

Venom looked to me, and I grabbed the ring, putting it on my own finger.

"Yes! Yes!" I yelled, jumping up and down.

Later that evening, we all went out to celebrate my engagement. I was forcing myself to eat because food didn't taste the same. I would rather have had some blood, but I couldn't do that in front of my mom without her having a heart attack, so I had to settle for a rare steak. Venom thought it would be better if we told them later about what we really were, and I agreed it would be better to ease them into it. I was glad to see my mother and Talia getting along so well, just like Venom said they would.

"I still can't believe you!" I whispered to Venom, while still admiring the rock on my finger, set off by my fresh manicure.

"Believe everything, baby. I'mma give you the world before it's all said and done," he said, gripping my fingers.

"I hope not on a silver platter," I joked.

He immediately scratched his chest, "Nah! Fuck that shit!" he laughed.

EPILOGUE

Six months later...
  JULES

I HAD OFFICIALLY BEEN a married woman for a month and life was great! Venom ended up signing with a different label, and his dreams were coming to fruition. Kember ended up singing the hook on his song dedicated to Val, and she was blowing up fast, like I knew she would! Nowadays you couldn't turn on the radio without hearing a record from one of them!

I was in the middle of starting my own public relations firm after becoming in high demand from the work I'd done for Venom and Kember. Especially handling the media frenzy that came about from Venom's burned vehicle abandoned on the highway. Almost everyday new rumors swirled, but I squashed them all when I released evidence from a *family doctor*. The only rumors I couldn't kill were those damn YouTube conspiracy people who claimed Venom was in fact, a real vampire. Luckily, no one believed them.

Nikki had started her classes and was doing amazing! She was turning out to be the best big sister ever. We'd been through so much, and it was funny how we could sit back and laugh at our previous arguments. Well, everything except her time with Rich. That was still traumatizing for her. I finally had the talk with her and my mom. My mother wasn't even surprised. She said she knew there was something different about me and when I questioned her, she explained that she pushed me out and she knows me inside and out and as long as I was happy, she was happy.

Nikki thought I was pulling her leg, until she watched me feast one night. Now she was a believer. Tash's rich ass ended up moving her and her grandmother to a giant house in Cherry Hill and placing her mother in an expensive rehab facility. I hoped for Tash's sake that her mom could get her act together. My boo was a sweetheart deep, down inside and she deserved happiness. I loved how she refused to let shitty circumstances define her. I was glad that she accepted my offer to do the books for my company.

She had her pick of men too, since Sypher and Millennium were both still competing for her affections. She liked to pretend that it got on her nerves, but I know she lowkey was living for it! That girl cracks me up! I was team Sypher all day. Millennium is a hoe! I don't care, I don't care! Plus, her and Sypher's crazy asses together always made for a fun time.

But let's get on some not so fun times. That asshole Clay's reach ran deeper than we thought. He had dirty cops, politicians, doctors, and lawyers in his pocket! All filthy and all vamps. One by one, we killed them off. It took awhile, but it was finally done! The Court did its own internal investigation finding that Clay was a lone snake.

No one had heard a peep from Lexi. She'd closed her boutique and was only offering online shopping for the time being. I really wish she would have spoken up sooner about Serina. She really wasn't a bad person, but she couldn't be trusted, and as long as she stayed away from me and mines, she would remain safe. As for some of these groupies that's been trying me, I can't say the same! If one more of these hoes hopped in his inbox or tried to talk more shit about me, I was gonna have her for breakfast, lunch, and dinner! But that's a story for another time.

THE END!

COMING 03/21!

CPSIA information can be obtained
at www.ICGtesting.com
Printed in the USA
LVHW031820100419
613666LV00004B/350

9 781090 981004